Robert Rankin... ...e attended variou... ...o study Graphics... ...h blah. Numerou... ...n Residence at Waterman's Art Centre, where he founded Brentford Poets, which soon became the largest weekly poetry group in England. Blah blah blah blah blah. Sexual athlete? Lives in Sussex. Blah blah blah . . .

P.S. He is the author of *Snuff Fiction, Apocalypso, The Dance of the Voodoo Handbag, Sprout Mask Replica, Nostradamus Ate My Hamster, A Dog Called Demolition, The Garden of Unearthly Delights, The Most Amazing Man Who Ever Lived, The Greatest Show Off Earth, Raiders of the Lost Car Park, The Book of Ultimate Truths,* the *Armageddon* quartet (three books), and the *Brentford* trilogy (five books), which are all published by Corgi books. Robert Rankin's latest novel, *Sex and Drugs and Sausage Rolls,* is now available as a Doubleday hardback.

What they say about Robert Rankin:

'One of the rare guys who can always
make me laugh'
Terry Pratchett

'To the top-selling ranks of humorists such as
Douglas Adams and Terry Pratchett, let us
welcome Mr Rankin'
Tom Hutchinson, *The Times*

'A born writer with a taste for the occult.
Robert Rankin is to Brentford what William
Faulkner was to Yoknaptawpha County'
Time Out

'One of the finest living comic writers . . . a
sort of drinking man's H. G. Wells'
Midweek

Also by Robert Rankin:

ARMAGEDDON THE MUSICAL

THEY CAME AND ATE US,
ARMAGEDDON II: THE B-MOVIE

THE SUBURBAN BOOK OF THE DEAD,
ARMAGEDDON III: THE REMAKE

THE ANTIPOPE

THE BRENTFORD TRIANGLE

EAST OF EALING

THE SPROUTS OF WRATH

THE BRENTFORD CHAINSTORE MASSACRE

THE BOOK OF ULTIMATE TRUTHS

RAIDERS OF THE LOST CAR PARK

THE GREATEST SHOW OFF EARTH

THE MOST AMAZING MAN WHO EVER LIVED

A DOG CALLED DEMOLITION

NOSTRADAMUS ATE MY HAMSTER

SPROUT MASK REPLICA

THE DANCE OF THE VOODOO HANDGAG

APOCALYPSO

SNUFF FICTION

and published by Corgi Books

The Garden of
Unearthly Delights

Robert Rankin

CORGI BOOKS

THE GARDEN OF UNEARTHLY DELIGHTS
A CORGI BOOK : 0 552 14212 3

Originally published in Great Britain by Doubleday,
a division of Transworld Publishers

PRINTING HISTORY
Doubleday edition published 1995
Corgi edition published 1996

3 5 7 9 10 8 6 4

Set in 10/11¾pt Monotype Plantin
by Kestrel Data, Exeter, Devon.

Corgi Books are published by Transworld Publishers,
61–63 Uxbridge Road, London W5 5SA,
a division of The Random House Group Ltd,
in Australia by Random House Australia (Pty) Ltd,
20 Alfred Street, Milsons Point, Sydney, NSW 2061, Australia,
in New Zealand by Random House New Zealand Ltd,
18 Poland Road, Glenfield, Auckland 10, New Zealand
and in South Africa by Random House (Pty) Ltd,
Endulini, 5a Jubilee Road, Parktown 2193, South Africa.

Printed and bound in Great Britain by
Cox & Wyman Ltd, Reading, Berkshire.

For my dear little
white-haired old mother
who can flick past
the rude bits

love and laughs
and
Rock 'n' Roll
Oh yeah!

1

'Rock 'n' Roll,' said Maxwell Karrien, as he opened the official-looking envelope. 'This is something of a great surprise.'

He called out to his wife of some years' standing. 'Wife,' called he, 'come look at this.'

'Whatever is it, dear?' the dear one answered.

Maxwell scratched his head. 'It would seem that I have been awarded The Queen's Award for Industry award.'

'The saints preserve us all,' said his voluptuous spouse, her bosoms entering the sitting-room before her like a dead heat in a Zeppelin race. 'And you never having done a day's work in your life.'

' 'Tis true,' said Maxwell, giving his head another scratch for luck. 'And it would appear that I have dandruff also.'

'All in one day.' His wife smoothed down her satin housecoat and shuffled her pompommed slipperettes.

Maxwell dropped into his favourite armchair. 'I suppose I shall now be called upon to officiate at Council functions, open fêtes and jumble sales, kiss babies and give talks at the Women's Institute.'

'I never knew dandruff made one so important,' said his wife, whose sarcasm had got her into trouble on more than one occasion.

Maxwell kicked her playfully in the ankle. 'Limp off

7

and make my breakfast,' he suggested. 'I have some serious thinking to do.'

'Your day for the use of the family brain cell then, is it?' whispered his wife, between gritted teeth, as smiling sweetly she hobbled away towards the unfitted kitchen.

It was *not* a marriage made in Heaven.

What with *her* hating *him* and *him* hating *her*.

And everything.

Maxwell took his tin and liquorice papers, rolled himself a ciggy and composed his handsome features into a look of grave concern. 'This must be a mistake,' he told himself.

'It is probably meant for Mr Camp next door,' he continued.

'That would be it,' he concluded.

But upon once more examining the gilt-edged certificate, these thoughts were forced to flee. There were the letters which formed his name. Bold as brass in copperplate.

'Papyrophobia,' said the fearful man. 'This is *not* Rock 'n' Roll.'

After a breakfast of egg, bacon, sausage, baked beans and a fried slice that the not-so-dear one had stubbed her cigarette out on, washed down with two cups of Earl Grey, Maxwell decided that he would take his certificate around to Father Moity at St Joan's to get an unbiased opinion.

For he reasoned thus: if I ask Duck-Barry or any of the lads at The Shrunken Head, they will say, 'Well done, Maxwell, get the drinks in.'

And if I ask the man in the cardy at the Job Centre, he will say, 'Queen's Award for Industry award, eh? Then we're stopping your dole money, mate.'

And if I ask at the Police Station, the policemen will

become embittered that I received it rather than they and they will smite me with their truncheons, as they do every time they see me anyway.

And so by such reasoning, ten o'clock of the morning hour found Maxwell in a confessional box, his Queen's Award award upon his knee and his chin upon his chest.

To the eastward side of the grim little grille, Father Moity seated himself, mumbled holy words and pecked at his crucifix.

'Spit it out,' said he.

'Bless me, Father, for I have sinned, it has been seventeen years since my last confession.'

Father Moity put on his most professional face (which he kept in a jar by the door) and scratched at his old white head. This was going to be a baddie, he thought, and, I seem to have dandruff, he discovered.

'It all began this morning,' said Maxwell in a reverent tone.

'You have not been to confession for seventeen years and you have the nerve to tell me that it all began *this morning*?'

The priest coughed into his cassock and marked out a cross on his chest.

'I have been awarded The Queen's Award for Industry award (award),' said Maxwell.

'Blessed be,' said the priest. 'And is it for seventeen years of sinlessness that this award has been awarded?'

'Sinless towards industry,' said Maxwell. 'For I have never done an honest day's work in my life.'

'Then isn't it a wonderful world that we're living in today and I don't think that our likes will ever be here again,' said the priest, who feared not the sin of plagiarism.

'I was hoping for some advice, Father,' came the voice of Maxwell to his ears.

'Advice is it you're wanting? Well, here's some now for you to be going on with.' The priest coughed once again.

'I should *cough*?' asked Maxwell, somewhat bewildered. 'Is that the advice you're offering?'

'Not a bit of it. I recently had a bad asthmatic attack.'

'I'm sorry to hear that.'

'Indeed,' said the priest. 'Three asthmatics attacked me outside Budgen's. Was my own fault, I should have heard them lying in wait.'

Maxwell scratched once more at his head. His dandruff had cleared up, at least. 'About the advice,' he adventured.

'Lead by example,' said the priest. 'By your deeds let others know you. These Queen's Award award awards are not handed out willy-nilly to any old Tom, Dick or Harry. It has probably arrived in the wrong post, for some service to industry that you have yet to perform.'

'You think that might be it then?'

'Seems obvious to me, my son.'

'Well thank you very much, Father.' Maxwell rose to take his leave.

'Will you not be after confessing any of your sins then?' asked the priest, in a sing-song Irishy kind of a way.

'No, I think not.'

'Then go with God, you capitalist bastard.'

'Thank you, Father.'

'Bless you, my son.'

Maxwell slouched from the church and took to plodding homeward, the heavy weight of his potential responsibilities pressing down upon his shoulders. As he crossed the canal bridge, he considered tossing his Queen's Award award into the murky depths. But on a second thought he didn't and continued on his way.

On the corner of Maxwell's street stood the *Tengo Na Minchia Tanta* Café. Right where it had always been. Maxwell stepped inside to take some beverage and think things through.

The new girl behind the counter knew Maxwell by sight alone. 'What would you like, sir?' she enquired, and there was more heaving sensuousness, more unabashed eroticism, more blatant vibrating sexuality in those few words, than could ever really happen in real life.

'Pardon?' asked Maxwell, whose life was real enough to him.

'Tea or coffee, sir?'

'Coffee, black, no sugar, please.'

The new girl liked male customers who took their coffee black with no sugar. Very manly, she thought. Very *machismo*.

Those who knew Maxwell through introduction rather than by sight alone, might well have scoffed at this, for Maxwell was no great man for the ladies.

The Maxwell these folk knew was a decent enough chap on the whole, but with that said considered by some rather *dull*, if not *stupid*.

The looks of himself were fine enough. Nearing the magic six feet in his height and in the middle of his twenties, he was gaunt of frame and square about the shoulders. Well favoured in the face department, with kind grey eyes, a happy mouth and a nose like a friendly arrow head. His hair was black and well quiffed back and his mood was, in general, hearty.

But.

Maxwell did have his foibles, his choice of dress being one such. Maxwell held in high favour the America of the nineteen fifties, the America of Wurlitzer Jukeboxes and Chevrolet Impalas and Danny and the Juniors. And this holding in high favour had a tendency to reflect itself in his day wear.

Maxwell sported Oxfam zoot suits, slim Jim ties and bowling shirts. Shirts whose collars had no 'stand-up', large, substantial, crêpe-soled boots. And as those who have ever sought to make a statement of their individuality through their choice of apparel will readily affirm, eccentricity of dress rarely fares well in societies where conformity is considered the standard by which others judge you.

Those who fail to conform are at best mocked and ridiculed, at worst, ostracized or injured.

If you are wealthy you can do as you damn well please. But if you are not, and Maxwell most definitely was *not*, then *pleasing* is something you must do for other people.

The rich can dress *up* to impress, the poor must dress *down* to survive. Maxwell dressed as he pleased, Maxwell was poor, hence to the world that Maxwell inhabited, Maxwell's appearance was 'stupid'.

And it had to be said, his habits did not exactly aid his cause (if cause he had, which actually he didn't). When not in the company of his beautiful wife, whom he had married in haste to repent about at leisure, Maxwell could, like as not, be found in the public library.

Here he passed away much of his life, deeply engrossed in the science fantasy novels of P. P. Penrose*, thrilling to the daring exploits of Sir John Rimmer, Dr Harney and Danbury Collins (the psychic youth himself) as they locked in mystical conflict with the evil Count Waldeck.

Maxwell seriously 'got into' these books. They were

*Better known to all as the creator of Lazlo Woodbine, Private Eye.

escapism nonpareil. And though, to the outward world, his dress code offended many and his conversation was at best uninspired, in that personal inner world of fantasy fiction, he was up there with the best of them, often solving some inexplicable conundrum pages before Sir John and his loyal companions caught on.

So this was the Maxwell that those who knew him knew. Dull, said some, and stupid, others, and Maxwell alone knew himself.

Maxwell paid for his coffee, took it to a window seat and sat down miserably.

The new girl behind the counter smiled him a smile. Here is a fellow, she thought, who needs a shoulder, nay a breast, to rest his weary head upon. A handsome fellow. A shame about the stupid clothes though.

Sandy the sandy-haired manager stood at the new girl's shoulder. Making one of his rare appearances at the *Tengo Na Minchia Tanta*, he had been examining the till roll upon Maxwell's arrival, and now felt it the moment to confront the new girl with his findings. 'Surely,' said Sandy, 'I spy a deviation here.'

The new girl's eyes left Maxwell, toured the café, took in the window view and finally met up with those of her employer.

'You what?' she asked.

'The cash in the register and the takings logged upon the till roll vary to the tune of twenty-three pounds, two and threepence,' said the manager called Sandy.

'What is that in new pee?'

'It is instant dismissal.'

'Stick your job then,' said the new girl, divesting herself of her gingham serving smock, slipping on her crushed-velvet coat and finding herself the new girl no longer.

Sandy stroked his sandy-whiskered chin and watched her stalk off through the doorway. 'While I labour away to grow this beard,' he exasperated, 'mere slips of gals rip me off for twenty-three pounds, two and three, old money. We should never have gone decimal in the first place.'

Maxwell stirred his unsweetened coffee with the wrong end of his spoon and wondered, perchance, if the Queen's Award award award had been intended for his father, who presently laboured industriously on the sewing of mailbags, at the pleasure of Her Majesty. Most likely not, was his conclusion.

'I'll have to ask you to drink up, sir,' said Sandy, vacating the counter to approach his single customer. 'This embezzlement of funds has sorely tried my nerves and I feel a headache coming on.'

Maxwell drank up his coffee and continued on his way.

When he arrived at the marital homestead he was most surprised to see a man of Romany stock carrying his favourite armchair to a waiting cart and returning to Maxwell's front door with a goldfish in a plastic bag.

'Blessings, ma'am,' said the gypsy, presenting this to the dear one.

'Hold on there,' cried Maxwell, storming up his garden path. 'Surely that is my favourite armchair.'

The gypsy shrugged, muttered 'Barter' into Maxwell's ear and then took flight. Maxwell put his weight against the door his wife was closing and entered his hall. 'What is the meaning of this?' he demanded to be told.

The dear one explained to him that it was 'barter' and all quite legal and above board.

Maxwell took the plastic bag his wife was holding and examined its carrot-coloured contents. 'This fish is dead,' he declared.

The dear one sighed and rolled her eyes. 'Of course

it's dead, Maxwell. It would be cruel to keep a live goldfish in a plastic bag, wouldn't it?'

Maxwell raised his hand to scratch his head again.

'For God's sake, don't,' his wife told him. 'It is becoming a habit and there's no telling where it will lead.'

Maxwell returned the bag of fish to his wife and placed his hands safely into his trouser pockets. 'I shall miss that armchair,' he said. 'It was my favourite.'

'You'll get over it. How did you get on with the priest?'

Maxwell closed the front door and leaned back upon it. 'Father Moity thinks that the Queen's Award award must have arrived early by mistake. That it's for something I have yet to do.'

'You've yet to wallpaper the spare bedroom,' the dear one suggested.

'I've yet to own a house that has a spare bedroom.'

'Good point.' Maxwell's wife put down the plastic bag which contained half a pint of water and a dead fish. She took up her handbag, opened this, removed a number of cosmetic accoutrements and began to worry at her face with them. 'I had a thought while you were out,' she said, examining her progress in the hall mirror. 'Would you like me to tell you what it was?'

'I don't know,' said Maxwell. 'What do *you* think?'

'I think you would.'

'That's a relief then.'

'You could sell it.' The dear one viewed her own reflection. 'Sell it for money. To buy things for me with.'

'Sell it?' Maxwell's face lit up like a Blackpool skyline. 'Sell it! You are a genius.' He almost kissed the dear one there and then. Almost! 'You're right. It's mine. I'll sell it. Rock 'n' Roll be praised.'

*　　*　　*

The slim legs of Maxwell carried him at speed towards The Shrunken Head. As every boy must have his dog and every dog its day, so every tale must have its pub and every pub its tale.

The Shrunken Head lurked at the bottom of Horse-ferry Lane. Long gone, of course, the horseferry, but the lane remained the same. And so the pub.

A venerable oak-framed edifice, daub and wattle; bottle glass. Dungeon door and spittled floor. Close on by the river's bank, its kegs to slake the thirst of lighterman and big bargee and grizzled tattooed salt.

Very close on by the bank. So close, in fact, that each high tide gave cause for great alarm. But just far enough up the bank for there not to be a single decent view of the river from the beer garden.

Such, they say, is life.

Those who know The Head know of its jazz nights and of these they speak in tones akin to awe. For when the moon is in the seventh house and Jupiter aligns with Mars, then do Papa Legba and his Voodoo Jazz Cats set the joint a-jumping. But of them, more, and later.

Elderly, low beamed, well cellared, was The Head and run by Sandy, who had business interests here and there and all about the borough.

Maxwell strode up to the saloon bar door, the blakeys on his substantial boots raising a fine shower of sparks on the cobblestones. From within came the carefree chatter of happy tongues. The gay badinage of good friends well met. The swell of piped music. The rustle of crisp packets. The tang of nectarines. That hint of Monday lunch-time in an otherwise month of Sundays. And the like.

Maxwell pressed open the door and entered The Shrunken Head.

'Good day to you, sir,' said Sandy, grinning from behind the bar counter.

'Good day to you,' said Maxwell, 'and a pint of your very best.'

As Sandy did the business, Maxwell gazed about the saloon in search of some likely fellow who might be all the better for having a Queen's Award for Industry Award award.

The voice of Duck-Barry Ryan reached him from the public bar where drinks were a penny cheaper and swearing was not only allowed, but encouraged.

'The worm is the gardener's friend.' Duck-Barry was telling a small and uncommitted audience of one. 'The wiggly worm digs tunnels which help irrigate the soil when it rains. He also eats woodlice and ticks, and, if left undisturbed, would live to be one hundred years of age.'

'Cobblers,' Maxwell recognized the voice of Jack 'The Hat' Cooper. 'The wiggly worm eventually turns into the bluebottle, from which spring all the evils of the world. Don't tell me about wiggly worms, I've bred more of the blighters than you've had pimples on your bum.'

Duck-Barry resented that remark.

'I resent that remark,' he said.

Sandy presented Maxwell with a well-drawn pint. Maxwell counted change onto the counter. 'What is all this talk of wiggly worms?' he asked.

'Please do not mention wiggly worms in the saloon bar,' said Sandy. 'I fear that the wiggly worm, its habitat and habit are doomed to be the major topic of conversation in this public house until the Government decides the matter one way or the other.'

'I am perplexed,' said Maxwell. 'Please explain.'

'The Government is putting a tax on worms,'

explained Sandy. 'Such will the high-rise dweller benefit and the rich land baron pay dearly.'

'I am astonished by this news,' said Maxwell, sipping at his pint.

'The discussion in progress', Sandy gestured towards the public bar, 'is between our two resident wigglyworm experts and is basically aimed in the direction of: how can one's wiggly worms be persuaded to vacate one's garden, during the period when the Worm Tax Inspectors call to make their tail-tally.'

'My astonishment becomes tempered by suspicion,' said Maxwell. 'Surely this is some April first tomfoolery or suchlike.'

'Scoff if you will.' And Sandy made a sombre face. 'But those of us with eyes in our heads and fire in our bellies can see nineteen eighty-four approaching in high-heeled jackboots.'

A man of Romany stock now entered the saloon bar in low-heeled gumboots. He was burdened by the weight of an armchair.

'Ah, excuse me,' said Sandy, and to the gypsy, 'Kindly put it by the fireside if you will.'

The gypsy did so. 'Blessings, sar,' he said, presenting Sandy with the bill.

The landlord raised his sandy-coloured eyebrows, cashed up no-sale and drew the sum of twenty-three pounds, two and three pence, old money, from the cash register. 'Easy come, easy go,' he said, as the money left his hands.

The gypsy tugged upon his forelock, then once again took flight.

'How do they fly like that?' Sandy asked Maxwell, who was staring at the armchair and making small choking noises from the back of his throat.

'Nice chair, eh?' said Sandy. 'That's a Dalbatto. Not to be confused with a Dalberty, of course. I've a member of the peerage lined up for that chair. Worth a king's ransom is a Dalbatto nowadays.'

Gag and croak, went Maxwell.

'Two more pints over here,' called the voice of Duck-Barry, 'and stick a couple of worms in Jack's.'

'Coming,' said Sandy.

Maxwell picked up his pint of best, took himself over to the armchair, which up until so recently had been his favourite, and sat down heavily upon it.

'Don't sit there!' cried Sandy, from the bar. 'Are you mad, or what?'

'I'm beginning to wonder.'

Maxwell removed himself to a table near the window, sat down upon a low stool and glowered into his beer. A hand touched him lightly on the shoulder and a soft voice said, 'Hello, it's you again, isn't it?'

Maxwell looked up to find the ex-new girl from the *Tengo Na Minchia Tanta* smiling down at him. 'It's me,' she smiled, 'remember?'

'Oh yes,' said Maxwell. 'At the café. What are you doing here?'

'I work here. Sandy's just taken me on as a barmaid.'

'Eh?' said Maxwell. 'But I thought he—'

'Ssh,' said the new barmaid. 'It will be all right as long as he doesn't want to take up a reference from my last employer.'

Maxwell shook his well-befuddled head. 'You deserve the Queen's Award for Industry award,' he said.

The new barmaid made a wistful face. 'What wouldn't I do for one of those?' she said.

'Oh yes?'

'Get a move on, Sandra,' called Sandy. 'There's empties to go in the washer.'

'Well, I can't stand around here chatting all day,' said Sandra, the new barmaid. 'I won't get The

Queen's Award for Industry award doing that, will I?' And with those words said, she was gone.

Maxwell drank his beer in silence, glanced furtively about the crowded bar, and when he felt assured that he was unobserved, took to a violent bout of head scratching.

It didn't help.

The day was wrong. Everything about it was wrong. Everything that had happened. The way people were behaving. All of it.

Perhaps he was dreaming. Or going mad. Or perhaps the dear one had slipped a tab of bad acid into his breakfast for a bit of jolly.

Maxwell rooted in his zoot suit pocket and pulled out his Queen's Award for Industry Award award. *This* was somehow at the back of it all. *This* was somehow the culprit.

Maxwell spread the thing before him on the table and gave it a good looking over. It did look good and though he had certainly never seen one before, he felt certain that *this* was the real McCoy.

A sudden lull in the general saloon bar conversation caused Maxwell to look up from his looking down. The lull was a silence and a most intense one at that. Everyone was staring. At him. At his Queen's Award for Industry award award award.

Maxwell gazed from one face to another. Stern the faces looked. Hostile. Definitely hostile.

'Ah,' Maxwell snatched up the certificate, rolled it between his fingers and thrust it back into his pocket. Someone muttered something. Whispers broke out here and there, like little charges of electricity. Elbows were nudging. Fists were being formed.

'Excuse me please.' Maxwell rose and made towards the door.

'He's got it,' said someone. 'He started it.'

'What?' Maxwell thrust into the staring, muttering, menacing crowd and battered his way towards the door.

And he was through it.

Outside.

And it had grown somewhat dark.

Maxwell blinked and rubbed at his eyes. It couldn't be much past midday. What had happened to the light? He blinked and squinted. The lane was blurry. Indistinct.

Dreamlike.

Dreamlike.

Maxwell made for home. He forced his way along. His boots, substantial as they were, seemed sticky about the soles. They clung to the pavement, making every step an effort.

Ahead was confusion. Police cars. Flashing lights. Shouting.

Crowds of people.

A policeman stepped forward. Barred his way.

'You can't go any further,' said the officer of the law.

'I live down there,' said Maxwell. 'Let me by.'

'No, sir. There's a fracture in the reality of that street, we can't let anyone past.'

'But my house is there.' Maxwell almost said, 'My wife is there.' But he didn't.

'There's nothing we can do about your house, sir. You'd better get out of town quickly. Go abroad. Go to Patagonia.'

'Let me through, please.' Maxwell raised a fist towards the policeman.

'I can shoot you for that, sir. It's allowed now, you know.'

'What's going on? You have to tell me.'

'It's a reality fracture, scientists are working on it.

Someone moved the chair. You'd better go, sir, before you arouse suspicion.'

'Yeah, go on. Bugger off.'

Maxwell turned. A policewoman sneered at him. It was his wife. The not-so-dear one. But then she was also the new barmaid! It was the same person. Maxwell couldn't understand how he'd never recognized her in the *Tengo Na Minchia Tanta* and in The Shrunken Head.

'Go on, Maxwell, sling your hook. Bugger off. Don't look back. Don't come back. Don't *ever* come back!'

Maxwell turned, ran blindly. Tripped. And fell.

And vanished.

2

And then awoke.

In his favourite armchair.

And groaned mightily.

'Oh I do hate that.' Maxwell reached to scratch his head but thought better of it and rubbed his eyes instead. 'Drop off back to sleep in your armchair, dream a lot of gibberish and think you're still awake. Horrible.' He shuddered briefly. 'Still, at least I didn't dream I was walking around the streets in my pyjamas this time.'

'Oh dear,' said someone in a tired and languid tone. 'I had hoped so much that we might simply skip over this sequence. It is *such* a cliché.'

'You can't skip over it just like that.' This voice was sharp and foxy. 'There has to be a process of adjustment and explanation.'

'And acceptance.' The third voice had a youthful quality to it. 'For him to function of his own free will.'

'What is *this*?' went Maxwell, opening wide his eyes. Then, 'Aaaaaagh!' he continued.

'Why is it always "Aaaaaagh!"?' asked he of the tired and languid tones.

'Because it *is*,' said foxy. 'Let him get it over with. Someone pour him some coffee.'

'Aaaaaagh!' went Maxwell, which wasn't a new

23

'Aaaaaagh!' but a continuation of the original. 'Who? What? Where? How? Why? Aaaaaagh!'

'Take some coffee, Mr Carrion. It contains a mild soporific. It will calm you down.'

'*Calm me down?* I don't want—' Maxwell jumped up from his favourite armchair. 'Who? Where? How?' He gaped all around and about. This wasn't his front room. He wasn't home. But where was he? And was he actually awake?

'You *are* awake,' said languid-tones.

Maxwell gaped now at the speaker. A long tall speaker, towering before him. Somewhere near to seven feet in height, he was. A bony frame shrink-wrapped in a suit of bottle-green velvet. The head was narrow, long, its facial features all pinched in together. A great red beard, a fantastic embroidery of tortured plaits, depended to the chest. Thick-lensed, horn-rimmed spectacles bridged a hatchet nose. The mouth beneath pursed quizzically, then spoke again. 'Try to remain calm,' it said.

'Calm? I?' Maxwell's eyes went flashing round this room that wasn't his. And 'wasn't his', it was, to a most notable degree.

This room was long and wide, yet low of ceiling, each wall bricked with books of ancient leather. Dusty cabinets displayed a wealth of *outré objets d'art*. Glass domes sheltered beasts and birds and insects, fruit and flowers. There were reliquaries of burnished gold on chiffoniers of satinwood, and deeply buttoned chesterfields and escritoires and astrolabes. What floor was seen was rich with rugs, of Soumak, Shirvan, Susani, Senneh and Savonnerie.

'Enough,' croaked Maxwell, gazing this way and the next, yet seeking only the door. 'If I'm not dreaming, let me out.'

'You're free to go,' said the long tall figure in the

bottle green. 'But I would not advise you so to do, quite yet.'

'It wouldn't go well for you if you did.'

Maxwell swung about to view the speaker with the foxy voice. A man of medium height (to those who dwell amongst the very tall and the very short in approximately equal proportion), broad of freckled, smiling face, with a nimbus of white hair rising airily above a forehead of considerable span. This chap was all in green tweed. Watch-chains swagged the waistcoat that curtained his luxurious paunch. Tiny hands toyed nervously on the mount of a lacquered cane. 'Drink some coffee, compose your thoughts, relax yourself, it's for the best.'

A third fellow offered a tiny Copeland coffee cup upon a delicate saucer painted in the Imari palette, with gilt line and dentil rims.

'And who are you?' asked Maxwell, declining the proffered cup.

The third fellow simply grinned. Young and elfish, he wore a black T-shirt printed with the words 'FAST AND BULBOUS' across the chest area. A black leather jacket, soiled Levis and Doc Marten boots completed the ensemble. He had a rather unfortunate cold sore on his upper lip. 'Sugar?' he enquired.

'I'm out of here,' Maxwell pushed his chair aside, took half a step and fell flat on his face.

'I took the liberty of tying your boot laces together,' said red-beard of the bottle green.

Maxwell glared up bitterly from the Soumak, Shirvan, Susani, Senneh and Savonnerie rug-bestrewn floor. 'Thanks a lot,' said he. 'But hold on there.' He glanced from standing figure to standing figure and back again. 'I know you, don't I?'

'He's getting there,' said foxy voice.

'I knew he would,' said FAST AND BULBOUS.

'You know us,' said red-beard of the bottle green. 'You do, go on.'

Maxwell fumbled with his boot laces. As with his boots, they were substantial. They would not be untied without effort.

'Help Mr Carrion back into his armchair,' said red-beard, and the others hastened to oblige.

'It's *Karrien*,' said Maxwell, sitting down once more. 'It's Maxwell Karrien. But . . . it is *you*. Yes it is.'

'It is,' the tall man nodded curtly from the waist.

'Then I *am* dreaming. You're not real.'

The tall man shook his head. 'This isn't helping. Who are we? Go on, say it. Tell us.'

'You're *them*,' said Maxwell. 'The characters in the books I read. You're Sir John Rimmer, fifth Earl of Boleskine.' The tall man winked an eye behind a pebbled lens. 'You're Dr Harney.' Fox-voiced freckle-face fluttered tiny fingers. 'And you're the psychic youth himself, Danbury Collins.'

'I'm that fellow,' said the psychic youth himself.

'The paranormal investigators in the P. P. Penrose novels.'

'We are they,' quoth those who were.

'And you *do* look very good.' Maxwell made a most approving face. 'Just as I imagined you to, in the novels. Except,' he peered at Danbury Collins, 'you never had a cold sore. In the novels.'

'Would *you*?' the lad asked.

'Quite so. Well, brilliant. I'm very impressed.'

'Good,' said Sir John. 'We hoped you would be.'

'Impressed by my own imagination,' said Maxwell. 'That last dream was crap, but this one is a killer.'

'This one is for real,' said Danbury Collins.

'Oh yeah, sure.'

'What happened yesterday was real,' said Sir John. 'That's why we're here.'

Maxwell glanced up, about, from face to face, around the room. It did all look so very real. And feel so very real. It even *smelled* so very real. Musty. Musky. A hint of armpit issuing from Danbury's direction. Sir John's beard lotion and the beeswax on the doctor's shoes.

So very real indeed.

'It *is* real,' said Maxwell. 'But it can't be.'

'Things have changed,' said Sir John. 'The times have changed. Perhaps I might explain. To spare much later anguish. To elucidate.'

'To allow for the process of adjustment,' said Dr Harney.

'And acceptance,' said Danbury Collins, offering the coffee cup once more to Maxwell.

Maxwell took the dainty thing and put it to his lips. 'Go on,' he said, suspiciously. 'Elucidate. Explain.'

'Good.' Sir John lowered his gauntness onto a chesterfield sofa and extended his long legs before him. 'Have you ever asked yourself why the Old Testament just sort of petered out at the end?' he enquired.

'No,' said Maxwell, sipping coffee. 'Can't say I ever have.'

'Or why the cycle of Greek myths simply finished?'

'No.'

'Or why Columbus never sailed over the edge of the earth when he went off in search of the New World.'

'That's because the earth is a sphere, I think you'll find.'

'Is it indeed?'

'Well, it was yesterday.'

'Ah,' said Sir John. 'Yesterday.'

'You mean it's not *today*?'

'Very possibly not. I've yet to find out.'

'Hold on there,' said Maxwell.

'I'll keep this as brief as I can.' Sir John twiddled

27

here and there about his beard. 'And as simple. The history of this planet, the history of man, is composed of "ages". From the age of chaos to the age of the dinosaurs, to the age of the dawn of man. The Stone age. The Bronze age. The Iron age. The age of myth and legend. The golden age. The dark ages. The middle ages. The age of reason. The age of steam. The technological age. The age of Aquarius. The new age. Ages, cycles, times, durations. Units of measurement, flowing from one into another, but always in the same direction: forward. Why does the Old Testament simply peter out? Because the biblical age came to an end. The age of the prophets and of those who walked with God was over.'

'Where is all this leading?' Maxwell asked.

'Quite simply, Max, the age you knew two days ago has *simply* ceased to be. The planet earth has moved into another age.'

'And so what's this age then? The age of fictional characters?'

His hosts exchanged glances.

'Leave it out,' said Maxwell.

'No-one has had a chance to give it a name yet,' said Sir John. 'But if I might make so bold, I should call it "The Age of Almost Infinite Possibility".'

'Really?' said Maxwell, most underwhelmed. 'But surely every age is of *almost* unlimited possibility.'

'I'll take your word for it, Max. You're the hero, after all.'

'The *hero*?' Maxwell choked upon the grouts in his coffee. 'I'm no hero. I'm just Mr Me. And I'm Maxwell, not Max.'

'You *were* Maxwell. It will all become clear quite soon. Does any of this make the vaguest sense to you so far?'

'You might try to be a bit more specific about this

28

new "age" you say the earth has moved into. How did it move into it anyway? And why?'

'There were signs of its coming. A shadow cast before, as it were. Prophecies, predictions.'

'You're saying that it's the Apocalypse then? Or Armageddon?'

'I am saying that the Age of Technology is no more. If you like, the earth has moved into a period of non-causality. Reality would appear to have fractured. A new age of myth and magic has dawned upon us.'

'Magic doesn't work,' said Maxwell. 'I've tried it.'

'Magic didn't work in the Age of Technology, how could it? It works again now though.'

'You are pulling my plonker, surely?'

'Pardon me?'

'Sorry. Something hung over from the age of slang colloquialism.'

'Perhaps you should let Max take a look outside,' said Dr Harney.

'It's *Maxwell*,' said Maxwell. 'After *Maxwell* House. My mum had this new neighbour move into the flat upstairs. And he came down to borrow some coffee one evening. And . . . you know . . .'

'You have much to be grateful for,' said Sir John.

'I do?'

'Well, he could have come down for some *Domestos*.'

'Or some *Ovaltine*,' said Dr Harney.

'Or a packet of *Durex*,' said the boy Collins.

Three scathing glances turned his way.

'Sorry,' said the lad. 'It just slipped out. Er, the *Durex* I mean. Not the willy in the *Durex*. Er—'

'Actually he's a bit of a prat in the books,' said Maxwell.

'Comic relief,' said Sir John.

'Hang about. Hang about,' said Maxwell. 'Before this goes any further. Say I accept that something really weird has happened and the earth *has* moved into some new cycle or age or something. How does this explain you lot being here? This room being here? This is *your* room, isn't it? Your study in the Hidden Tower? "The location of which is known to yourself alone." Explain to me how I'm *here* talking to *you*. How you, a bunch of fictional characters, exist?'

'In all truth,' said Sir John, 'it is *you* who should do the explaining. As you say, you are *here* in *my* study, conversing with *myself* and *my* trusted companions. How do *you* explain that?'

'I don't,' said Maxwell. 'But then, frankly, I don't give a toss.'

Sir John made tut-tut-tuttings with his tongue.

Dr Harney pulled a pocket watch from his waistcoat and made a worried face at it.

Danbury Collins moved nervously from one foot to the other.

Dr Harney spoke. 'The last reader is almost halfway through the final chapter,' he said. 'We have hardly any time left. Max must know what he has to do before the book closes for ever upon us.'

Maxwell looked from face to worried face. 'What *is* going on?' he asked.

'All right!' Sir John leapt from the chesterfield. 'Max, you must know this. My companions and I *are* fictional characters. We have no objective reality. We only live within our readers' imaginations. But there we have life. There we exist. We have our adventures. We engross our readers. We become real. At this very moment, someone is reading this. Imbuing us with reality. Soon, however, they will become aware of the great change that has overtaken the planet. They will put down the book, never to open it again. Then we will cease for ever to be.'

'That's tragic,' said Maxwell.

'I do so agree. But there it is. That's why it is so important that we pass on to you our knowledge. Pass on the books of magic, which, though before had only power within the imagination of the reader, can, in this new world, bend space and effect change. Pass on the techniques and skills you will need to survive and succeed in this strange new world.'

'I'm very touched,' said Maxwell. 'But why *me* of all people? I'm just a work-shy bum. I have no special talents. Quite truthfully, I'm really rather dull.'

'Quite truthfully, you're really *very* dull.'

'Oh, thanks a lot.'

'But we have no choice in the matter. Dull old Maxwell Karrien will soon cease to be.'

'He will?'

'He will. To be replaced by Max Carrion, Imagineer.'

'Max Carrion,' said Maxwell. 'I quite like the sound of that. But what's an imagineer, for Goddess sake?'

'A kind of cross between Bladerunner, Terminator, Darkman and Doctor Strange.'

'Sounds a bit derivative.'

'You'll put a new slant on it.'

'I'm sure I won't.'

'I'm sure you will, Max. But listen, we must be quick. We can only talk to you like this because the reader is daydreaming for a moment. In a minute he will continue reading and then we must continue to act out our roles. We are powerless to alter the plot. We must pass on our skills to you now.'

Maxwell shook his head. 'But you still haven't told me why you've chosen *me* of all people for this.'

Sir John Rimmer sighed deeply. 'Because, my dear Max, it is *you* who are reading the book. *You* are the last reader.'

'*Me?*'

31

'You.'

'Oh.'

'You see,' said Dr Harney, 'fictional characters can't choose their readers. Would that they could. But as you are our final reader, to you we bequeath our knowledge. And . . .' He paused, his mouth hanging open, and ceased to move.

'Go on,' said Maxwell. 'What?'

'He . . .' Sir John half turned and then froze to a statue.

'What's happening? Danbury?'

Danbury Collins managed to say, 'The book is being read again. Now *he* comes.'

'*He?* Who?'

A violent knocking now came upon the chamber door that Maxwell had sought earlier to escape by, but failed to locate.

Dr Harney became galvanized into action. He twisted the pommel of his lacquered cane and drew from the shaft a shining blade.

Sir John was moving once again, this time towards the door.

'What's going on?' asked Maxwell, knowing something was and fumbling to free his bootlaces.

'Have a care,' called Sir John. 'He will not have come alone.'

'Who's he?' Maxwell slipped forward from his armchair and fell once more to the floor.

Elm splinters, shards of aspen inlay, fractured gilded bolts. The study door lurched from its hinges, smashed into the room.

Two monstrous forms – distorted heads with quills for hair and light bulb eyes, snapping jaws and pointed tongues, great barrel chests in leather harness and hands that reached down to the knees – charged forward, tumbling priceless antiques, elbowing aside the library globes and statuary. Roaring, yelling. Terrifying.

Maxwell took shelter beneath one of the satinwood escritoires and looked on fearfully as an alarming scene began to unfold.

'Back, foul spawn of Satan's bed-sit.' Sir John raised up his hands, uttered syllables, formed enigmatic figures with his fingers. Maxwell's ears popped as waves of pressure buffeted the room. Sparks crackled from Sir John's hands. Beams of energy flew from his contorted fingers and smote the monsters, fiercely, thus and so.

The things cried out in anguish, backed away and cowered. Then they shrivelled, guttered like two dying candles, and were gone.

'Rock 'n' Roll,' whispered Maxwell. 'Was that something else, or what?'

'Dr Harney, the scroll,' cried Sir John. 'He must not have the scroll.'

What scroll? thought Maxwell. And what *he*?

The doctor patted at his pockets. 'I don't have the scroll. It's gone from where I put it.'

'What?' whispered Maxwell, keeping his head down and struggling to untie his laces.

Sir John's face was grave. 'The scroll holds all the power,' he said. 'He that can decipher it will have ultimate control. It must never fall into the hands of the count. If it did, all would be lost.'

'Not for me it wouldn't.'

Maxwell jerked his head towards the speaker and was quite impressed by what he saw. Framed in the doorway was the very picture of evil: big and bald and bad to the bone; skin bone-white and clothes of graveyard black; the face, that mask of hatred and contempt that villains wear. The overall demeanour one of menace. Sinister and cruel.

'Count Waldeck,' said Sir John. 'We meet at last.'

'It's the count,' whispered Maxwell to his boots. 'Sir John's arch enemy. The Moriarty to his Sherlock Holmes. This must be the big confrontation scene in the final chapter of the book. The book I'm supposed to be reading at this very moment. And somehow I'm in it too. Because I'm so engrossed in it, or something. I suppose it makes some kind of sense, if you're prepared to let it. And I *am*.'

Maxwell's boots had no comment to make.

'You know what I've come for,' said the count. 'If you wish me to spare your lives, hand it over.'

'Never.' Sir John crooked his fingers, uttered words. Power welled. Light blazed. Then faltered. Fizzled. Fluttered and melted away.

'Bugger,' said Sir John.

The count dusted specks of white from night-clad shoulders. 'You would appear to have given me dandruff,' he said. 'But no matter.' He flung up his hands. Golden cords snaked across the room, whipped about Sir John, bound him fast.

Sir John fought and wriggled but to no avail.

'My magic is more powerful than your own,' sneered the count. 'The day is mine, I think.'

'But how did you find this place?' Sir John squared up in his bondage. 'Its location is a secret, known only to myself and my loyal companions.'

'Loyal?' The count raised an evil eyebrow, laughed an evil laugh.

'No.' Sir John turned his eyes to his companions. Dr Harney was bound fast. Danbury, however, was not.

'*You* told him?'

Danbury shuffled his DMs and giggled ghoulishly. 'Yeah, that's right.'

'But why?'

'Look, I didn't ask to be written. And it's more fun being the bad guy. Everyone knows that.'

'The scroll,' said the count. 'Where is the scroll?'

'Max has it,' said Danbury.

'Max? Who is this Max?'

Maxwell, who had finally freed his bootlaces, was edging towards the door.

'That Max,' said Danbury, pointing to the Max in question.

'Oh dear,' said Maxwell, climbing to his feet.

'Give me the scroll.'

Maxwell grinned a sickly grin. 'I don't have any scroll. And I'm really not supposed to be in this. Would it be all right if I just sort of slipped away?'

'No it would not. Give me the scroll.'

'I don't have any scroll.'

'He does,' said Danbury. 'I sent it to him in the mail yesterday, after I stole it from Dr Harney.'

'In the mail?' Maxwell dug into his inner pocket, pulled out a roll of paper. The Queen's Award for Industry Award (award). 'You don't mean this?'

'That's it. Give it to me now.' The count took a step forward.

Maxwell took one back. 'Not a chance,' said he.

'Give it to him.' Danbury made urging gestures. 'He'll let you join his gang.'

'I don't want to join his gang. He's a right bastard.'

'Bastards have more fun,' said the count.

'Surely that's *blondes* have more fun.'

'You could dye your hair,' said Danbury.

'You're a right little shit, you are.' Maxwell clutched the scroll of paper to his bosom. 'I'm not giving this to anyone. In fact, I'm going to rip the bloody thing to pieces.'

'You won't do that.'

'Oh no, and for why?'

Danbury smiled. 'Because you haven't the strength.'

'I have, you know.' Maxwell gripped the scroll between both hands and struggled without success to rip it up. 'I haven't,' he concluded, somewhat puffed. 'I wonder why that is.'

'Because I poisoned your cup of coffee. You have only moments to live.'

'You thorough going swine!'

'So I'll take *that*.' Danbury reached forward and tore the scroll from Maxwell's fingers. 'You can't change the plot. The count wins this time.'

'No.' Maxwell's fingers were turning numb. His mouth was growing dry.

'But yes.' Danbury knelt down before the count and offered up the scroll.

'Good boy, my loyal servant, now take this.' The count placed a silver pistol into the upraised hand. 'And kill them all.'

'Yes, my lord.' Danbury rose, turned and aimed the gun at Sir John.

'No,' croaked Maxwell. 'You can't do that. The series can't finish this way. It just can't.'

'It can, you know.' Danbury Collins cocked back the hammer and pulled the trigger. Maxwell turned his face away. Another shot rang out and Dr Harney too fell dead.

'No, no, no, no, no, no,' gagged Maxwell, slumping down onto his knees. 'It's all wrong. The bad guys can't win. By the Goddess, I feel sick.'

'That will pass,' said Danbury. 'Then you'll just feel dead.'

'Danbury,' said the count.

'Yes, master?'

'Shoot yourself in the head, will you?'

'Certainly, master, anything you say.'

Danbury put the pistol to his temple and shot his brains out. 'I think I might just have taken loyalty to extremes there,' he murmured, as he crumpled, lifeless, to the floor.

'Good lad.' The count made free with the evil grins and unrolled Maxwell's certificate. And then a look of some concern appeared upon his face. 'What is this?' he muttered. 'WHAT IS THIS?'

'It's a Queen's Award for Industry Award,' said Max, 'award.'

The count spun round.

And Maxwell raised his head.

There in the doorway stood himself, though looking somewhat better than he'd ever looked before. His hair was combed high into a shining crest. The face was tanned, corded with muscle about the hard-set mouth. The eyes were glinting beneath down-curving brows.

His hands were thrust deeply into the pockets of a simply splendid coat of black leather that reached almost to the ankles of a similarly splendid pair of riding boots. This coat hung open to reveal a cravat of dark material, secured by silver pins, a rich crimson brocade waistcoat and a number of belts, which holstered pistols, daggers and a samurai sword in a polished scabbard. His corduroy trousers bulged at the knees with pockets, which no doubt harboured further fearsome armament.

This Maxwell looked like he meant business.

'So,' said the count, 'I don't think we have been introduced.'

'The name is Carrion,' said Carrion, 'Max Carrion, Imagineer.'

'You don't look particularly imaginative, Mr Carrion. More like a cross between Bladerunner, Terminator, Darkman and Doctor Strange.'

37

'He looks bloody good to me,' croaked Maxwell, making unpleasant death-rattle sounds in his throat. 'But then, I am rather dull.'

'And you'll soon be rather dead,' said the count.

'But not before *you*,' said Max Carrion.

'Oh, don't waste my time, please.' Count Waldeck flung up his hands and made mystical passes. A stream of purple energy arced towards the chap in the simply splendid coat.

The chap moved not an eyelash.

The gush of power engulfed him. Stinging. Blistering. Consuming.

Max Carrion stood, cool and unconcerned.

The count's face contorted, he rocked upon his heels, ground his teeth, cast further bolts of force.

Max took a packet of Woodbine from his pocket, withdrew one, held it towards the flames that engulfed him and drew a puff or two.

'What?' The count grew purple in the face. His body rocked and shivered. More light came, but weaker. And then none at all.

'All done?' asked Max Carrion.

'What?' The count examined his fingers. They were a bit charred about the tips. He looked all done.

'I think he's all done,' said Max.

'I think he *is*,' said Maxwell.

'What?' went the count once more, turning to the seated poisoned fellow.

'You've run out of steam,' said that man, rising to his feet, then stooping to pluck the pistol from Danbury's dead hand.

'*What?*'

'You're all used up. And now you're dead.' Maxwell turned the pistol on the count, pulled the trigger and shot him.

'Nice one,' said Max.

'Thanks,' said Maxwell, blowing into the barrel.

'Congratulations,' said Sir John, dusting fragments of the golden bonds away from his person.

'A first-rate job,' agreed Dr Harney, jumping up and aiding the long man into the vertical. 'Most skilfully performed.'

'Thanks too,' said Maxwell.

Groan and croak, went the count. 'You shot me.'

Maxwell grinned down at him. 'Well, I couldn't have you win, could I?'

'But how did you do it? How did you change the ending? I was supposed to win.'

Maxwell's grin turned towards Sir John. 'Should I tell him?' he asked.

'I think you should,' said the long man. 'The villain always gets an explanation from his Nemesis. It's a tradition, or an old charter, or something.

'All right.' Maxwell looked down at the count. 'How are you doing for time?'

'I'll last about another minute, get a move on.'

'Right. OK. Well, it's all quite simple really. You see, under normal circumstances, a reader can't change the ending of the book he's reading. Even if he could, it wouldn't make any difference, because there'd be thousands of other copies around, being read by thousands of other people.

'But you see, this is different. As Sir John explained to me earlier, *I'm* the last reader. So I can do whatever I want. I read the book right through to the end. And I didn't like it, not with you winning and everything. So I flicked back a few pages, got a bottle of *Tippex* and made some changes. I wrote myself in. That's how I came to be here, you see. I wrote myself in as Sir John's new apprentice. I already knew of Danbury's treachery, so I took a few precautions. Like equipping Sir John and the doctor with bullet-proof vests and switching the poison Danbury put in my coffee for harmless sugar.'

'But who's the bastard in the simply splendid leather coat?' The count made feeble gestures towards Max Carrion.

Maxwell's grin was still on full. 'He's a figment of my imagination. Your powers were greater than Sir John's, so I had to have you use them all up. Then I could simply shoot you. Which I did.'

'Oh,' said the count. 'Well, fair enough. I suppose in the long run, it really doesn't matter which one of us wins. When you close the book we'll all cease to exist anyway.'

'True. But as the last reader, I felt it fitting that the book should end the way I wanted it to end.'

'Then I suppose I'm dead.'

'I suppose you are.'

And he was.

'Bravo,' said Sir John, adjusting his beard. 'You have certainly proved yourself an imagineer of the first order, Maxwell. What do you plan to do now?'

Maxwell scratched his head without shame. 'Close the book, then venture out into this strange new world, I suppose.'

'A sound idea. Our thoughts go with you.'

'So I trust will whatever books of magic spells you possess. Along with any powerful talismans and protective amulets. If magic works in this new age, then *I* shall be the one to work it.'

Sir John pursed his lips and shivered his beard. 'I regret to disappoint you there,' he said. 'Such items are beyond price and could never be considered as largess to propitiate a total stranger who just happened by through fortuitous circumstance.'

'What gratitude is this?' cried Maxwell. 'I am appalled by what I hear.'

'I promised you knowledge,' said Sir John. 'And knowledge I impart. It is the knowledge that you now possess a creative imagination sufficient to perform remarkable deeds. The knowledge that, should you choose to apply yourself to just causes, you will ultimately triumph over all who would prevail against you.'

'Such knowledge is no doubt profound,' said Maxwell uncheerily. 'But your propositions I believe to be somewhat quixotic. Perhaps you might spare me some minor spell from one of your great tomes to aid me on my way. One to instantly disable a potential enemy, multiply gold or indefinitely postpone the ravages of old age would not go unappreciated.'

'Cast such frivolous notions from your mind,' said Sir John. 'You are now Max Carrion, Imagineer. Think only of noble deeds and high moral standards. Dr Harney will show you to the door.'

'I won't stand for this,' declared Maxwell. 'I will rewrite it all. Where is my *Tippex*? Where's my Biro?'

'Many leagues away from here.'

'I have been shabbily used,' protested Maxwell. 'Don't think you can simply cast me out in such a churlish fashion. Am I not Max Carrion, Imagineer?'

'You certainly are,' said Sir John. 'Now Dr Harney, please, the door.'

3

Although Maxwell put up a respectable resistance, he was no match for Sir John and Dr Harney, who, at length, with the aid of sword stick and cricket bat, drove him from the premises.

Outside, with the great tower door now firmly slammed upon him, Maxwell fumed and cursed his erstwhile hosts, reserving especial tirades of condemnation for the infamy of his imaginized double. He of the simply splendid coat who had, throughout the uneven struggle, stood passively by, smoking a Wild Woodbine and showing not the least concern for the welfare of his creator.

When finally he had run himself dry of invective and bruised many toes through futile door-kicking, Maxwell marshalled his thoughts. It was time to go home.

Now the first of Maxwell's marshalled thoughts was that, as he was now no longer in the book he had apparently been reading, he should therefore be back in his own front room, sitting in his armchair, the very book upon his knees and *Bic* and *Tippex* close to hand. A glance about at his alien surroundings, however, assured him that this was not, in fact, the case.

Maxwell stood upon a promontory of tended grass that rose from picturesque foundations. Story-book meadows and cultivated pasture lands spread from near to far away.

Above, Sir John's Hidden Tower reared in Gothic splendour, a babble of carved pink stone, helmeted by turrets and cupolas that blinked in the golden sunlight. All very nice if you like that kind of thing. But Maxwell did not.

'I must imagine that I'm home,' Maxwell told himself. 'And then I will be. Imagine that I have closed the book and that I am home. And then I will awaken from this daydream or nightmare or whatever.' Maxwell closed his eyes, screwed his face into an expression of deep concentration and thought himself back home.

'There,' said Maxwell, opening his eyes. Then, 'By the Goddess!' he continued.

He was still where he had been a moment before. But now the vista had drastically changed. The grass about him rose in course blades almost to his waist, the story-book meadows and cultivated pasture lands had become gorse-grown moorlands, the Hidden Tower was nothing but a jumble of fallen stone.

Maxwell made a rueful face and hugged his arms. There was a definite chill in the air, and the reason for it was all too plain to see. Above the barren landscape, in a clear and cloudless sky, the sun hung nearly at its zenith. But the sun was strange: swollen, bloated, ruby red, as if about to set. A thin black line was evident about the solar disc.

Maxwell made a sullen sound to go with his rueful face. '*That* is not my fault,' he murmured. '*I* did not do *that*.'

Maxwell gazed about the cheerless panorama. Where was he? Still in England? Perhaps not. Was there somewhere in the world where the sun looked like that? Greenland? Iceland? Tierra del Fuego? Patagonia?

Maxwell sniffed the air. Did it smell like England? What did England smell like anyway? An American he'd once met had told him that France smelled of garlic and *Gauloise* and England smelled of stale beer and boiled cabbage. Maxwell recalled that the American smelled of cheese, but couldn't remember why, although it had been explained to him at the time.

'Wherever I am, I have no wish to be here.' Maxwell took half a step forward and fell on his face. Tied boot laces again? It was far from amusing. Maxwell struggled with his feet. They were literally grown over, knotted with ground weed and stinkweed. He kicked and thrashed and fought himself free. Two dark dead patches of soil remained to mark the spot where he had been standing. 'I'm out of here,' said Maxwell.

He trudged down the promontory, hands deep in trouser pockets, jacket collar turned up to the chill. Out onto the gorsy waste. But which way? 'South,' he decided and trusting to that in-built sense of direction that all men claim to possess, struck off towards the west.

The going wasn't easy and neither was it pleasant. Small stinging beasties of the gnat persuasion swarmed up to feast upon his exposed fleshy parts. Something howled ominously in the distance and the dreariness of the gorsy waste relieved itself periodically by suddenly giving way to a boggy morass into which Maxwell stumbled without let or hindrance.

The sun moved on before him, which puzzled Maxwell who found himself hard put to calculate which portion of the globe it was, where the sun set in the south.

It was with no small sense of relief therefore that he finally tripped through a ragged overgrown hedge and fell onto the side of a road.

Though it wasn't much of a road.

More of a track.

It had the look of having once been a road and by its width, one much travelled. But now it was gone to fragmentation, burst through by beggarweed and spark heather. Maxwell looked up the road and down and consoled himself with the traveller's verity that 'A road always leads to somewhere'.

'Hm,' went Maxwell. 'West or east? West, I think.' And so saying he began to plod northward.

He had plodded for more than an hour, blessing, with almost every step he took, the substantial nature of his substantial boots, when he saw it.

Away in the distance.

But bright as a shilling in a sweep's behind and beautiful as Bexhill was to Betjeman.

A bus-stop.

With a shelter.

And, by all the grace of the Goddess herself . . .

With people waiting in it!

Maxwell's plod became a walk, his walk a stride, his stride a springing, joyous goose-step prance.

As he drew nearer, Maxwell became aware that this was not just any old bus-stop with a shelter. This was the mother of all old bus-stops with shelters. It was painted in rich hues of orange, green and gold and decked all around and about with garlands of gazania, olive branch and bulbous reticulata.

Three persons stood within this colourful bower of a shelter. Next to the stop itself, which was adorned with yellow ribbons, stood an old dear clutching two Budgen's carrier-bags, next to her a grim-looking youth with a six-hair beard sprouting from a flock of pubic chin-blossoms and next to him a lady of middle years clutching the remnants of what once had been one of those impossible-to-foldaway foldaway buggies. All looked sorely down at heel and all looked towards

Maxwell with expressions which could best be described as doubtful.

Maxwell made a cheery face and approached with a waving hand. The three persons acknowledged his waves with troubled twitchings of the shoulders and then turned down their eyes.

Maxwell chanced to glance down and noted with no small degree of puzzlement that the section of road which lay before the stop and shelter had been carefully weeded, filled, restored, swept clean and painted over in a glossy black.

Maxwell shrugged. These folk obviously were hoping to gain a first in the Best Kept Bus-Stop of the Year Competition. Thoughts of competitions and awards suddenly drew Maxwell up short. He had all but forgotten about his Queen's Award for Industry Award (award). He had left it behind in Sir John's now-vanished Hidden Tower. Maxwell gave his lip a curl. When he got home he would certainly put things right. Phrases such as 'his massive piles made his every waking minute a hell on earth' would be inserted into the paragraphs referring to the ungrateful Mr Rimmer. Oh yes indeed!

The three persons had now returned their gaze to Maxwell, who hastily uncurled his lip, resumed his cheersome grin and said, as he drew near, 'I cannot tell you just how happy it makes me to find this stop and shelter here.'

Two of the three faces lit up like Swan Vestas. The youth, however, remained disposed to gloom.

'Then you are of The Queue?' asked the old dear.

English bus-stop, English speech – I'm in England! thought Maxwell. 'Praise be,' he said aloud.

'Praise be indeed,' said the old dear. 'Welcome, brother.'

'Thank you,' Maxwell stepped up to take his place

behind the lady of middle years, who clutched the non-foldaway foldaway.

She looked him up and down. 'Make the sign then,' she said.

'Pardon me?' replied Maxwell.

The lady extended her arm, as one would when hailing a cab, or stopping a bus.

'Oh I see. Request stop, yes?' Maxwell extended his arm in a likewise fashion, then tucked both his hands into his trouser pockets.

'Praise be,' said the old dear once more.

Maxwell offered her a smile. 'Been waiting long?' he asked.

'We are here for the afternoon wait, yes.'

Maxwell nodded. 'I confess that I'm a stranger to these parts. Where do we go to from here?'

The three persons now cast Maxwell mystified expressions. 'To Terminus, of course!' spat the dour young man. 'Where else?'

'Where else indeed. And in which town would the terminus be?'

'Town?' The young man looked long and hard at Maxwell. 'Are you sure that you are of The Queue?'

'Here I stand,' said Maxwell, 'as your eyes will testify.'

'Then where is your token of penance?'

'I am perplexed,' said Maxwell. 'Would you care to explain?'

The young man glared at Maxwell, then, as if resigning himself to the fact that he was clearly addressing a simpleton, said, 'None may travel to Terminus without their token of penance. See the old woman carries the *get-a-move-on-with-those* shoppering sacks. This lady holds the *I-can't-let-you-on-with-that-thing* wheel-about, and I . . .' The young man removed a crumpled piece of paper from his pocket and flourished it before Maxwell's eyes. 'I have the *I-don't-have-change-for-anything-that-big-you'll-have-to-get-off* parchment.'

Maxwell viewed the item being flourished before him. It was *not* a money note. He looked from one to another of his fellow queuers, then he looked once more up and down the road. And then a thought entered his head, which really should have entered it earlier.

There was no possible way that any bus could ever travel along this ruined track! Something was very very wrong about these folk.

'Ahem.' Maxwell cleared his throat and sought to compose questions which might evoke clear and unambiguous answers, whilst offering no offence. He addressed his first one to the old dear.

'Good woman,' he said, 'I observe that you are at the head of the queue. Might I enquire as to just how long, overall, you have waited here?'

The old dear smiled a proud smile. 'I have observed the morning wait, the afternoon wait and the "last one cancelled", three times a week for the past forty years. When I am finally taken up to Terminus, my son Kevin here will have my place.'

Maxwell's throat made a gagging sound. '*Forty years?*' he said in a harsh whisper. '*Forty years?*'

'As my mother did before me and hers before her, dating back to the Time of Transition.'

'The time of transition?'

'When the old aeon ended and the new one began.'

'But . . . but . . .' Maxwell now had a serious shake on. 'But that was yesterday, surely?'

'Yesterday?' The young man guffawed. 'You are a buffoon and no mistake. The old aeon ended a century ago.'

'No,' said Maxwell. 'No, no, no.'

The lady of middle years stretched out a hand to finger the fabric of Maxwell's jacket. 'This antique costume the buffoon wears is of royal stuff. Such a jacket would suit you well, Kevin.'

'Much so,' said Kevin, affecting a covetous leer.

'Stop!' Maxwell tore himself away from the lady's tightening grip. He was now in a state of confusion and alarm. A century gone since the earth left the Age of Technology and passed into whatever it had? A century? Then everyone he knew ... everyone he loved ... his wife ... well, he didn't love *her*. He was glad to see the back of *her*. But he'd never have wished her *dead*. This was terrible ...

'What fleeting reason he had, has now deserted him,' said the lady. 'Mark well that I claim his boots.'

'Stand aside!' Maxwell reached forward, grabbed the youth by the ragged collar of his rustic coat and drew him almost from his feet. 'Questions,' said Maxwell, 'to which you will furnish answers.'

The youth's head bobbed up and down. 'Yes, sir,' said he.

'Firstly, what year is this?'

The youth looked hopelessly towards his mum. Maxwell gave him a teeth-rattling shake. 'The ninety-eighth year, sir,' he said.

'And no bus has been along this road for ninety-eight years?' There was much desperation in Maxwell's voice. It was not lost upon the youth.

'It will come,' cried the old woman. 'Varney will come and carry the faithful to Terminus. We tend the shrine. There will be room for us on top.'

'It's a bloody cargo cult,' declared Maxwell. 'And Varney? Who's Varney?'

'Varney is the driver,' said the old dear – she didn't look quite so dear now – 'who is also known as Butler.'

'*Reg* bloody Varney?' Maxwell let the youth go limp.

'This shelter, this stop, is a shrine to Reg bloody Varney?'

'Blasphemer!' The old woman threw up her hands, dropping her shopping bags, which spilled out stones and clods of earth. 'I declare the afternoon wait at an end. Slay the heretic!'

'You're all barking.' Maxwell gave the youth a shove, propelling him onto the section of blackly painted road where he fell in a heap. 'Barking mad.'

'Outrage!' The old woman covered her face with her hands. 'Sacrilege! The Highway to Heaven is despoiled.'

'Cease this madness now.' Maxwell shook his fists in the air. 'There is *no* bus. There is *no* Varney. You're wasting away your lives. Ninety-eight years, waiting for a bus that will never come, to carry you off to some terminus in the sky. How long must you wait to learn the folly of your ways?'

The old woman crooked a finger at Maxwell. 'Unbeliever, iconoclast, son of some faithless harlot.'

'How dare you?' said Maxwell. 'My mother wasn't faithless.' And the cold shiver passed through him once more for the mother he would never see again. 'My mother was a Christian,' said Maxwell.

'Oh yes?' The old woman gave a mocking laugh. 'My grandmother told me of that sect. You scorn a wait of a mere ninety-eight years. Then tell me how long your mother's lot waited in vain for their deity to make his second coming?'

Good point, thought Maxwell. 'That is neither here nor there,' he said.

The youth had now raised himself from the painted section of road. He snatched up a rock from the selection which had spilled from his mum's shoppers and brandished it menacingly. 'I must bear a mighty penance for soiling the sacred tary-mac. The-case-

of-suits-which-is-not-allowed-on-the-top-deck.   Your
broken bones will fill this case.'

Maxwell took a smart step backards. 'This is a
theological discussion,' said he. 'There is no cause for
violence.'

'The violence is all of your making. You began it.'

Good point also, thought Maxwell. 'Now see here,'
he said, as the two women began to sort amongst the
stones. 'Now see—'

'Stone the heretic!' cried the old woman.

Maxwell weighed up his chances. They weren't
good. He could strike the surly young man, but
hardly the two women. And if he simply turned tail
and ran there was the strong possibility that he might
be brought to book by a well-aimed stone to the skull.

Well, thought Maxwell, if you're going down in
flames, try to hit something big. 'Cease this behaviour
at once,' said Maxwell, in no uncertain voice. 'Do you
not recognize me?'

'No!' agreed the three, hefting their missiles.

'I am The Inspector.' Maxwell uttered this with such
authority that he almost surprised himself.

'You are *who*?' The old woman halted in mid swing.

'The Inspector,' said Maxwell. 'Surely you have
heard of The Inspector.'

Heads nodded. They had *indeed* heard of The
Inspector.

The young man's head ceased to nod first. 'Hah,'
said he. 'If you are The Inspector, where is your
uniform?'

'This *is* my uniform.' Maxwell straightened the lapels
on his Oxfam zoot suit.

'He lies.' Kevin raised his stone once more.

'You have seen an Inspector's uniform before?'
Maxwell ventured. 'How, then, does it differ from my
own?'

'I . . .' Kevin did not have a ready answer to this question.

'And let me ask you this: do you know the role of The Inspector?'

'Of course. He judges all who enter Terminus.'

'Thus and so,' said Maxwell, who had been hoping for such a reply. 'And thus you *are* judged.'

'*Judged?*' Young Kevin almost raised his stone once more.

Almost, but not quite.

'Judged,' said Maxwell. 'And *not* found wanting. I, The Inspector, came to test your faith. Ask yourself, would any ordinary man dare what I have dared?'

'Well . . . no . . .' said Kevin. 'I suppose . . .'

'No indeed.' Maxwell thrust out his chest. 'I mocked your beliefs. I blasphemed the holy name of Varney. I cast you down onto the sacred tary-mac. And why did I do this?'

'To test our faith?' asked the old woman.

'Correct,' said Maxwell. 'And I am greatly pleased. Pleased with how well you have tended the shrine. Pleased with how stoically you bear your penances. Pleased that you would not be moved from your faith. And as such I now reward you.'

'We shall be taken at once to Terminus?' The old woman thrust out her arm towards the road. Her son and the lady with the non-foldaway foldaway thrust theirs out also.

'Hold very tight please,' they chorused. 'Ding ding.'

Maxwell raised a hand as in benediction. 'All will be rewarded in Terminus,' he said kindly. 'Varney will call for each of you when the time is right. You have no further need to wait here. Return to your homes. Live useful and caring lives. Tell others of the faith that The Inspector came unto you and that no longer need any serve at the shrines.'

'What? No more waits?' A look of transcending relief appeared upon the old woman's face. 'No more must we stand throughout the wind, rain and chill?'

'No more. I hereby relieve you of all such obligations. And through my relief of you, so also all others of the faith. No more waits for anyone. Any more. Ever.'

'We can just go home and live caring lives? This is enough?'

'More than enough. You have kept the faith well. Such is your reward.'

'Gosh,' said the lady with the non-foldaway foldaway.

'Such is as Varney wills it.' Maxwell mimed a little steering-wheel motion. 'Now be gone.'

The queuers looked at Maxwell, looked at each other, opened their mouths to speak, closed them again and began to sink to their knees.

'No kneeling,' Maxwell told them. 'No more worshipping of any kind. Varney has had worshipping enough. This is his message that I pass on to you.'

'Thanks be. Thanks be,' was the general feeling all round.

Kevin said, 'What of you, Inspector? Will you not come with us? Spread the word to all yourself?'

Maxwell gave this a moment of thought. As a visiting god he might expect to receive a great deal of hospitality at the tables of his worshippers. Comfy beds would be offered and possibly young maidens to share them with. Maxwell came within a gnat's organ or saying, 'Yes indeed,' but did not.

It occurred to him also that a visiting god would like as not be expected to show some proof of his divinity, such as turning water into wine, for instance, or munching hot coals. A god who failed to perform such trifling feats might well find himself called upon

53

to demonstrate his invulnerability to shotgun shells.

'No,' said Maxwell firmly. 'I must travel on. To other shrines.'

'Pity,' said Kevin. 'I'd have liked to have seen you swallowing hot coals.'

'Another time perhaps,' Maxwell breathed an inward sigh of relief. 'So farewell. Farewell. And don't forget what I have told you.'

The lady offered Maxwell her non-foldaway. Maxwell took it. 'Go in peace,' he said.

And so they drifted off across the wretched moorland. Maxwell watched them, waved when they turned to wave to him, then flung away the non-foldaway and resumed his trudge to the north.

The troubled sun was heading down the sky as Maxwell struck off once more along the ruined road. But it didn't detract from the curious sense of well-being he felt.

True, he was all alone in this strange new world and true and terrible the knowledge that his loved ones were now nothing more than memory. And the anger he felt towards Sir John had not died away.

· For surely it was he who had somehow bucketed Maxwell into the future by nearly one hundred years – a somewhat drastic course of action to insure that Maxwell did not get home and change the ending of the book. An efficient one also.

But, of course, that was all now in the past. Considerably so in fact. Sir John would now be long dead, but here was he, Maxwell, in the present. And, if he was to be honest with himself, well pleased to leave the past behind him. Especially *the wife* behind him. He was here, now, in the new world, with everything to look forward to and not very much to look back on. And he felt very much alive. He, Max Carrion,

Imagineer. He had performed his first noble deed, freed a group of people from the yoke of superstition. He'd done well and it was only his first day on the job.

Maxwell drew back his shoulders, stuck out his chest and put a new spring into his step.

He had just begun to whistle when he heard it: a low rumble. Not thunder? thought Max. That's hardly fitting.

The rumble grew into a growl.

Not some wild beast?

Max turned in his tracks and stared back along the ruined road. Something large was heading his way. Something large and red, swelling in size as it drew nearer and nearer.

Maxwell's eyes widened.

It was a bus!

It was a big red London bus!

Maxwell's eyes became very big and wide indeed. The bus bore down upon him. Accelerating. Maxwell dithered, knowing not which way to flee. Certainly not forward. To the side then. Into a ditch. Maxwell made to take that dive, but tripped over an untied bootlace and fell once more onto his face.

The bus rushed forward, nearer and nearer. As Maxwell fell he caught a fleeting glimpse of the driver's face. For a split second they faced each other, eye to eye. The driver had a smiley face. There was no doubt at all in Maxwell's mind as to whom that face belonged.

'Reg . . .' Maxwell screamed and tried to roll himself into a ball. But the big red bus was on him.

Maxwell held his breath and awaited the hideous life-stopping crunch.

But the hideous crunch didn't come.

Maxwell opened his eyes and looked up.

And up.

The bus had risen from the road and was sailing into the sky.

And there wasn't just one bus.

There were three of them. One behind the other.

And they were all empty!

Maxwell gaped, open-mouthed, and watched as they ascended into the heavens, bound, no doubt, for Terminus.

'Well I'll be . . .' But Maxwell said no more, for to his ears there now came shouts and screams. Glancing once again along the way that he had come, Maxwell spied three figures running towards him. One old, one young and one of middle years. They were picking up stones as they ran.

'Bastard!' they cried, and names far worse. 'You made us miss it! You made us miss it!'

Sensing that further theological debate would probably serve no positive purpose at this time, Maxwell took to his substantial heels and fled towards the north.

4

The travelling TV was a large and histrionic affair, solidly constructed of worthy oak and elaborately embellished in alliterative *découpage*. Sundry smiles smothered its sides. Scandalized statesmen and seductive super models. Sensational sports folk and sullen serial killers. Scathing satirists and sedentary scientists. Sober scholars and the scabrous singers of scatological songs.

A somewhat staggering sight.

This whole was mounted upon four sturdy wheels and furnished with a towing bar and ox harness. A zany, done up in the multi-hued costume of his calling – long-billed cap of tawny red, green felt tunic with slashed sleeves and blue silk cummerbund, pink tights and blue suede brothel creepers – pranced about amongst the viewing public who had gathered in the town's square, soliciting alms and acting the warm-up man.

Having finally satisfied himself that he had wrung from the gathering all he was likely to wring, he pranced up to the travelling TV and made much of polishing the screen and carefully adjusting the knobs.

Now he hushed the crowd to silence with a finger to his lips, counted down the seconds on a Goliath pocket watch, flipped the set's *on* button and, bowing, backed away.

The screen cleared and lit up to reveal the face of Dayglo Hilyte, news teller. Dayglo wore a pale grey skin toner, dark eye shadow and black lip gloss. His bald head had stencilled curls snaking down each cheek. The widow's peak which began an inch above his pencilled eyebrows made his face appear an ungodly chimera of Mickey Mouse and Bela Lugosi.

At the sight of Dayglo Hilyte, several small children amongst the viewing public began to weep and bury their faces into their mothers' laps.

Dayglo Hilyte opened his mouth, spoke words, but said nothing. The zany hastened to adjust the sound control.

Dayglo made himself heard. '. . . in a heated exchange during Prime Minister's·question time today, the leader of the opposition, Pasha Ali Ben Jumada described the Government's devolution policy as ill-conceived and indefensible. The granting of home rule, not only to Scotland and Wales but also The Isle of Wight, each separate county, each borough, city, town and village, each street, shop and individual home, was, he said, a move taken to confuse the general public and distract them from noticing that the Government had now lost all control and was utterly incapable of maintaining any rule whatsoever over anything.

'The Prime Minister responded to this allegation by stating that he had pledged himself to the policy of home rule. That home rule should exist in every home, especially his own, and that the leader of the opposition, Pasha Ali Ben Jumble Sale, was an unscrupulous mischief-maker with the libido of a March hare.

'The leader of the opposition, Pasha Ali Ben Jumbo Jet responded by describing the Prime Minister as a pot-walloping parvenu and drew the analogy that, as water always found its own level, so too did scum, which inevitably rose to the very top.

'At this point swords were drawn on both sides of the House and the speaker cried out for order. The member for Brentford North elicited much laughter by calling back that "his was a pint of Large please". The speaker, through tears of laughter, demanded that the leader of the opposition, Pasha Ali Ben Jump Suit, apologize at once to the Prime Minister. Pasha Ali Ben Jock Strap declined to do so and said that, for the record, if it wasn't for the vacuum in the Prime Minister's head, his bowels would fall out of his bottom. And that if the Prime Minister was a quarter of the man the Prime Minister's wife knew the leader of the opposition to be in bed, he would step outside and settle the matter with his sleeves rolled up. Highlights from the fight will be brought to you during our evening broadcast.

'Science news now and Greenwich Observatory has confirmed the findings of the Royal Astronomer Sir Patrick Moore, that the earth is no longer revolving about the sun, nor spinning on its axis. Sir Patrick described the planet as being in stasis, with the sun now orbiting it once every twenty-four hours. He also endorsed the statement recently made by the Archbishopess of Canterbury, that the sun was not a great big ball of fire, because, if it was, then where was all the smoke? The Archbishopess's pronouncement that the sun was, in fact, a very large lens, which focused the radiance of heaven onto the earth, was, Sir Patrick said, probably not far off the mark.

'And now the weather.' A little hatch opened in the side of the travelling TV and Dayglo Hilyte stuck his hand out. 'Dry,' said he. 'And that is the end of the news.'

The crowd in the town square clapped enthusiastically, then dissolved into its component parts and drifted away.

Dayglo Hilyte climbed through a doorway to the rear of the travelling TV, stretched, cursed and then set to examining the contents of the contributions sack.

'Mostly parsnips again, I'm afraid,' said his zany.

'Parsnips, bloody parsnips.' The news teller made and raised fists. 'Back in the days of the station, it would have been account lunches at Soho Soho. Pigging it out on Italian designer dishes. A starter of sun-dried tomatoes and focaccia, with lashings of fresh basil and virgin olive oil. Then—'

'Spare me,' said the zany. 'It is parsnips again today, and that's all there is to it. Had you not elected that we eat the ox, we would not be trapped in this godless hole, living on naught but parsnips.'

'I cannot survive upon a diet of vegetables,' whinged the news teller. 'They are affecting my metabolism, I find myself leaning towards the sun.'

'Get a fire going,' said the zany. 'Unless you would prefer to eat them raw.'

'Outrageous.'

A pale shadow, cast by the troubled sun, fell across the zany causing him to look up from his parsnip-sorting and offer a curt, 'What of you?'

The owner of the shadow inclined his head and grinned a cheersome grin. 'Pardon me,' said this body, 'but I couldn't help but overhear your conversation.'

'You are pardoned,' said the zany. 'Now be on your way.'

'The name is Carrion,' said Carrion. 'Max Carrion, Imagineer.'

The zany looked Max up and down. 'You look like a beggar man to me and you twang like a cow's behind.'

Max examined the soles of his substantial boots. 'Pardon me once more,' he said, scraping something smelly from the left.

It had been a month since Maxwell's unfortunate

60

encounter with the followers of Varney. An instructive month, and one which had determined him upon a course of action.

Maxwell had travelled north, seeking refuge where he could amongst the hamlets he chanced upon. He earned victual and shelter by entertaining his hosts with antique songs of the 'doo wop' persuasion and tales of days gone by. The story telling was well received and with an unlimited fund of movie plots to draw upon and the entire Walt Disney catalogue at his disposal, Maxwell had left more than one farmstead with a well-stocked rucksack on his back and a tuneless rendition of 'When You Wish Upon a Star' harassing his ears.

He had learned to avoid the use of words which provoked looks of stupefaction and bafflement. Among these were 'electricity', 'telecommunications' and any reference to the internal combustion engine and what was now considered its improbable applications.

As he moved from place to place, Maxwell sought to tease from his hosts what histories had been passed down to them, regarding the time of the great change. Those who would speak muttered only of terrors and tribulations that were better left beyond the reach of memory. They then demanded to hear once more the adventures of Winnie the Pooh.

Maxwell's wanderings, though ever north, were aimless and he was irked by the lack of purpose. Although in his former life he had been content to summer his time reading fantasy in the public library, now he was an adventurer himself, cast adrift in a fantastic realm, and he just wasn't making the best of it. He had to find some goal. Some *raison d'être*.

Some noble cause.

Any noble cause!

And so, in search of this, Maxwell's wanderings had

brought him at length to Grimshaw, the largest town in the principality.

Grimshaw was a market town, home to some nine hundred souls, and raised in the nouveau-medievalist style which prevailed everywhere. Maxwell had seen little or nothing in the way of extant twentieth-century architecture and he surmised, correctly enough, that without electricity, most twentieth-century habitation soon became uninhabitable.

In Grimshaw Maxwell determined that he would set himself up as *Solver of Problems Supremo*, accepting any challenge that would offer him scope to flex his mental muscles. Discarding modesty and bashfulness with the ease of one casting out those nasty advert enclosures that clog up the pages of a new *Radio Times*, Maxwell envisioned himself as some kind of twenty-first-century consulting saint. A cross between Sherlock Holmes and Gandhi, slicing through Gordian knots, bringing succour to the downtrodden, deftly defogging the most mysterious of mysteries, innovating social reform and, in short, sorting out all the problems of the new world.

Having made scrupulous checks that he infringed no local bylaws, Maxwell set up a booth of bartered canvas in the town square. This served him as business premises and sleeping quarters and before it he hung a sign which read, simply:

MAX CARRION
IMAGINEER
ALL PROBLEMS SOLVED

And then he awaited the rush.

And waiting it still was he.

So far he had been called upon to solve only two problems. The first being to trace the whereabouts of a lost dog, the second to seek the cause of blockage in the town's latrine. Although hardly grist to the thought-mill of an imagineer and sadly lacking for chivalrous adventure, Maxwell had accepted both commissions, working on the 'great oaks from little acorns grow' principle.

And he had been successful in both commissions, hauling, as he did, the corpse of the lost dog from the sewage outflow pipe.

One party had defaulted in payment, however.

But the mayor of the town had paid Maxwell handsomely.

In parsnips.

The arrival of the travelling TV had raised Maxwell's spirits no end, and, as the Imagineering business was a bit slack, he had taken to viewing the daily performances. And while so doing, a grandiose scheme had entered his mercurial mind, which he now felt he should translate into deeds for the benefit of all.

Good chap.

'Are you still here?' asked the zany. 'Bugger off, will you?'

'I have come to offer you my services,' said Maxwell.

'Now that is pleasing to my ears.' The zany sliced parsnips into an earthenware casserole. 'Hitch yourself to the towing bar and be prepared to pull us out of town once we have eaten.'

'Your humour is well received.' Maxwell squatted down beside the zany. 'But the services I offer are more cerebral in nature.'

'Who is this clod?' asked Dayglo Hilyte, shambling over with a bundle of kindling.

'This is Max Carrion, Imagineer,' explained the zany. 'He has come to proffer his services.'

'Splendid, then hitch him up to the towing bar.'

'Your servant has already split my sides with that particular witticism,' said Maxwell. 'However, I have a proposition to put to you which I think you will find most beneficial.'

'Oh yes?' Dayglo raised a pencilled eyebrow. 'How much will this proposition cost us?'

'It is utterly free of charge. I act through altruism alone.'

'Then we will be most pleased to hear it.'

Max sat down on the ground and looked on whilst Dayglo and his zany continued with the preparation of their bleak repast.

'It is regarding this news of yours,' said Max.

Dayglo made a proud face beneath his make-up. 'It is fine news, is it not?'

'Fine news indeed, but somewhat out of date.'

'Out of date?' Dayglo puffed his cheeks. 'How can such fine news ever date?'

'It hardly addresses current issues.'

Dayglo Hilyte laughed. 'My news is the last news ever to be broadcast upon the networks before they closed down for ever at the time of the great transition. This news is the property of my family. It has been handed down from generation to generation.'

'So much I surmised,' said Max. 'But I feel that you are somehow missing the point of what news is actually supposed to be.'

'Oh yes? And what is *that* then?'

'Well, as I said, news should address current issues. It should relate information about important or interesting recent events.'

'Tish and tosh.' Dayglo laughed once more. 'This is archaic thinking. I am a learned man and possess books dating back to the former aeon. In those benighted times, although the food was perhaps more varied, the news was never the same two days running. It was forever changing, here today and gone tomorrow. You could never take hold of it, be secure with it, say, this news I like and this news I will keep. Happily such times are dead and done with.'

'Perhaps so,' said Maxwell. 'But consider this. You have now been here for a week, telling your same piece of news, and daily your audience diminishes. How would you explain that?'

'In truth I am at a loss to explain it.' Dayglo arranged kindling beneath the casserole pot. 'Although we have observed this phenomenon repeatedly in other places.'

'Perhaps if you had different news to offer each day, folk would hurry in droves *each day* to hear of it.'

'Had you been listening more carefully,' said the zany, 'you would have noticed that we already do this. The leader of the opposition's name is changed several times at each telling, to provide novelty and extra amusement.'

Maxwell shifted to another tack. 'Do you never tire of reciting the same pieces of news again and again, year after year?'

'I never tire of eating,' replied Dayglo. 'My eating and my news telling are inextricably bound together.'

Maxwell peered into the pot. Dayglo did likewise. Thoughts were possibly shared.

'But surely,' said Maxwell, 'during your constant travels you must pick up all manner of information that would interest your viewing public.'

Dayglo made an outraged face. 'I am not some disseminator of rumour and gossip. I am a teller of news, which is a noble calling.'

'Quite so,' said Maxwell. 'And few nobler. Before the time of the great transition it was well known that the reason there were so many corrupt politicians about was that all the good and true men of noble calling and unimpeachable morality worked as journalists.

'But casting aside rumour and gossip, as one naturally would, surely you have heard hard facts, genuine information, that might be passed on to your viewing public in order to enrich their lives.'

Dayglo gave this matter some thought. 'I did hear something last week,' he said.

'Go on.'

'In the lands to the south I heard that an iconoclast had defiled one of the shrines of Varney and that the worshippers have put a bounty on his head. Is this the kind of information you have in mind?'

Maxwell made an involuntary croaking sound. 'Not specifically. Something of more local interest perhaps.'

'I have it on good authority that the mayor's wife is enjoying a sexual relationship with another man.'

The zany, who had been chewing on a raw parsnip, now made an identical croaking noise to that just made by Max. 'That would certainly be rumour,' he gasped, when he could find his breath. 'And should *not* be broadcast abroad.'

Dayglo smiled warmly upon his servant, then not quite so warmly upon Max. 'So there you have it,' said he. 'The reinstatement of your archaic principle could never work successfully. I have suggested two items of current interest and both have been immediately censored. The telling of different news every day would be fraught with such difficulties and be open to all forms of corruption and abuse.' The news teller fixed Maxwell with a most meaningful stare. 'Let us say, out of idle speculation, that I chose to relate the icono-clast news to the viewing public and, say, that the iconoclast himself learned in advance of my intention. Do you not think he might seek to *bribe* me in order to preserve my silence?'

Maxwell returned the news teller's meaningful stare. 'Clearly *I* cannot imagine what thoughts go on in the mind of such a maniac. Out of similarly idle speculation I feel it more likely he would *slit your throat*!'

'No doubt aided by the lover of the mayor's wife,' the zany added, 'out of fear that similar exposure awaited him.'

'Ahem.' Dayglo massaged his throat. 'I am, of course, merely hypothesizing. But you take my point, I'm sure.'

'Indeed I do.' Maxwell rose and stretched. 'So we are agreed then. I will provide you with good and wholesome news which will educate, instruct, inform and satisfy. No sleaze, no rumour, no gossip. Fine news, but new news.'

'Stop right there.' Dayglo Hilyte leapt to his feet. 'I agree to no such thing. My news is the finest news there is, unsullied by the vagaries of day-to-day existence. Although . . .' And here he paused once more for thought. 'Should I consider such a radical departure from the norm, would I be provided with a news crumpet?'

'A news crumpet?' Maxwell asked.

'A news crumpet. It is my understanding, that the news tellers of ancient times were always assisted by a news crumpet. A glamorous young woman who provided for the sexual fantasies of the male viewing public and dealt with the second-rate news items that were beneath the dignity of the male news teller to relate.'

'That's not quite how I would have put it,' said Maxwell. 'But it is in essence correct.'

'And I would get one of these?'

'Well,' said Maxwell, 'I don't see why not.'

'The mayor has a most attractive daughter,' said the zany, 'or so I've heard, anyway.'

'That's settled then,' said Maxwell. 'Now listen to what I have in mind. Picture, if you will, a year from now. Imagine, as I have, a network of news gatherers covering the country. An information supertrackway.

Each town and village with its own permanent TV set. You at the head of a mighty organization dedicated to education and instruction, to engender progress, to raise standards. To—'

'Hold hard,' cried the news teller. 'Although wildly ambitious, there is much here to inspire one of noble calling such as myself, *but* I spy a very large flaw in your concept.'

'Which is?'

'Which is, who is going to pay for all this? The takings from the contributions sacks could at best support only the news teller and his crumpet. Who would pay these seekers after news who must scour the countryside?'

'You would,' said Maxwell. 'Out of the huge revenues you would receive.'

'Huge revenues? From what?'

Maxwell grinned his winning grin. 'Have you ever heard of something called a TV commercial?' he asked.

5

Over what was possibly the first business lunch to be
held in nearly one hundred years, Maxwell explained
the principle of advertising and the power of the TV
commercial.

'The substance of the thing is this,' said Maxwell.
'You are a respected man, are you not?'

Dayglo Hilyte nodded proudly and munched upon
a parsnip.

'You represent authority, someone who can be
trusted.'

'I pride myself upon this.'

'So if you were to recommend a specific product, for
instance, one particular baker's bread, which you considered superior to that of his rivals, your viewing
public would respect your opinion.'

'I should expect nothing less.'

'Is there anything in this town you would recommend to me?'

Dayglo pursed his lips. 'The apothecary at the end
of the river lane produces a most efficacious laxative.'

'Hm,' said Maxwell. 'But all right. So if you were to
approach the apothecary and tell him that for a small
fee you would be prepared, during one of your broad-
casts, to sing the praises of his laxative—'

'Sing?' Dayglo fell back in horror. '*Sing?*'

'Only a turn of phrase. *Recommend* then, to your

viewing public, thereby creating what is known as "product awareness". Folk who heard your recommendation, who trusted you, would thereafter purchase their laxative from this apothecary.'

'But they would anyway. He is the only apothecary in town.'

Maxwell sighed. 'There is more than one baker's shop.'

'Agreed.'

'And more than one grocer, and more than one tavern and more than one inn and more than one butcher—'

'Aha,' said the zany. 'I follow this reasoning. If, for a small fee, Mr Hilyte was to broadcast that "Bulgarth the butcher's beef is the best", then folk who previously purchased their beef elsewhere, might be persuaded to shop at Bulgarth's instead.'

'You have it,' said Maxwell. 'For the small fee Bulgarth has paid you, his trade increases manyfold.'

'I see a problem here,' said Dayglo Hilyte. 'What of the other butchers who now lose trade?'

'This brings us to what is called "the spirit of healthy competition",' Maxwell told him. 'For example, I myself have looked into the window of Leibwitz. His hams appear eminently superior to those of Bulgarth.'

'I see it, I see it,' said Dayglo. 'Thus for a small fee from Leibwitz, I would recommend the quality of his hams.'

'Precisely. And soon each butcher will try to improve the quality of his meat. Each will seek your endorsement of this improved quality. Trade will increase for all, as you spread the word and folk rush to sample the improved products. The buyer will receive better meat. The butchers will enjoy greater custom. You accrue more fees. All are ultimately satisfied. Thus is financed the entire grand scheme.'

70

'There is sound logic to this,' said Dayglo, shaking Maxwell by the hand. 'I should have thought of it myself.'

'*You* are the eminent and noble news teller. *I* am the imagineer. And *this* is how we go about it.'

And *this* Maxwell now explained.

'I shall undertake the job of news gatherer,' he said. 'I will interview folk of the town, learn what is to be learned, cross-referenced to ensure clarity and lack of bias. I shall seek out and document all I can of recent events and events yet to come; fêtes, fairs, weddings, funerals; anything that might coalesce into worthy news, to be of interest and instruction.'

Hearing this, the zany now volunteered to take on the role of advertising rep, visiting all the local business premises to explain the new scheme and solicit fees from anyone who wished to have their products endorsed in the first commercial break.

'Excellent,' said the news teller. 'Then I shall dedicate myself to the thankless task of selecting a suitable news crumpet.'

'Shortly,' said Max, with a knowing smile. 'But first I suggest you visit the nearest carpenter's shop and commission the building of a spectacular new two-person TV set.'

'They will want a down payment,' said the news-teller, gloomily.

Maxwell shook his head. 'By no means. Outline our grand scheme to them. Stress that many TV sets will need to be constructed in the future. Stress also the prestige of their name being emblazoned across the front of every one.'

The news teller now shook *his* head. 'Is there nothing you have not thought of?' he asked.

'Nothing,' Maxwell said.

But on this surmise he was incorrect. Because here

a spanner, or more aptly a chisel, introduced itself into the otherwise smooth-running works: the news teller, having scuttled off to the carpenter's shop, shortly returned with some discouraging 'news'.

'They will supply the wood free of charge, but not the labour,' he said.

'No matter,' said Maxwell, as ever optimistic. 'Accept the wood with thanks, then construct the TV yourself.'

'*What?*' The news teller stepped back in outrage. 'Surely all hinges upon my reputation and social standing. I cannot descend to the humble role of carpenter. The zany must build it.'

'Would that I could,' said the zany. 'But I must solicit fees, without which the project cannot be financed. Max must build it.'

'Gladly,' said Maxwell. 'But I must gather news. Without news there *is* no project.'

'I have a suggestion to make,' said the zany. 'Clearly Mr Hilyte must remain aloof from manual labour in order to preserve his dignity and esteem. Why should I not gather news as I do my rounds of the business premises? Mr Hilyte could accompany me, showing his face as it were, absorbing news—'

'And interviewing likely candidates for the position of news crumpet,' said Mr Hilyte.

'Then you', the zany told Maxwell, 'could use your imagineering skills to great advantage, designing and constructing the new two-person TV set.'

Maxwell chanced a thoughtful scratch at his head and a wonderful vision swam into his mind.

'Rock 'n' Roll,' said Maxwell. 'Rock 'n' Roll.'

And so began a week of much industry on the part of Maxwell, the news teller and his zany. It had been agreed that the first two-person commercial newscast

72

would be scheduled for six o'clock on the coming Saturday night. Maxwell laboured long into each night on the construction of the TV set. It was to be a thing of great beauty and he lavished much tender loving care upon its every detail.

The news teller and his zany went about their sides of the business with considerable vigour and although Maxwell wished to consort with them each day, regarding what news had been gathered and what advertising commissions received, their paths rarely crossed his and Saturday drew ever close.

On Friday night the news teller did happen by for a moment, but only to try out his seat in the TV and insist upon an additional feature or two being added.

'This is the most amazing thing I have ever seen,' he told Maxwell, who grinned proudly as the news teller scuttled off with talk of a pressing meeting with the mayor, concerning proposed improvements to the town's sewage system, which Dayglo considered worthy news.

On Saturday Maxwell rose before dawn. Such was not the normal way with him, as he preferred to begin his mornings at a more civilized hour. But today was special. If all went well today he would have done his part in bringing a new age to this new age. He might well be written up in future books of history.

Throughout the week he'd hardly left the yard of the carpenter's shop, where he had been constructing the TV set. Now he flung wide the gate and applied himself to dragging his brainchild, shrouded as it was by a canvas cover and mounted upon wooden trolley wheels, out into the square. It was somewhat weightier than he had accounted for and by the time Maxwell reached the centre of the square he had a fine sweat on and was panting not a little.

But this was the moment. *His* moment.

As the sun began to rise, he tore aside the canvas and positioned the TV set 'just so'. The moment was for he alone. The moment was now.

The sun's first rays struck down upon the two-person TV.

With that full *2001* effect.

Maxwell whistled the strains of *Also Sprach Zarathustra* and then said 'Rock 'n' Roll' in a voice of no small awe.

The red sunlight glancing down held his masterpiece to full glory. Glimmering about its polished edges, reflecting in its painted panels, highlighting this detail and that.

A thing of great wonder it truly was. And Rock 'n' Roll indeed.

Maxwell had fashioned the TV into the semblance of the classic nineteen sixty-one *Rock-Ola* Regis Model 1495 stereo jukebox.

He had, as they say, 'gone to town on it'.

As *aficionados* of the now legendary *Rock-Ola* will not need reminding, the 1495 model was the first to feature the finless button bank, the rounded top valance and the streamlined body shape that would later become the standard design carried through the *Rock-Ola* range, to *The Empress, The Princess* and even the nineteen sixty-four *Rhapsody*.

Maxwell had hobbled it together from everything he could lay his hands on. Strips of tin beaten from old cooking pots, painted canvas, as many different varieties of timber as he could coax from the carpenter's assistant (which was a considerable number, as the carpenter himself had gone out of town for a few days).

It was a veritable stonker. Maxwell had even acquired the windscreen from a century-defunct

Renault 4, which was serving as a cold frame in the carpenter's kitchen garden, to provide the panoramic wide screen. Two speaking tubes within the cabinet led to a pair of commandeered ear-trumpets positioned beneath the wide screen to amplify the news teller's words to the viewing public. The entire ensemble was painted in as many colours as there had been paint pots in the carpenter's shed.

It could be truly said that no such item had ever existed before and that all who saw it would be truly amazed.

If there was one small fly in the Rock 'n' Roll ointment, it was the matter of the carpenter's name. The carpenter's assistant had been ordered by his departing boss to stand over Maxwell to ensure that he did not renege on his promise to emblazon the name in letters big and bold across the front. Maxwell had carved the carpenter's name into a fair approximation of the famous *Rock-Ola* lettering. But the name FUT-TUCK just didn't have the same wop-bop-a-loo-bop ring to it.

Maxwell sighed deeply, looked upon all that he had made and found it good. Now he re-covered the TV and set to erecting the posts and curtains which were to screen it from the viewing public until the final moment of the first commercial newscast. It was also imperative that Maxwell stand guard over his wonder, to protect it from prying eyes and wandering hands.

And so began the day for Maxwell.

And so went the day.

The town square became busy, stallholders plied their wares, folk came and went, children played. The grim red sun offered its mysterious light and Maxwell, his labours done, sat and watched it all go on.

It was certainly a strange old business, watching

these folk, dressed in the garb of medieval peasants and living the lifestyle. To think that several generations before, their ancestors had driven about in cars and enjoyed the benefits brought by electricity; sat before real television and viewed news from every part of the world.

'I will improve your lot,' said Maxwell. 'I, Max Carrion, Imagineer. You see if I don't.'

And then the day passed into afternoon and then towards evening. The stallholders packed their remaining wares away and departed. And Maxwell began to grow uneasy.

There had been no sign of Dayglo Hilyte and his zany.

As the town hall clock, a water-powered contrivance, struck five-thirty, Maxwell felt those seeds of panic taking root in a stomach which had survived yet another day upon the ingestion of parsnips alone.

Folk were now strolling into the square. They were all done up in their finest attire. They had brought cushions, hampers of food, flasks of wine. They were taking up positions before the curtains. They were evidently looking forward to the broadcast.

Maxwell looked this way and that amongst them.

Where was Dayglo Hilyte? Where was the zany?

'Hello.'

Maxwell turned.

'Are you Mr Carrion?'

Maxwell blinked and stared. 'I am.'

'I'm Miss Tailier.'

'Yes,' said Maxwell. 'Indeed.'

She was 'simply stunning'. Young and fresh and slim and shapely. Her face a most vivacious instrument of expression. Great dark eyes fringed by curling lashes, tiny upturned nose, wide and sensuous mouth. All framed by flocks of amber curls.

76

She wore a black figure-hugger of a dress that almost reached her knees, and soft gold slippers. Golden rings sheathed her elegant well-manicured fingers.

'Miss Tailier,' said Maxwell, shaking the pale hand that was offered.

'I'm the new crumpet. You can call me Jenny.'

'Jenny Tailier. *Jenny-Tailier?*'

'Yes, what about it?'

'Oh nothing.' Maxwell shook his head. 'Nothing at all.'

'I was supposed to meet Mr Hilyte at five-thirty. I'm a little late.'

'He's not here,' said Maxwell. 'In fact, I have no idea what's happened to him. Oh, hang about.'

Through the growing crowd came the zany. He waved to the right and left, uttered greetings, but as Maxwell watched him approach, it was quite clear that something was terribly wrong.

'What has happened?' Maxwell asked, when at last the zany reached him.

'Something terrible. Terrible.' The zany hopped from one foot to the other.

'What is it?' Maxwell pulled him through the curtains and beyond the view of the crowd. 'You look dreadful.'

'It's Mr Hilyte,' the zany wrung his hands. 'He's collapsed. He's in a terrible state – pale as death and burning with fever. He worked himself too hard, got too carried away with the excitement of it all. I think the parsnips have done for him also.'

Maxwell stared aghast. 'This is appalling. Have you called a medic?'

'A what?'

'A doctor. The apothecary.'

'Oh yes, he's in capable hands. But what are

we going to do about the broadcast. We'll have to cancel it.'

'No.' Maxwell shook his head fiercely. 'We can't do that. There's a hundred people out there, we can't let them down.'

'But we can't do the broadcast without Mr Hilyte. This is terrible, terrible.'

'Just calm down.' Maxwell gripped the zany by his trembling shoulders. 'There must be a way. The show must go on.'

'I could go on by myself,' said Miss Tailier, in the manner of one who most definitely could.

Maxwell made a doubtful face. 'I don't think it would do. *You* could go on in Mr Hilyte's place,' he told the shivering zany.

'I can't go on. I can't even stay here for long. I must go back to Mr Hilyte, I'm his oldest friend. We'll have to cancel the broadcast. Unless . . .'

'Unless what?'

'Well,' said the zany. 'Perhaps, but no . . .'

'Go on,' Maxwell demanded.

'*You* could go on in Mr Hilyte's place,' the zany blurted out.

'*Me?* That's ludicrous.'

'Well, no it's not. I could make you up to look like Mr Hilyte. Through the glass of the screen and with the number of men concentrating on Miss Tailier . . .'

Maxwell scratched at his head. This moment of hesitation caused further distress to the zany.

'You're right,' he all but wept. 'It would never work. We'll have to cancel.'

'No we won't.' Maxwell's voice was very firm indeed. 'All right, I'll do it. Make me up.'

'What a hero,' said Miss Jenny Tailier, squeezing Maxwell's hand.

'I'll have to shave your head,' said the zany.

'Forget it,' said Maxwell.

The zany chewed upon his finger nails. 'Oh calamity,' he said.

'All right, all right,' cried Maxwell. 'Shave my head, apply the make-up. By the Goddess, the things I do to make this world a better place.'

6

To the zany's credit, he was skilful in the art of make-up.

Not quite so skilled in the barbering department, however: his trembling hand almost cost Maxwell an ear.

Maxwell examined himself in the zany's hand mirror and the artist returned his make-up sticks to the pouch he wore on his belt. A horrible sight met Maxwell's eyes, but a fair enough facsimile of Dayglo Hilyte.

Maxwell shook his now bald head. 'So,' said he. 'The all-important matter. The news script. I haven't even seen it yet.'

'It's here,' the zany thrust a wad of papers into Maxwell's hand. 'Mr Hilyte has been working on it all week.'

'What about the one for Miss Tailier?'

'I've learned mine off by heart,' said the beautiful young woman, fluttering her gorgeous eyelashes.

'Well done,' said Maxwell.

'Now quickly,' said the zany. 'Into the TV. I will take the collection and make the introductions. Oh dear, oh dear.'

'Don't worry,' said Maxwell. 'We can handle it.'

The zany opened the rear doors of the wonderful wide-screen two-person TV and assisted Maxwell and Miss Tailier inside.

'Everything OK?' he asked.

'Just fine,' said Maxwell, making himself comfortable. The TV set was roomy enough. But now, with the doors firmly closed, rather intimate. Knees were touching and shoulders too. Maxwell could smell the young woman's hair. It smelled quite wonderful.

A lump came to Maxwell's throat. Maxwell prayed this lump would be the only one that came.

From beyond the curtain came the murmur of the crowd. Gay voices, much laughter. Maxwell heard the zany as he moved amongst the merry throng, joking, 'warming up', passing the contributions sack. Silver collection only, this time.

Maxwell suddenly felt a growing sense of terror. Stage fright! He glanced at Miss Tailier, but she was cool, aloof, a real professional. Maxwell steadied his nerves. If she was up to it, so was he. The dawn of a new age of enlightenment was about to begin, and he, Max Carrion, Imagineer, was to be the rising sun of this new dawn.

Oh yes!

'My lords, ladies, grandees and duchesses, Mayor and lady Mayoress, town's folk of Grimshaw, welcome.' The zany's voice rang out in a confident tone. 'Tonight the first ever, the never seen anywhere before, all new commercial newscast. Put your hands together for your own, your very own Mr Dayglo Hilyte and his lovely assistant Miss Jenny Tailier.'

The crowd gushed out applause. The zany yanked upon the rope, the curtains parted. The jukebox TV took centre stage.

The applause was veritable thunder. Maxwell and Miss Tailier smiled out at the multitude. And some multitude.

Several hundred at least.

'Will they all be able to hear us?' Miss Tailier asked.

'Speak loudly and clearly into your speaking tube. Are you ready?'

Miss Tailier squeezed his hand once more. 'I'm ready.'

'So be it.' Maxwell raised his other hand and the eager crowd stilled to its raising.

'Good evening,' said Maxwell, in a voice which might almost have passed for Dayglo Hilyte's. 'And here is the six o'clock news.'

'*Bong!*' went Miss Tailier.

'Bong?' asked Maxwell, turning in immediate confusion to the news crumpet.

'Bong,' whispered Miss Tailier. 'Mr Hilyte said I should go *bong* when you announced the news. It's a tradition or an old charter or something. It's the chime of Big Dick.'

'Oh, I see.' Maxwell coughed politely. 'Big Ben,' he whispered.

'I prefer a big dick any time.' Miss Tailier fluttered her eyelashes.

Maxwell made that croaking throat sound of his. 'Here is the six o'clock news,' he went once more.

'Bong!'

Maxwell read directly from the first sheet of paper. 'Hundreds feared dead as God accidentally drops his toothbrush on village.'

'Bong!'

'Hundreds *what*?' Maxwell's jaw was hanging slack. 'What is this rubbish?'

'Bluff it,' whispered Miss Tailier between the perfect teeth of a big broad smile. 'Everyone's watching you. Just read the script.'

And everyone was watching Maxwell. And watching very closely. And being very very quiet about it too.

'Bong!' went Miss Jenny Tailier once more for luck.

'Blind farmer wears out fingers trying to read cheese grater,' read Maxwell.

'Bong!'

'Mayor's wife comes second in beauty contest. A pig wins it.'

'*What?*' cried the Mayor, who was right at the front.

'Oh my Goddess.' Maxwell fumbled with his script. 'It's a misprint,' he blurbled. 'I'm sorry. A misprint.'

'Get a grip of yourself,' whispered Miss Tailier. 'Introduce me.'

'Indeed,' Maxwell grinned goofily at the now murmuring crowd.

'Over to you, Jenny,' he said.

Jenny Tailier smiled a sensational smile. The crowd cheered and clapped with great enthusiasm.

'Thank you,' said Miss Tailier primly. 'I always appreciate a warm hand on my opening.'

'*What?*' went Maxwell, turning ever paler beneath his make-up.

'This week I've been out and about on the streets of Grimshaw talking to the men who have been making the news.'

Ah, thought Maxwell. Not bad.

'I spoke to a man with a foot-long penis, who told me, "It may be twelve inches, but I don't use it as a rule." '

The crowd erupted in laughter.

Maxwell sank down below the level of the screen. 'No,' he implored. 'Not knob gags. Anything but knob gags.'

'Also,' Miss Tailier went on, when the laughter had died away, 'the vicar who caught his plonker in the bell rope and was tolled off by the verger.'

'No!' Maxwell raised a hand and clapped it over Miss Tailier's mouth.

'Boo!' went the crowd.

'What is going on?' muttered Maxwell through seriously gritted teeth. 'What is happening here? My news is all rubbish and you're telling dirty jokes.'

'That's what I do', said Miss Tailier, wrenching Maxwell's hand away, 'where I work in the town's bordello. I'm a star round these parts, everyone knows me.'

'What?'

'Boo, boo,' and 'hiss,' went the crowd, and 'get on with it.'

'Back to you, Dayglo,' said Miss Tailier.

'Ah . . .' said Maxwell. 'Oh Goddess!'

'Go into the commercial break. I'll do it if you like.'

'No you will not.'

'Please yourself then.' Miss Tailier folded her arms and made a huffy face.

'And now', said Maxwell, 'the moment that many of you have been waiting for. The commercial break.' He rummaged about amongst his papers. But for the single sheet he had been reading from, all others were uniformly blank. 'Oh dear,' said Maxwell. 'Oh dear, oh dear, oh dear.'

The crowd was now becoming very restless indeed and through it there came a large man. He was hauling behind him an even larger young woman. 'Hold up there,' he shouted. 'Just what is going on?'

Maxwell blinked at the new arrivals. 'Excuse me,' he asked, 'but who are you?'

'I am Rushmear the horse trader and this is my daughter.'

'Pleased to meet you,' said Maxwell.

'The pleasure is yours alone. Why have you begun half an hour early?'

'The news began sharp at six,' said Maxwell.

'Then we were misinformed.'

'My apologies.'

'Apologies are not sufficient. What is that woman doing in there with you?'

'This is Miss Jenny Tailier, the news crumpet.'

'The town strumpet you mean, I know her well enough.'

The crowd cheered somewhat at this, but, now eager to learn what the fearsome Rushmear had to say for himself, soon quietened down.

'Get that woman out of there and put my daughter in at once,' was what he had to say.

'Impossible,' said Maxwell. 'Miss Tailier has been accepted for the post.'

'Swindler and cheat,' bawled Rushmear. 'I paid your zany two fine white horses on the understanding that my daughter would be given the job.'

Maxwell viewed Rushmear's larger daughter. She was well-knit and muscular. She had a small black moustache and an interesting line in tattoos. 'Two fine white horses?' Maxwell turned to Miss Tailier. 'Did your father pay any such, er, fee?'

'Certainly not. I was picked from dozens of other applicants who auditioned on the "casting couch" at the inn.'

'Casting couch?' Maxwell let out a mighty groan. '*Inn?*'

'My inn,' cried another large man, elbowing space beside Rushmear. 'As *you* know well enough.'

'*I?*' asked Maxwell.

'*You,*' said the innkeeper. 'My inn where you and your zany have been enjoying first-class accommodation for the entire week on the understanding that you would "sing the praises" of my establishment. So go on, *sing.*'

'There seems to be some mistake,' Maxwell chewed upon a thumb nail.

'Enough of this,' shouted yet another large man. 'What singing there is will be done for my beef.'

'Your beef?' Maxwell asked.

'My beef. I am Bulgarth the butcher and you . . .' Bulgarth stared in at Maxwell. 'You . . . Who in the name of the deity are you anyway? You're not Dayglo Hilyte.'

Maxwell gagged and spluttered. The crowd erupted. 'What?' they went. '*What?*'

'There is duplicity here,' yelled Bulgarth. 'Give back my money whoever you are.'

A woman close at hand peered in at Maxwell. 'It's that arrow-nosed scoundrel who calls himself an imagineer. He pulled my dog Princey from the sewage pipe. I reckon he stuck him in there too.'

'Boo!' went the crowd once more.

'What of all this?' cried Bulgarth and the innkeeper and Rushmear and Rushmear's daughter also. And a lot of the crowd too.

'Mr Hilyte was taken sick,' whimpered Maxwell. 'I am standing in for him.'

'Hilyte promised that *he* would recommend my beef. Give me back my money. I paid out ten pieces of gold for my commercial.'

'Only ten?' This voice came from Leibwitz who, although not quite so large as Bulgarth, was respected for his hams. 'Hilyte told me the fee was fifteen, for the exclusive recommendation of *my* beef alone.'

'I paid seventeen,' shouted Grimshaw's third butcher.

'Shut up, the lot of you!' Rushmear pushed folk to either side. 'Get that prosie out of the box and install my daughter at once.'

'Do nothing of the kind,' ordered Bulgarth. 'Hilyte's zany promised that the news crumpet would be singing the praises of my beef without her top on. No offence to your daughter, Rushmear, but if she'd lived in old India she would have been sacred.'

As Rushmear's daughter raised a fist the size of a Leibwitz prize ham, yet another voice rose to join the others.

'Where are my fireworks?' this one wanted to know.

'Fireworks?' gagged the sweating, shaking Maxwell.

A pale thin man had been allowed to push his way forward. 'I am Clovis the banker. My guards and staff were all invited here to witness the spectacular firework display that would emblazon my name across the sky. For the fortune I paid, it had better be worth it. I—'

But he said no more. The mighty fist of Rushmear's daughter caught him by accident and felled him to the ground. A bit of a rumpus then occurred.

Maxwell eased himself back in his seat and sought to take his leave. He pressed upon the rear doors, but they seemed disinclined to open. Maxwell pushed harder. The doors held fast. With heart now sunken into his substantial boots, Maxwell recalled that one of the additional features Mr Hilyte had insisted upon the previous night was a big sturdy bolt that fastened from the outside.

As he watched the fists beginning to fly, Maxwell viewed yet another large man forcing his way forward. 'What is this abomination that bears my name?' he barked.

'Who?' managed Maxwell.

'Futtock, the carpenter,' came the reply. 'Who designed this atrocity?'

'Well . . . you see—'

'Outrageous! I offered to have my finest craftsmen construct a beautiful cabinet at no cost. But Hilyte told me that he had an imagineer whom he personally wished to take charge of the project. Now I return from my holiday to find this . . .'

Maxwell made further groanings. It all fell so neatly into place, he wondered just how he had failed to see it coming.

But now others were coming.

The first of these was a pale thin man, the dead spit of Clovis the banker. He looked somewhat battered and the worse for wear.

'Robbery,' he cried, pushing into the circle that was widening about Rushmear's daughter who was laying into Bulgarth with a vigour.

'Help, help, robbery.'

'What has happened, brother?' shouted Clovis, struggling to his feet.

'Two masked men entered the bank shortly after you and the guards left. They tied me up and beat me. They have taken everything.'

'What?' wailed Clovis. 'Everything?'

'And they rode away on a pair of fine white horses.'

As Maxwell had a further groan left in him, he used it now.

And it was well timed for into the growing mêlée came the sound of chanting. Maxwell could make out robed figures armed with flaming torches, marching through the crowd. Now who might these be? he asked himself.

'And who might you be?' demanded Rushmear.

The leader of the advancing legion was an old woman who looked vaguely familiar to Maxwell. 'We are the Queuers who wait upon Varney!' she bellowed. 'We have paid our bounty and now we demand the head of the iconoclast in a bucket.'

'Whose head is this?'

'His!' A young man with a torch, pointed the accusing finger towards Maxwell. 'Disguised, though locked in the box, as Mr Hilyte promised when we paid him the bounty.'

'You can damn well wait your turn for his head,' bawled Rushmear buffeting the young man in the ear.

'How dare you hit my Kevin!' shrieked the old woman, clouting Rushmear with her flaming torch.

'Guards. Arrest the malcontents in the travelling TV,' ordered Clovis the banker.

'Not till the tart's got her kecks off,' called Zardoz the baker. 'I paid for an exotic dance involving a pair of baps and a french stick.'

'So did I!' called one of his rivals.

'And me!' called another.

Maxwell was now in the foetal position, chewing his nails to the knuckles. 'For Goddess sake, whip out your charlies before we're both killed,' he told Miss Tailier.

'How dare you.' Miss Tailier kicked Maxwell in the head. 'I'm a star of the small screen now and—'

It was good night from her.

The crowd surged forward. The followers of Varney set to smiting all about them with their flaming torches. Butchers, bakers and no doubt the manufacturers of candlesticks, drew out all manner of concealed weapons and entered into the fray.

The arrival of several more large men with equally large and star-struck daughters, to whom much had been promised in return for large sums received, did nothing to quiet the riot. Spleens were being vented, old scores settled. Anarchy prevailed.

The maelstrom of struggling bodies swept into the glorious *Rock-Ola*-style two-person wide-screen travelling TV set, overturning it and bursting it asunder. In pandemonium the mob fell upon Maxwell and Miss Tailier. Many seemed particularly anxious to fall upon Miss Tailier . . .

These who fell upon Maxwell had a more violent intent. Dragged from the wreckage of his masterwork, he was yanked this way and that. Maxwell struck out with his substantial boots, shattering shinbones, knackering kneecaps. The howls of the wounded were lost in the hullabaloo.

Kevin rose up before him. 'So die, idolater,' said he, raising a mattock.

'Sorry,' said Maxwell, punching Kevin's lights out, then diving low to scramble through the shambles.

Certain images of mayhem would remain to haunt young Maxwell and disturb his sleep for many months to come.

There are few things quite as frightful as the madness of a mob and, as brother beat on brother and the butcher struck the baker and the Varneyites and carpenters and traders and their daughters raged and rampaged, fought and forayed, beat and bludgeoned, mashed and mangled . . .

Maxwell quietly quit the scene and slipped away.

He ran for several miles along the road that led north out of Grimshaw before he dared to stop, draw breath, drink from a stream and wash the make-up from his face and scalp.

The sun was setting now, its bloated red orb wallowing on the horizon to the west. Sounds of violence and carnage drifted across the barren landscape and looking back, Maxwell could see that much of Grimshaw was now fiercely ablaze.

With a rueful shake of his shaven head and a deep and heartfelt sigh of regret, Maxwell gathered wits and breath together and fled once more.

7

Maxwell marched north.

He slept in ditches and maintained the communion of body and soul through a meagre, though nourishing, diet of fruit and berries. Once he snared a rabbit, but the beast did the dirty and stared at him with big brown reproachful eyes. Maxwell let it hop upon its way.

His vegan repasts left him in no need of the apothecary's laxative that Dayglo had recommended and hourly bush-squats punctuated each day's journey.

It was during one of these, that he viewed riders pounding from the south. Peeping from the safety of his gorse privy, he glimpsed the face of the turbulent Rushmear, bruised but determined, as the riders thundered by. Ahead the road forked and they took the left. His ablutions completed, Maxwell took the right.

He felt hollow inside, and it wasn't just for the lack of food. The appalling devastation wrought upon Grimshaw had been of his making. In his zeal to bring enlightenment to this new world, he had unleashed horrors from the old upon it.

No news was good news here, and as for advertising . . . Maxwell shuddered. Certainly Hilyte and his zany had brought new meaning to the words treachery and deceit, but Maxwell still felt wholly to blame. If he hadn't interfered, none of it would have happened.

His vision of being written up in future history books

had now acquired a nightmare aspect. He envisioned generations to come pointing to engravings of a Rock-Ola-style TV set from which sprang all the evils of the world and speaking not of Pandora's infamous casket, but of *Maxwell's Jukebox*.

'I shall make amends,' Maxwell told himself. 'But through small acts of charity rather than grandiose gestures.'

And with this said he pressed on. His wish was to put many miles between himself and Grimshaw. Let no grass grow beneath his feet, while the hair grew back on his head.

The landscape was dull as a duffle-coat, sardine-grey and just went on and on and on and on and on and on (like that).

Once he viewed the ruins of a village, which lay shattered beneath what appeared to be a gigantic golden toothbrush, but other than that, he didn't see much of anything.

After a week of thin feeding, gorse-bush visiting and troubled nights, Maxwell's substantial footwear carried him to a low range of hills, beyond which rose a mighty forest. Without the aid of a map to guide him, or a destination for it to guide him to, Maxwell left the moorland track, which probably wasn't even on a map, and entered the forest, which probably was, but not in any great detail.

It is said that travel broadens the mind.

But not whether it lengthens it also.

Somewhere in the forest Maxwell lodged for several days at the hut of a charcoal burner. Here he earned his keep by chopping wood. And, through the exercise of almost super-human self-control, resisted the temptation to advise the humble forest dweller how, by means which sprang immediately to Maxwell's mind, he might increase his scope of operation and branch out into other fields of enterprise, that would, in due time, see him at the head of a major nationwide logging industry.

Maxwell kept his mouth shut and his chopper sharp and when his hair had risen to a My-Boy-Flat-Top, he bid the charcoal burner goodbye, accepted a satchel of food and the generous gift of a fine woollen cloak and set out once more on whichever was his way.

A day later, or it may have been two, but it doesn't really matter, Maxwell left the forest and joined a rugged road that led towards a village.

As he approached its outskirts he passed between two stone columns, each surmounted by a metal sphere. These evidently marked a boundary, because there were others at regular intervals leading off in either direction encircling the rich cultivated fields that surrounded the village. The folk here evidently took great pride in their horticulture, as the fields were impeccably kept and flourished with exotic fruit and vegetables, many varieties of which were completely foreign to Maxwell. There wasn't a parsnip in sight.

The village itself presented an equally respectable face. The high street, cobbled over, led between shops, houses and inns, almost twentieth century in appearance. To Maxwell's amazement there was even a Budgen's supermarket. The plastic sign had been weathered down to blurry indistinction but it was still recognizable as the shopper's paradise it had once been.

As Maxwell drew near he spied through the plate-glass window that the supermarket had been stripped of its once proud shelving and now housed booths and stalls. Which seemed reasonable enough.

As Maxwell gazed in, the door to this emporium swung open and a young man, wearing a cloak not dissimilar to Maxwell's, issued into the street. He was a handsome fellow, spare framed, brown eyed, with drapes of yellow hair swinging to his shoulders.

He carried a pair of shopping bags and offered Maxwell a toothy grin as he passed him by. He had not gone two steps further, however, when a small animal, appearing as if from nowhere, darted between his legs, causing him to sprawl headlong into the road.

Maxwell hastened to assist the young man to his feet and help rescue the shopping, that was now liberally distributed about the cobbles.

'My thanks,' said the young man, dusting himself down.

'You're not injured?'

'No. I'll survive. I always do.'

'Can you tell me the name of this village?' Maxwell asked.

'Of course I can, I live here.'

'So what is it?'

'Oh, I see. It's MacGuffin.'

'Ah,' said Maxwell. 'Then perhaps I am in Scotland?'

'No,' said the young man. 'You are in MacGuffin.'

'Yes, but *where* is MacGuffin?'

'You have me puzzled now,' said the young man. 'I always thought it was *here*.'

'Then you're probably right.'

The young man weighed this up. 'Have you ever seen me before?' he asked.

'No,' said Maxwell.

'Then how do you know it's me?'

'I think I should be going now,' said Maxwell.

'Are you looking for work?'

'Yes, I am actually.'

'Then come with me while I drop my shopping off.'

'Wonderful,' said Maxwell.

94

'Oh, it's not all that. I drop my shopping off every day.'

The young man, who, after much prompting with specific questions, revealed that his name was Dave, led Maxwell to a cottage which huddled at the rear of the bygone Budgen's. They arrived by a somewhat circuitous route, but Maxwell made a point of not asking why.

Within, a cozy sitting-room showed a fire in its hearth, a comfy box ottoman, a carpet bare of thread, but with a nice pattern, a few sticks of furniture and a few extra sticks for the fire. Maxwell hung his cloak upon a cloakhook and sat down in a rocking-chair.

'Be careful on that,' Dave advised. 'It has a tendency to move back and forwards in an arc.'

'Thanks,' said Maxwell, shaking his head.

Dave tossed both bags of shopping straight into a cupboard, then turned to Maxwell. 'I have trouble with my trousers,' he said. 'Every time I shake them, something flies out.'

'What, moths, do you mean?'

'No, sea fowl, curlew, birds of the air.'

'That sounds somewhat unlikely,' said Maxwell.

'But nevertheless it's so.' Dave gave his left trouser turn-up a shake. 'There you go,' he cried. 'That's a sparrow hawk, if ever.'

Maxwell stared up at the bird, now flapping about the ceiling. 'Looks more like a kestrel to me,' he ventured. 'By the plumage.'

'But you see what I mean?'

Maxwell nodded dubiously. 'They are without doubt most unusual trousers.'

Dave pulled gingerly upon the knees of his trews and sat down on the box ottoman. 'It is the curse of the Wilkinsons,' he explained. 'Some say that one of my forefathers fell out with whichever god was then in fashion. Some say.'

Maxwell asked, 'Why don't you just get rid of the trousers?'

Dave laughed a hollow laugh. 'If only it was that easy. You didn't come to my wedding, did you, Maxwell?'

'I've only just met you, I thought we'd established that.'

'Well, it was a grim day for the Wilkinsons, I can tell you.'

'Really?' said Maxwell, wishing he hadn't.

Dave now sighed a sigh. 'I had postponed putting on my wedding suit until the very last moment. Then, feeling it was safe to do so, foolish foolish me, I togged up and set off to the church. All went well for a while. I stood at the altar, my fragrant Mary at my side. The sky pilot read the service. The choir sang, "Oh Come All Ye Faithful".'

'It was a Christmas wedding then?'

'Christmas? What's Christmas?'

'Never mind,' said Maxwell. 'You've started, so you might as well finish.'

'Yes, well, the choir sang. The sun beamed rouge rays through the old aeon stained-glass windows, lit upon the gilded ornamentation of the rood screen, brought forth mellow hues of—'

'And?' Maxwell asked.

'And I was about to slip the ceremonial wedding sprout into the head band of my fair one's bonnet—'

'When?'

'When okapi!'

'Okapi?'

'*Okapi!* Dirty great okapi came roaring out of my waistcoat.'

96

'Okapi don't roar,' said Maxwell. 'But otherwise it was not a bad yarn.'

Dave looked defeated (but he wasn't). 'No yarn, my friend. No yarn. Here, take a look at the wedding photo.'

'Photo?' Maxwell leaned forward in his rocker. A smile appeared on his face. 'There is still photography?'

Dave tugged a well-thumbed item from his trouser pocket and thrust it into Maxwell's hand.

Maxwell's face fell. 'This', he said, 'is a photograph of the March of the Wildebeest. Cut, if I'm not mistaken, from a now ancient copy of *The National Geographic*.'

'So how do you explain that?' Dave indicated the top of a church spire, clearly visible in the background. 'That's St Wilko of Feelgood's in the high street, you must have seen it when you entered the village.'

Maxwell parted with the photo. 'They used to do that sort of stuff with things called computers. You have my admiration none the less.'

'And the sparrow hawk?' Dave pointed to the bird, now quietly roosting on the mantelpiece.

'Kestrel, you mean.'

'The kestrel then?'

'It's a conjuring trick. You're winding me up. An uncle of mine could poke a pencil up his nose and make it come out of his ear. That was a conjuring trick also.'

'We have a woman in the village who can . . .' But Dave left the sentence unfinished. 'This kestrel business is no trick, I can assure you of that.'

Maxwell shrugged. 'I have heard of ferrets in the trousers. But of okapi in the waistcoat, I remain unconvinced. Sorry.'

Dave threw up his hands in despair. Two squirrels emerged from his left shirt cuff and scrambled onto the curtain pelmet.

'There,' Dave cried. 'Explain that, if you can.'

'You might perhaps open a zoo,' said Maxwell, who still had his doubts.

'What's a zoo?'

'A place where you keep a collection of interesting animals. People pay to come and view them and—' Maxwell halted before he reached full flow. Zoos were perhaps not the best idea in the old world.

'Pay?' Dave laughed. 'Pay to see my animals? And what if some visitor steps up to bid me good morning and a venomous cobra darts out of my buttonhole and sinks its fangs into him?'

Maxwell rocked backwards with such vigour that he nearly fell off his chair. 'That sort of thing doesn't happen. Does it?'

'No. Not as such. It probably depends on the season and where I happen to be. It is summer in MacGuffin, hence the squirrels and the sparrow hawk.'

'Kestrel,' said Maxwell.

'Kestrel then.'

'So what about the okapi?'

Dave now shrugged. 'The exception that proves the rule, perhaps?'

'Perhaps.' Maxwell rose and stretched. Enough was quite enough. 'I think I'll just take a little stroll around the village,' he said.

'But what about the job? You wanted a job.'

'I'll get back to you on that.'

'No, really, please don't go.'

'Things to do, people to see.' Maxwell snatched his cloak from the cloakhook and made hastily through the door and into the little lane beyond.

At least he thought it was *his* cloak.

A moment passed, the way some of them do. Then Dave heard a startled scream, followed by a great trampling sound and the distinctive baritone snort of a Tibetan yak.

'There,' said Dave to the squirrels. 'Let's hear him talk his way out of that.'

As he spoke, a rabbit appeared from his right trouser cuff, twitched its nose nervously and scurried away to take shelter beneath the box ottoman.

Where a fox ate it.

8

Cocking a snook at the now traditional, 'Where am I?'
Maxwell awoke from unconsciousness with a cry of,
'Dave, you *BASTARD*!' This cried, he blinked his eyes
and asked, 'Where am I?'

He was lying on a couch. It was an over-stuffed
leather jobbie of the type once favoured by psy-
chiatrists, for putting patients at their ease, while they
were relieved of their cares and cash. This stood in a
pleasant enough room, about as broad as it was long,
and bathed in the red sunlight which washed through
two high arched casement windows.

This room owned to a multitude of glass-fronted
showcases containing many stuffed beasts: rabbits,
hares, minks, ducks, geese and others arranged in
tableux of imaginative depravity.

Maxwell, as a lad, had, as most lads have, pored
breathlessly over a many-thumbed copy of the *Karma
Sutra*. And he might well have lingered long in
appreciation of the taxidermist's skill at depicting
such wonders as a ferret 'splitting the bamboo' of a
toad, or an otter 'taking tea with the parson' in the
company of not one but three French hens, had it
not been for the mind-grinder of a headache he now
possessed and the all-over nature of his aches and
pains.

Maxwell ached in the manner that only one who has

recently received a sound trampling from a Tibetan yak can.

Or possibly one run over by an articulated lorry.

Or crushed beneath a fall of dumbbells, which had been carelessly stacked in a high cupboard, usually reserved for the storage of books such as the *Karma Sutra*.

Or even having been remorselessly beaten with ball-pane plannishing hammers, wielded by a sheet-metal worker named Brian and two of his drunken mates, outside a pub in Camden Town at closing-time, because he mistook you for the bloke who had been splitting his wife's bamboo while he was on the nightshift.

No, actually the last one is somewhat different, as the blows rained are aimed towards a specific area of the body.

Maxwell groaned and felt about his person. 'By the Goddess,' he mumbled, 'I feel as if I've been remorselessly beaten with ball-pane plannishing hammers, wielded by—'

'A sheet-metal worker named Brian?' asked a voice.

Maxwell turned his aching head to view its owner and was impressed by what he saw.

In the doorway stood a figure of heroic proportion. His broad shoulders almost filling the entrance span, his head bowed to avoid contact with the lintel. This man was a veritable giant.

And he was marvellously dressed.

All in red. Every inch. His costume was intricate, highly decorated and many layered. Over a ruffled shirt with four collars, flounced sleeves and gathered cuffs, he wore a number of sleeveless garments, graduating in length from the innermost, which reached nearly to the floor, to the outermost, which was little more than a skimpy bolero.

His baggy trousers were tucked rakishly into red leather kneeboots with stylish double toes.

All in all this outfit created a most singular and dashing appearance, but one somewhat at odds with his face. This was a bloated affair, big as a pig's bladder balloon, all puffs and rolls of flesh. The eyes, black points, were scarcely visible, the nose was a dab of putty, the hair a red ruff teased into a thousand hedgehog quills.

Returning to the nose, which Maxwell had no particular wish to do, but did, none the less, this nose was pierced through the centre cartilage between the nostrils, by a huge golden ring which encircled the mouth and reached almost to the first of several chins. From this ring hung two slender golden chains, one of which looped up to the left ear lobe, the other to the right.

'Are you feeling yourself?' asked the big red man.

'No,' said Maxwell. 'It's just the way I'm sitting.'

The big red man nodded thoughtfully. 'This is *my* house,' said he. 'And anyone who engages in cheap *double entendre* here receives a smack in the gob. Do I make myself clear?'

'Certainly,' said Maxwell. 'You have no need to press home your point.'

'Good,' said the big red man. 'So what do you feel like?'

'I feel like shit, as it happens.'

'Well, that's a pity, because I only have cornflakes.'

Maxwell shook his aching head.

'Just my little joke,' said the big red man.

'Really?' said Maxwell.

'Of course. I have eggs, bacon, sausage and toast also. Follow me.'

*   *   *

With a great deal of groaning and creaking and cracking of joints, Maxwell followed his enormous host from the room of rude animals, across a hallway lined with statuary of equal rudeness, up an elegant sweep of stairs and into a wonderful circular room.

This had a high domed ceiling, decorated with a *trompe-l'œil* of rich blue sky, dappled by scudding clouds. So cunning had been the hand which wrought this masterpiece, that the clouds appeared to drift free of the ceiling and hover in the room beneath.

The big man's tiny black eyes followed the direction of Maxwell's large round ones. 'An interesting piece,' said he. 'Although somewhat fanciful. A blue sky, who could imagine such a thing?'

'*I* could,' said Maxwell, wistfully.

'Look from the windows and tell me what you see.'

Glazed apertures, set between pillars which supported the dome, encircled the room, Maxwell limped slowly from one to another, peering out.

Beneath lay the village, petticoat-pretty and Queen-Mother-quaint; beyond, the cultivated fields and flower gardens, abruptly contained by the circle of raised columns with their spherical headpieces; beyond this, bleak moorland and the forest to the south.

'Should I be seeing something specific?' Maxwell enquired.

The big man in red stared over Maxwell's head. 'Something *most* specific,' he said. 'What you see, there below. All around, thus and so. Is no jest and no joke. But a conclave of folk. Self-sufficient, contained. Content and unstrained. Order from chaos, complete harmony. A delicate balance, *that's* what you see.'

'Most poetic,' said Maxwell. 'And very nice too.'

'I'm so glad you think so,' said the big red man. 'Because that's the way *it's ruddy well staying*!'

Maxwell smiled up at his host. 'Rock 'n' Roll,' said he, raising a thumb.

'Then let us eat.' Maxwell's host waved a great hand towards a circular table at the centre of the room. Its top was a mighty slab of clear rock crystal supported by the raised hands of a grinning naked satyr, carved from black basalt. The look of pleasure evident upon the face of this grotesque was in no small part due to the oral homage being paid him by the kneeling figure of a woodland nymph. This being, delicately wrought in white marble, was a thing of extreme beauty and Maxwell's eyes dwelt upon it for more than a moment.

'Sit down and get stuck in,' said Maxwell's host.

Maxwell glanced up at the big red man who was lowering his big red self into a big red throne-like chair.

A single other seat remained before the table, this was a knackered old bentwood number. Maxwell shrugged and sat down upon it.

'Eat,' said his host.

'Thank you,' said Maxwell.

The table was burdened by a bounty of local fare: pyramids of boiled goose eggs, a fine pink hock of ham, a tray of baked muffins, a pot of steamed mushrooms, jars of honey and pickled preserves, a silver samovar simmering tea, and a whole lot more, which without the aid of some cunning literary artifice would be far too tedious to list.

There were, however, white linen table napkins and ivory-handled cutlery of the 'Saltsberg' pattern. The china came as a bit of a body-blow though. It was that nasty fruit-spattered stuff that you get from the Argos catalogue.

'Careful with the china,' said Maxwell's host. 'Most valuable and antique.'

Maxwell ladled a helping of plump sausages onto his plate. He was *very* hungry indeed.

'So,' said the big fellow, delicately dispensing tea. 'You are Maxwell.'

'That's me.' Maxwell forked sausage into his mouth and began to munch.

'And you are an imagineer.'

Maxwell's munching ceased. 'Who told you that?' he asked.

'Never mind. But listen, how rude of me. I have not introduced myself.' The big man reached a big hand across the table for Maxwell to shake. 'I am MacGuffin,' he said.

Maxwell shook the big hand. It was soft as a spun-silk sporran, if such a thing exists. The nails were delicate and richly lacquered. The thumb was embraced by a golden ring clasping a jade disc, intagliated with an erotic device.

Maxwell's hand returned to his fork, his fork to his sausage. 'Then this village is named after one of your ancestors,' said Maxwell, before pushing the sausage home.

'Named after *me*,' said MacGuffin. 'It is *my* village. Within the circle of columns, all is *mine*.'

Maxwell nodded as he ate.

'I am known by many appellations,' the big man continued. 'MacGuffin the Munificent. MacGuffin the Merciful. MacGuffin—'

'The Maroon?' Maxwell asked.

'MacGuffin the Mage,' said MacGuffin, in no uncertain tone. 'And MacGuffin the Maleficent to any who dare rub me up the wrong way with duff remarks like that.'

Maxwell reached for a tomato ketchup bottle which had previously escaped mention. 'Mage, you say?' said he. 'Do you mean, as in magician?'

'You thought, perchance, that I was a plumber?' MacGuffin laughed.

'Pornographer perhaps,' said Maxwell, squirting ketchup on his sausage.

MacGuffin's laughter stilled away. 'Magician I am. And one of no trifling talent. I maintain absolute control within the environs of my domain. I am a benign despot. All who dwell here understand this and are employed in a useful capacity. They enjoy the benefits of my maintenance of their equilibrium.'

'Well,' said Maxwell. 'You would appear to be doing a splendid job and as I assume I have you to thank for nursing me back to health, I thank you. Very much.'

'Indeed.' MacGuffin passed Maxwell a cup of tea.

'I was hoping to take some kind of work,' said Maxwell, accepting the cup.

'There is no work here for a man like you.'

'Oh, Dave must have got it wrong then.'

'I said there is no work *here*. There is work for you elsewhere though. I divine in you, Maxwell, a man who lacks purpose. A man of great talent, but one condemned to put this talent to no good use, unless under the guidance of some leading light. Tell me, have you ever heard of a town called Grimshaw?'

Maxwell, who had been packing toast into his mouth, now spat this all over the table. 'Sorry,' he spluttered. 'Went down the wrong way. Grimshaw, you say? No, I don't think I know the name.'

'How strange,' MacGuffin dusted flecks from his layered leisurewear. 'Several riders came through here only yesterday. They spoke of a terrible disaster that had befallen Grimshaw and told of the three men responsible. One of these answered to your description and also, would you believe, your name.'

'Coincidences abound,' said Maxwell, dabbing at his chin. 'Many have sought to interpret them, all with an equal lack of success.'

'All, that is, before *me*,' said MacGuffin. 'But then I do not believe in coincidence. I believe in predestination. I feel absolutely certain that fate has taken you by the hand and led you directly to my door.'

'That's a cheering thought,' said Maxwell, who had the feeling that it was anything but. 'These, er, riders, are they still in the village?'

'No. They have departed on their way. All bar one, who has departed upon *mine*.'

The sinister emphasis laid on the word *mine*, was not lost upon Maxwell who now felt quite certain that it was time to say thank you and farewell. There was something deeply unsettling about this gargantuan figure with his love of the lewd and his taste for autocracy. 'Well,' said Maxwell. 'This has been a most marvellous meal and again I must thank you for looking after me and everything. But I'm sure your time is valuable and I must not presume to take it up in such abundance. Thank you and farewell.' He rose shakily to his feet.

MacGuffin fluttered his fingers. 'Stay, stay,' said he. 'I would not have you leave quite yet. Eat your fill. Sustain yourself for your journey.'

'All full up,' said Maxwell, patting his belly. 'Goodbye now.'

'*Sit down!*' MacGuffin fluttered his fingers once more and Maxwell's knees gave out beneath him. He sank back to his chair in an undignified heap. 'Comfy?' asked MacGuffin.

'No,' said Maxwell. 'What have you done to my knees?'

'A temporary disassociation of the muscular synapses. It will pass.'

'What do you want from me?' Maxwell asked in a quavery voice.

'All right,' said MacGuffin. 'Let us bandy words

no more. You are Max Carrion, the imagineer who brought chaos to Grimshaw.'

'It wasn't my fault,' complained Max. 'I was trying to help.'

'Well, you shall help me. I require you to perform a service. I have restored you to health and kept your whereabouts secret. Now you will repay my kindness. This is fair, don't you think?'

'I suppose so,' said Maxwell, plucking at his knees.

'Ungrateful bastard,' said MacGuffin. 'Free breakfast thrown in and all.'

'OK, I'm sorry. What is it you want me to do?' Maxwell shuddered. 'Nothing sexual, is it?'

'How dare you!' MacGuffin's nostrils flared. The chains on his nose-ring jingled.

'No offence meant,' said Maxwell.

'Nothing sexual,' said MacGuffin. 'I have all the women I need. All the men too, as it happens. And the sheep and—'

'What do you want me to do?'

'In Dave's company you used the word "computer".'

'Dave told you that?'

'A sparrow hawk has ears.'

'It was a kestrel.'

'No matter. Its ears were my ears.'

'Then those animals that plague Dave – *you* cause them.'

'My subjects must be kept on their toes. Dave's job is to keep watch on the high street, greet all strangers and direct them here, by one means or another.'

Maxwell's knees showed no signs yet of supporting him, which was a shame, considering how dearly he wished to put them into service.

'Interesting things, computers,' said MacGuffin the mage.

'I never found them particularly so.'

'It is said that they caused the downfall of the old aeon, you know.' MacGuffin dipped a bread soldier into his tea and sucked upon it. 'Formed a global link, hard-wired the planet. Blew its natural fuse.'

'That wouldn't surprise me one bit.'

'I have one,' said the mage. 'Well, half a one. Your mission, should you choose to accept it – and you will – would be to supply me with the missing half.'

'Have you ever heard of the word, *electricity*?' Maxwell asked.

'Of course. Have you ever heard of the word, *iconolagny*?'

'No.'

'Good. This computer does not require electricity. It requires its other half. Let me show it to you.' MacGuffin clapped his hands together. 'Aodhamm, come,' he called.

There came the sounds of movement on the stairs beneath: dragging footsteps. Frankensteinian dragging footsteps, horrible monstrous Frankensteinian dragging footsteps.

Maxwell shifted uneasily on his knackered bentwood.

'Get a move on, you idle bugger,' called MacGuffin.

The horrible monstrous Frankensteinian dragging footsteps drew nearer and nearer.

Something entered the room.

Maxwell gawped.

This something was no graveyard nasty. This something was a something of such rare and almost unutterable beauty, that a man might expect to view such a something only once in his lifetime.

Or twice if he was very lucky.

Or three times, if he was Mr David Doveston of Bronwyn Terrace, Harlech, who is blessed of the gods and regularly has Jesus round to tea.

Maxwell might have managed 'Rock 'n' Roll', but he was speechless.

The something of rare and almost unutterable beauty shuffled into the high-domed room, bringing with it a golden radiance that seemed to make the very air vibrate.

It was a man. But such a man. A man of bronze (though not Doc Savage). A man of burnished bronze, of metal. Perfect in form. An Adonis. Quite naked. Embarrassingly so.

Maxwell turned away his face. This wonderful creation did not belong here, in this house of perversity. 'Who is he?' Maxwell asked.

'*What* is he. He is an automaton. A robot. A computer.'

Maxwell shook his head. 'But he lives, surely.' He glanced at the beautiful man, who stood with downcast eyes, exuding, for all his radiance, an aura of unbearable sadness.

'He is but a toy,' said MacGuffin the mage. 'An exotic toy. But he yearns for his mate.'

'His mate?'

'His other half; her name is Ewavett. You will reunite them.'

Maxwell tried to picture the other half. As beautiful as this? More beautiful by nature of its femininity? And he could picture, without difficulty and without going into detail, just what plans MacGuffin had for these two once they were reunited, what entertainments he might expect them to provide.

'He is no toy,' said Maxwell. 'No robot. Can he speak?' Maxwell glanced back up at the metal man. '*Can* you speak?'

The metal man just hung his head and stared blankly at the floor.

'He seldom speaks. He can perform a few basic tasks. He is made of metal, Maxwell. Come, Aodhamm, let Maxwell have a feel of you.'

The shining figure shuffled over to the table and reached out an elegant hand. It was clearly metal, although not jointed, or hinged, but flowing like mercury.'

'Go on,' said MacGuffin. 'Have a good feel.'

'No,' said Maxwell. 'Somehow it isn't right. I won't.'

'As you please. Aodhamm, be gone.'

Aodhamm turned away and left the room upon dragging naked feet.

'So,' said MacGuffin. 'You have seen him. You have seen his sorrow. You will restore his other half to him. Yes?'

'No,' said Maxwell. 'Well possibly,' said Maxwell. 'Well, yes,' said Maxwell. 'But I want to know a good deal more. If he is a robot, which I doubt, who made him? And where? And how did you come by him? And how did he get separated from his mate? And who has his mate now? And—'

'That's quite enough ands. You will restore Ewavett to him?'

'Yes,' said Maxwell. 'If I can.'

'Good,' said MacGuffin. 'Then you have at last found a purpose. That is good.'

Good for Aodhamm, thought Maxwell, but not good for you.

'But can you be trusted?' asked MacGuffin.

'To restore Aodhamm's mate to him? Absolutely.'

'But can *I* trust you, Maxwell?'

'I have said I will attempt to do what you ask. What more can I say?'

'You could say, to yourself of course, I will restore Aodhamm's mate to him, but not for the voyeuristic pleasure of the odious MacGuffin; him I will seek to slay, as soon as the opportunity presents itself.'

'As if I would,' said Maxwell.

'As if you would,' said MacGuffin. 'So I can trust you implicitly?'

'I swear that you can,' said Maxwell, crossing his heart with his right hand, and the fingers of his left beneath the table.

'Excellent,' said MacGuffin. 'Excellently excellent. Then the action that I now perform is nothing more than a formality.'

'And what action might this be?'

MacGuffin smiled through his golden nose-ring. 'I'm going to remove your soul,' said he.

9

'No!' Maxwell fought to bring life to his knees. 'Whatever you're going to do, don't!'

'Tut, tut, tut.' MacGuffin shook a big finger at Maxwell. 'You have sworn that I can trust you. So now, that the balance of equilibrium be maintained, I swear with equal sincerity that you can trust me.'

Maxwell made a bitter face. 'Irony, I can take,' said he, 'but death is quite another matter. Please let me go. I truly, truly promise you can trust me.'

'And I believe you, really I do. But I am an old-fashioned fellow and well set in my ways. So pardon me if I go about my own business in my own fashion. Radical changes rarely bring forth pleasing results. This lesson, I feel, is one that you yourself are coming to learn.'

'There is much I could learn from a man of your genius,' said Maxwell, putting his brain into first gear. 'Much that you could teach a willing pupil.'

'Much more than you could ever imagine.'

'A willing pupil, once taught, could manage the affairs of the village,' said Maxwell, 'giving his master more time to engage in his private pursuits. Such a pupil—'

'Maxwell,' said MacGuffin, 'don't bullshit the bullshitter, there's a good fellow. Now, let's get on with it.'

MacGuffin clapped his hands together. 'Come, cabinet,' he called, and at his calling, and to Maxwell's further amazement, a long glass-topped cabinet, ominously coffin-shaped and brass-bound at the corners, entered the room, floating several inches above the floor.

'Over here,' called MacGuffin the mage. 'And get a move on, do.'

The cabinet swung around and dropped to the floor with a thud.

'Careful,' said MacGuffin.

'Sorry,' said the cabinet.

Maxwell beat furiously upon his knees, but to no avail.

The magician flipped open the long glass top and explored the cabinet's interior. Upon velvet cushioning rested a number of crystal globes, each approximately the size of a small melon or a large orange or a very large grape or an absolutely enormous blackberry or a severely shrunken pumpkin, depending on your taste in fruit and your sense of proportion.

MacGuffin dipped in his prodigious fingers and lifted one out. He went 'Hhhh' upon it and buffed it gently upon his sleeve, before leaning across the table and placing it before Maxwell.

'What is this?' Maxwell asked.

'What do you think it is?'

'A crystal globe, exactly the size of a nineteenth-century French ceramic carpet bowl.'

'Is that supposed to be funny?' MacGuffin asked.

Maxwell shrugged. 'Search me.'

'Then look inside the globe.'

Maxwell leaned forward and peered in. 'By the Goddess,' said he, falling back in his chair. 'It's Rushmear the horse dealer. How did he get inside there?'

MacGuffin took the globe into his possession.

'This is not the flesh-and-blood Rushmear. This is his spiritual homunculus, his etheric stuff. His *soul*, if you like.'

'I do not like. Then Rushmear is dead?'

'No. He is very much alive for now. And working hard for me far away to the north. I hope he *is* working.' MacGuffin gave the crystal globe a sharp tap with the ring upon his thumb.

An agonized cry echoed about the room. It did not come from the crystal globe.

Maxwell made a frightened face. 'What was that?'

'Just a little reminder to Rushmear to keep on the job. Not that I think he needs one.'

'So Rushmear is away searching for Ewavett?'

'His physical self is. His soul remains here, under my control, to be returned to him should he successfully complete his mission.'

'I'm sure you can rely on Rushmear,' said Maxwell. 'He's a most determined fellow. With him on the case, you have no need to send me. So, shall we discuss what duties you would like me to perform about the house?'

'Such discussions can wait until *you* return.'

'Fair enough,' said Maxwell. 'But for all we know Rushmear might return at any moment with Ewavett by his side.'

'That is somewhat optimistic.'

'You're right. Let's give him a week, or perhaps two. Then if he has not returned, I will set out and see what's become of him.'

MacGuffin shook his head wearily. 'Spare me your wheedlings, Maxwell, you set out today and that is that.'

'But I—'

'Enough, Maxwell, or I seal up your mouth.'

Maxwell raised his hand politely.

'Go on then, but make it brief.'

'Look,' said Maxwell, 'I don't understand any of this. How can Rushmear be up north somewhere working for you, and his soul be here?'

MacGuffin returned the crystal globe to the cabinet. 'Through refined magic it is possible to separate a man's soul from his body without the man dying. Such magic calls for considerable refinement and much practice. I have slipped up a few times in the past. Well, a great many times. But I have the knack of it now. But body and soul can only be kept apart for a limited period: a lunar month. Twenty-three days.'

'A lunar month is twenty-eight days,' said Maxwell.

'I would not recommend that you put it to the test. So, as I say. If body and soul remain apart a day longer, then—'

'I get the picture. As a matter of interest, how many others are presently away seeking Ewavett for you?'

MacGuffin examined the rows of globes and shook his head sadly. 'Only Rushmear, I regret. As for the others,' he shrugged, 'you just can't get the help nowadays, can you?'

Maxwell shook his head dismally.

'But, if at first you don't succeed, and all that. Perhaps you will bump into Rushmear and the two of you join forces.'

Maxwell shook his head even more dismally.

'Allow me to tell you this. Ewavett is presently in the possession of a magician by the name of Sultan Sergio Rameer. He rules over a city called—'

'Rameer?' Maxwell asked.

'You've been there?'

'Just a lucky guess.'

'His influence extends over a considerable distance, so it will be necessary for me to set you down at the border of his kingdom.'

'Set me down?'

'I will arrange your transportation there. You must find your own way back. If you are successful, this should present no difficulty.'

'How so?'

'You'll find out. Now, let me give you this.' MacGuffin drew a small pouch from his pocket and tossed it across the table.

Maxwell took the thing between thumb and forefinger and examined it without a lot of interest. 'And what is this?'

'It's a bag with a hole in it.'

'Oh, thanks very much.' Maxwell made to fling the thing away.

'Not so fast. Put your hand inside.'

'Why?' asked Maxwell.

'Don't ask why. Just do what you're told.'

'There's nothing nasty in there?'

'There's *nothing* in there at all.'

Maxwell gingerly slipped his hand through the opening and felt inside the pouch. He could feel *nothing*. He slipped his hand in further. Up to the wrist. The forearm. Up to the elbow.

'By the Goddess,' Maxwell yanked out elbow, forearm, wrist and hand. 'How does it do *that*?'

'Never mind the how. Just be aware that it does. When you locate Ewavett, slip the bag over her head and draw it down to her feet. Whatever is contained within the bag loses its weight and so may be easily transported.'

'That's very clever,' said Maxwell, truly impressed. 'Did you give Rushmear a pouch like this?' Maxwell tucked the thing into his trouser pocket.

'What I gave or did not give Rushmear is no concern of yours.'

'Fair enough. But tell me, with all the magic at your

disposal, why do you not simply travel to Rameer and acquire Ewavett yourself?'

'I am too busy here. I cannot leave the village.'

'I suspect otherwise. I suspect that this Sultan Sergio, who rules a city rather than a village, is your superior in magic. I further suspect that it would be nothing less than suicidal to attempt *stealing* Ewavett from him. And I—'

'Enough, Maxwell. Enough. I have my people to care for.'

'Your slaves to rule, more like.'

'*Enough!*' MacGuffin snapped his fingers and Maxwell's jaw locked.

'Grmmph!' went Maxwell. 'Rmmph, mmmmph!'

'Will you hold your tongue?'

Maxwell nodded vigorously.

'Good.' MacGuffin snapped his fingers again and Maxwell's jaw unlocked.

'Now I shall remove your soul.'

'No,' said Maxwell. 'Listen.'

'Careful now.'

'I'm being careful. You don't understand. I'm not like others of this time. If you take my soul you will kill me.'

'That would be a shame. But no doubt I can put your body to good use. Or at least your skin. Stuffed and imaginatively mounted it can join the others in my private basement collection.'

'You vile bastard!' Maxwell lunged across the table.

The magician drew back and uttered certain words of power. Maxwell's hands became affixed to the table top.

'Now let this be done,' said MacGuffin, drawing a slim transparent tube from the glass-topped cabinet. 'Please speak no further words, or you go upon your way with a maggot for a tongue.'

What happened next happened horribly fast and was horribly horrible also. MacGuffin snatched hold of Maxwell's head, drew it up, rammed the transparent tube up his left nostril, pushed and pushed and pushed. Maxwell's eyes started from their sockets. Blood spurted from his right nostril. MacGuffin put the other end of the tube into his mouth and sucked. There was a terrible sound. A scream? A whine? A high-pitched sawing? MacGuffin lifted his nose-ring and took from his mouth a shining crystal globe which he examined carefully, nodded over, then placed in the cabinet.

Then he tore the tube from Maxwell's nose.

Maxwell's hands freed. He slumped back in his chair, gagging and wretching. He clutched at his head.

'Hurts, doesn't it?' said MacGuffin. 'But the operation was a success and the patient didn't die.'

Maxwell opened his eyes and stared at MacGuffin. Suddenly all had changed. If MacGuffin had seemed evil before, now he seemed something much more than that, a transcendent malignant horror. Evil beyond all evilness.

'You will experience a shift in your sensitivities,' said this loathsome beast. 'A man without a soul is a very angry man. A man bereft of scruple or conscience or compassion; a man driven by rage and motivated only by the desire to be reunited with his spirit.'

Maxwell foamed about the mouth. 'I will kill you,' he said.

'No, you will not do that. You will do what I wish you to do. Fetch me Ewavett or die so doing. I told you that fate led you directly to my door. Is not Carrion the perfect name for a man without a soul?'

Maxwell fought like a madman to rise from his seat.

'Know also this, Maxwell: I am ever alert. Do not think to return here empty handed. Do not think to sneak back and attempt to take me by surprise. This cabinet, for instance, opens only at my command. A word from me and it destroys its contents. Others have gone before you. Others who thought as you now think. They are gone into the nothingness that awaits us all. *I* am not.'

Maxwell glared with unbridled hatred at the magician and opened his mouth to speak curses.

The magician raised a hand. 'Though nothing would give me greater pleasure than to hear whatever it is you wish to say, as you have only twenty-three days in which to complete your mission, it would be churlish of me to keep you here chatting. So, Maxwell, farewell.'

MacGuffin rose to his feet and flung wide his arms. 'Horse and Hattock, Maxwell's chair,' he cried. 'To the outskirts of Rameer's kingdom at the hurry up. Be gone.'

The chair lifted from the floor. Maxwell tried to leap from it, but MacGuffin's magic was proof against that sort of thing. The chair swung across the room towards an open window and passed through it into the sky.

Maxwell, now clinging to the chair for what dear life remained to him, was only able to turn his head, glare back at MacGuffin and utter three small words.

But, though they were small, and only three in number, these were special words. Words which had brought untold joy to millions of discerning movie goers the old world over.

'I'll be back,' howled Maxwell.

'*I'll be back!*'

10

Maxwell clung fearfully to the flying chair.

With the red sky above, the grey earth below and himself lost somewhere in between, he sought to attempt the near impossible and collect his widely scattered wits.

He was angry. *Very* angry. A red-mist rage stormed around inside his head, kicking his senses all about. His nose was bleeding and his ears popped. His teeth rattled and his knees, now restored to power, knocked together violently.

Maxwell was in a bit of a state. What had MacGuffin done to him? Taken his soul? Impossible! Nonsense! You couldn't do a thing like that to someone. You just couldn't. There had to be a more logical explanation for the alarming situation he now found himself in. And the dreadful way he felt, wrung out like a jaded J-cloth, yet simmering as soup.

Perhaps he'd been hypnotized or narcotized, that was more likely. Bunged some dire hallucinogenic in his breakfast. Maxwell ground his rattling teeth. It was neither of those and he knew it. He'd had his first taste of magic in this new world of myth and legend and he was now in the worst trouble he'd ever been in.

He had to think his way out of this mess, and fast. Twenty-three days, MacGuffin had said. Twenty-three days, then wipe-out.

'I'll fix you, you BASTARD!' Maxwell raised a fist, the chair tilted alarmingly and Maxwell clung on once more for what was left of his dear life.

What did he know for certain? What could he cling to, mentally?

Well, he knew why MacGuffin had given him this crap chair to sit on. That was one.

And he knew what he was expected to do. Somehow steal Ewavett from the Sultan Rameer, pop her in her magical pouch and return with her to MacGuffin. That was two. Or twelve, or a hundred and seven. There was nothing certain at all there.

Kill MacGuffin. Yes, he was absolutely certain about that one. The evil MacGuffin must die.

Maxwell's teeth resumed their rattling. He *was* absolutely certain about that. Which was terrible. Murder somebody? He, Maxwell Karrien, murder somebody? Unthinkable. Up until now. But he, Max Carrion, man without a soul, man consumed by anger and hatred.

'Get a grip,' Maxwell told himself. 'You are the Imagineer. Cool reason. Strategy. Forward planning. Logic. Low cunning – lots of low cunning. Just get a grip. Don't go to pieces. And don't fall off.'

The chair flew on.

Maxwell set about the job of persuading it to land. He impersonated the voice of the magician and cried, 'Horse and Hattock, Maxwell's chair, and back to MacGuffin at once.'

The chair ignored him.

Maxwell locked his feet about the chair's legs, formed aerofoils with his hands and sought to steer the thing down.

The chair flew on regardless.

Maxwell took to wondering, as one would, just what held the chair aloft. Magic surely obeyed some scientific principles. Gravity *was* being defied here, after all. How was the magic done?

Did some invisible entity, summoned from the Goddess knew where and slave to the unspeakable MacGuffin, carry the chair upon its winged shoulders?

Was it a beam of force, possibly embodying elements of the transperambulation of pseudo-cosmic anti-matter?

Had the atomic structure of the chair been altered in some way that it was repulsed by the magnetic polarity of the planet?

Maxwell pondered upon the last possibility. What might occur if he could break the chair up, a bit at a time? Would its power slowly ebb away? Would it gently sink to the ground?

Or simply plummet?

With *his* luck?

Maxwell hunched on the chair and resigned himself to wait.

Onward flew the knackered bentwood. Onward ever onward.

Villages passed beneath. Rivers, streams, hills and mountains. A sea. Some dismal-looking islands. Maxwell recognized nothing.

Either the topography of the world had altered substantially when the great transition came, or he was simply flying over bits of it that he knew nothing of. One or either, both or neither, were as likely. There was no consolation to be had.

The chair moved at a fair old lick and Maxwell didn't have his cloak. It was bloody cold. By sunset he was hungry. And he needed the toilet. By sundown he was still hungry, but he had managed to piss on a fishing boat.

Whether the chair was offended by this, Maxwell didn't know, but with the coming of night it took to performing hair-raising aerial manoeuvres which seemed expressly calculated to dislodge him.

There was no sleep for Maxwell, and if it hadn't been for the thoughts which crowded his head, concerning the sequence of horrific tortures he would subject MacGuffin to prior to the slow and agonizing death, he would surely have nodded off and plunged to a swift one of his own.

By dawn Maxwell was grey-faced and crazy-eyed. Determination now held a rein to his fury. Revenge was ever uppermost in his mashed-about mind. Survival, at any cost, to satisfy this vengeance, the driving force of his being. And nasty stuff like that.

Shortly after sunrise the chair began to lose altitude. Maxwell could only guess how far he'd travelled, but it had to be many hundreds of miles. Far too many to walk back.

Maxwell recalled the magician saying that if he completed his mission successfully he would learn how to return. Learn how to activate the chair, perhaps?

But now was not the time for guessing. Now, Maxwell realized, was the time for praying. The chair was going down.

Fast.

Pell-mell.

And helter-skelter.

Maxwell's ears went, pop pop pop. A boiled sweet to suck on would have been nice. Down went the chair and up rushed the ground. Maxwell could hear it coming. And he could see it too.

It was a green and pleasant land. Far better looking than all that waste and moor he'd tramped across. But there was no joy whatever in the speed of its approach.

'Slow down!' Maxwell told the chair. '*Slow down!*'

The chair was deaf to Maxwell's pleas. It had

evidently reached its destination and was now eager to return to its natural habitat. The chair began to spin on its vertical axis, the dreaded 'Roman Candle', much afeared by parachutists. Round and round went Maxwell and down and down and down.

Blur, whirl, rush and scream.

And finally—

Stop!

The chair screeched to a halt. Maxwell caught his breath, gasped a gasp, thanked the Goddess, hailed Rock 'n' Roll, and cursed MacGuffin.

And then the chair dropped the final six feet.

Maxwell smashed down. Struck something, other somethings, further somethings. Rolled over and over and continued on down.

Then he came to rest in the dirt.

Winded, fuming, starving, bloodied, joint-stiff, sore-bummed, giddy-headed, Maxwell lay upon terra firma, a tangled heap of old grief and bad attitude, a sorry soul-less shadow of his former cheery self.

Hardly surprising really.

Groaning like a good'n and cursing fit to bust, the lad in the zoot suit, bowling shirt and fine substantial boots, raised himself to his knees and blinked around and all about.

And up.

Maxwell gazed up. And his jaw dropped down. Above him loomed the mountain, whose peak he had struck and whose side he had careered down. A fairly good-sized mountain, considering what it was composed of.

Chairs.

Bentwood chairs.

Hundreds and hundreds of broken, knackered, clapped-out bentwood chairs. Just like the one he had travelled upon.

'MacGuffin.' Maxwell shook his fist at the sky. 'I'll fix you, you fu—'

The word, whatever it might have been, probably 'Fuchsia-face' or 'Fumble-bottom', was cut short, however, by a clamouring of bells. Maxwell, senses tingling, lurched to his feet and gave his present surroundings a good looking about.

The mountain of broken chairs rose from a sort of plaza, paved with sandstone blocks, hexagonal in shape. The plaza too was hexagonal, high fence of iron staves running about its perimeter. Beyond this, clusters of houses, Mexican-looking. White adobe walls, tinged rose-pink by the wan sunlight. Shuttered windows. Dungeony doors.

Maxwell viewed the bell-clamourer. He was high atop a raised wooden tower, just beyond the perimeter fence. He was jumping up and down and pointing with his non-bell-clamouring hand.

He was pointing at Maxwell.

'Aw, sh—' This word, possibly 'Showaddy-waddy' or 'Shamrock' (but more likely 'Shit-a-bugger-bum-pooh'), was similarly cut short, as Maxwell now viewed the small dark running forms. They were carrying long poles with rope nooses attached to the ends. They were howling and whooping and hollering.

And yes, of course, they were running towards Maxwell.

They threw open gates in the perimeter fence and swarmed onto the plaza. Dozens of them. Dark and rat-like.

If they were men, then they were of no race Maxwell knew. Red eyes glared, sharp little teeth went snip-snap-snip.

Maxwell was in no fit state to fight, but he wasn't 'coming quietly'. He snatched up a chair leg, brandished it in a menacing fashion, weighed up the odds, found them not to his favour, and so set to scrambling back up the mountain of chairs.

The going wasn't easy, but the hollering mob, now ringed around the mountain, put a certain zest into Maxwell's climbing.

As he reached the summit, all torn fingernails and great lung-bursting gasps, a roar of applause rose up from below, followed by nothing but silence.

Hyperventilating and numb at the extremities, Maxwell peered down from his bentwood eyrie to see what was now on the go.

What was now on the go was a pathway clearing through the mob. Something tall and white was moving down it. Moving, of course, towards Maxwell.

Maxwell wiped sweat from his eyes. The tall white something was a man: a white man in a white suit and a white panama hat. He carried with him a long-handled fly whisk and an air of great authority.

At the foot of the mountain he paused, gestured. Little black forms scurried about, selected a serviceable chair, tested its strength, aided the white fellow onto it.

The white fellow gazed up at Maxwell and Maxwell in turn gazed down.

'Ahoy there,' called the white fellow in an upper-crust kind of a tone. 'Good day to you, sir.'

Maxwell glared him some daggers, irrational hatred knotting his stomach like a dodgy vindaloo. 'Kill him,' shouted Maxwell's senses. 'Go down there and rip off his head.'

''Spect you're feeling a bit squiffy,' called the white fellow. 'Fuming with rage and thinking you'd like to pluck out my eyeballs and drop red-hot coals in the sockets.'

'Eh?' managed Maxwell. The thought *had* crossed his mind.

'Perfectly natural, old chap. It's because of what MacGuffin did to you.'

At the mention of the magician's name the crowd shrank back, visibly cowed.

'What say you come on down and partake of a bit of brekky?'

Maxwell shook his head slowly.

'Pretty disorientated, eh? Understandable. Listen, haven't introduced meself. The name's Blenkinsop. Tim Blenkinsop. Chaps at the Colonial Club call me Tadger, but we needn't go into that here. I'm the Governor of these parts. Keep the natives in order, doncha know.'

Maxwell glared down upon the natives.

'Not a bad bunch. Bit rough around the edges. Pay'm no heed.'

Maxwell shook his head once more.

'Oh, I see. A bit perturbed about the numbers and the long sticks and all. For my own protection, d'you see? Think about the way you're feeling. Imagine yourself in my shoes.'

Maxwell weighed this up. The scales came down on the side of common sense.

'Tell them to go away,' called Maxwell. 'I'm feeling fine now.'

Governor Blenkinsop shook his panama'd head. 'No can do, old chap. Tried that once. Still walk with a limp when there's frost in the air. Listen, my old tum's crying out for a bowl of porridge and some rounds of toast and jam. Why don't you just sit up there and ponder the situation? I'll call back in a couple of hours, see which way your wind blows, what?'

Maxwell's hollow stomach gurgled noisily. 'Perhaps that would be for the best,' he called down. 'Until I get my senses straight. Would you be so kind as to send me up some food? One of your chaps could put down his stick and carry up a tray.'

The panama'd head shook again. 'Sorry, no can do, neither. Natives consider the pile of chairs taboo. Bad ju-ju to climb up. Superstitious bunch, but willing workers. Must adhere to local manners and customs, when in Romania and all that.'

'When in *Rome*,' Maxwell said.

'When in Rome, what, old chap?'

Maxwell shook his head. 'Never mind.'

'Quite so. Well, say toodle pip then, call back around lunch-time. Shouldn't climb down when I'm not about though. No telling what pranks this lot might get up to. Bye for now.' Governor Blenkinsop rose from the chair and turned to take his leave.

'No,' called Maxwell. 'Hang about.'

'Change of heart?'

Maxwell justly dithered. What to do for the best? Weather it out up here? For what? He was starving. A couple of hours up here and like as not he'd pass out. Or the mob would start chucking stones the moment the Governor's back was turned. 'I'm coming down,' called Maxwell. 'In the name of *MacGuffin*.'

'Ooooh!' went the crowd, shrinking back a little further.

'Stout fellow. Don't mind if I just walk on a bit. Really can't be too careful. Some of you blokes in absolute lather, frothing at the mouth and so forth. Have to play it safe. Hope you understand.'

'OK.' Maxwell climbed down the chairy mountain. It had been a lot easier climbing up. The chairs slipped and tumbled causing 'Ooohs' and 'Ahhs' from the swarthy crowd.

At last Maxwell found himself once more upon the ground.

'Follow me then,' called Governor Blenkinsop,

marching away. Little black figures fell in behind him, others now cleared a path for Maxwell, who dubiously followed the man in the white panama.

Across the plaza they went and out through one of the gates. A few yards beyond the Governor turned and winked back at Maxwell.

'Everything okey-dokey?' he called over the multitude of little black heads.

'Yes thank you.'

'So good. *Kakoo bee benado kunky.*'

'Pardon?' Maxwell called.

The man in white raised a pale right hand. '*Kakoo bee benado kundy!*' he shouted. And at this signal the mob fell upon Maxwell. He was dragged from his feet, hurled to the ground, stamped upon, then bound securely hand and foot and gagged about the mouth.

The man in white cleared a path once more and came to stand over Maxwell. 'Must apologize for the old subterfuge,' he said. 'Have it down to something of a fine art now. Practice making perfect and all that.'

Maxwell kicked and struggled but once again to no avail.

'Funny old lot the natives,' the Governor continued. 'Get things a bit arse about face. Believe in a sky god named *MacGuffin.*' (He whispered the hateful name.) 'Believe he sends down bounty from above. Human bounty. Human foodstuff, doncha know. Believe me to be a kind of high priest. Long as I keep'm supplied with din-dins, then they're nice as knitwear.'

Maxwell's teeth ground into his gag.

'Bloody furious, what? But you haven't heard the best bit yet. Told you I was the Governor. Didn't say Governor of where. Governor of this town Kakkarta. Which is in the province of *Rameer*! Close chum of the Sultan, me. Fraid old *MacGuffin*', the whisper again, 'got his calculations a bit skew-whiff. Should have dropped you a mile to the south. Bit of a bummer, eh? Still, you'll get plenty of grub to fill up the old tum-tum. Natives will want to fatten you up. Like their gifts from the god nice and fat. Big'ns small'ns, they can't tell one white man from another. But they do like them all to be nice and fat when they gobble them up. Must skedaddle now. Trust you won't take this personally. Only doing my job for the Sultan. You know how it is.' And with that said the Governor skedaddled and Maxwell was left to the untender mercies of the mob.

He really did his best, with the struggling and kicking and the swearing too, once he had bitten through his gag. But he was raised and dragged and buffeted and driven across the town.

The little shuttered windows in the pinky-tint adobes were open now and tiny black faces peeped down upon him. They certainly weren't human this lot. Black rat crossed with cockroach. Those darting red eyes, chitin wattles with awful furry parts. That it really didn't count as cannibalism if you didn't eat one of your own species wasn't a point at all, so as such it didn't enter Maxwell's head.

And why should it?

Beyond the town, a grey concrete area. The foundations of an ancient building perhaps. A big heavy iron grille was being unbolted and raised. Maxwell's hands and feet were untied, he was lifted into the air, flung forwards and down.

Down into a pit beneath.

As Maxwell hit rock bottom in a pile of manky hay, the grille clanged shut above and the bolt flew home. Evil black faces giggled and chattered gibberish, then drew back and were gone.

A dim red shaft of sunlight fell upon Maxwell as he thrashed about in the manky hay. Screaming and shouting.

131

Then, suddenly aware of the terrible stench, he shut his mouth and clapped a hand across his nose. The smell was appalling. The smell was of human excrement.

Maxwell slumped down in a wretched heap. This was it. The bitter end. The end to everything. Tricked once more. And this time, the last ever time. He was truly done for. To be fattened for the pot. The most ignominious end known to man. This was as bad as it could possibly get. No worse than this could there be.

'Well, well, well, well.' The voice wasn't Maxwell's, but it *was* one Maxwell knew. A friend! Dear Goddess, a kindred spirit. A soul with whom to spend his final days?

A movement and a big and bulky frame shambled into the shaft of light. The head was a mass of matted grime. The eyes shone a ghastly white. 'Well, well, well, well,' said Rushmear the horse dealer. 'What a pleasant surprise this is.'

11

'Now, Rushmear wait.' Maxwell scrambled into
the farthest corner he could scramble to. It was
the corner that served as latrine, quite naturally
enough. 'Urgh,' went Maxwell. 'Now don't do anything hasty.'

'Hasty?' The burly horse trader rocked to and fro
upon his heels. 'Hasty? Allow that thought to perish.
Slow and steady and one bone at a time.'

'Rushmear, you're making a big mistake.'

'Oh, pardon me,' said Rushmear, in an evil whisper.
'For a moment there I thought you were none other
than Max Carrion, Imagineer.'

Maxwell gave a foolish titter. 'Who?'

'Max Carrion, who tricked me from my horses, made
a laughing-stock of my lovely daughter and was party
to the riot that ended with my town being burned to
the ground. The same Max Carrion whom I swore
to track down and whilst so doing fell into the
clutches of a mad magician who stole my soul and cast
me halfway across the world that I might grace the
table for a hoard of Skaven rat ogres.'

'Easy mistake to make,' said Maxwell. 'I've been told
I do bear a passing resemblance to the man you speak
about.'

'Even down to the big substantial boots. You are that
man. And now you die.'

133

'Can't we talk about this?' Maxwell cowered and flinched.

'My brain burns,' said Rushmear. 'It may cool a little once I have disposed of you.' He swayed forwards, crooking the fingers of his mighty hands. 'Recommend yourself to your maker, for in minutes you will meet Him face to face.'

Maxwell sought invisibility. And in the seeking thereof, and what with death definitely now being only moments away, a thought entered his head, which was swiftly joined by another and yet another. Until, and all this occurred in but a single nanosecond, these thoughts melted themselves into one mighty thought.

Rushmear lunged forward, grasped Maxwell by the throat and hauled him up the stinking wall.

'Let me go,' gagged Maxwell. 'I know you hate me, but you hate MacGuffin more. *Croak-gag-cough.*'

'I hate all,' said Rushmear, tightening his hold.

'I can get you out of here,' choked Maxwell. 'I know of a way. You could revenge yourself on MacGuffin, reclaim your soul. *Gag-choke.*'

'There is no way out of here, the grille is beyond reach.'

'You could revenge yourself on the Governor too. *Gasp-gag.*'

'I'll pluck out his eyes and—'

'If you kill me now you'll never know how.' Maxwell's senses were departing him fast. 'What have you got to lose?'

The grip slackened. Not a lot, but sufficient to allow a modicum of air to pass down Maxwell's windpipe.

'Speak,' said Rushmear. 'Speak quickly and clearly. And precisely.'

Maxwell opened his mouth and began to speak.

*　　*　　*

It was nearly ten of the morning clock before breakfast arrived. And when it did, it looked far from appetizing. A pail-load of vegetables, emptied without ceremony down through the grille.

Rushmear held Maxwell back with one big hand whilst sorting through the tumbled veggies with the other.

'Let me eat,' implored Maxwell. 'If I die of starvation, you will never get free.'

'Of this I am aware. But if you eat without care you'll suffer for your folly.'

'How so?'

'There are little seeds amongst the vegetables. Seeds of the blow-gut bush. They look harmless and wholesome, but when eaten they swell in your belly, puff you out.'

'How do you know that?'

'I am Rushmear the horse dealer. I know how to fatten cattle. Here, chew on this.' Rushmear handed Maxwell a parsnip.

The day then passed without a happy interlude to call its own. Maxwell explained the more subtle details of his scheme to Rushmear. Rushmear chewed upon them and spat faults from each, so that Maxwell was put to the further effort of consoling the truculent horse dealer, who seemed at every moment on the point of losing all control, and simply splaying him there and then.

It was a long day and made singularly hideous by Rushmear's not infrequent visits to the latrine corner.

By sunset Maxwell's nerves were in the final phase of decomposition and he felt certain that his nose would never function properly again.

The sun vanished away, and the moon, the one with the new improved twenty-three-day cycle, rose into the sky. It flung a sheet of whiteness into the black hole of Kakkarta.

'Hand me the string,' said Maxwell. Rushmear, who had been unravelling his woollen smock all day and knotting the lengths of yarn together, handed the coil to Maxwell.

'Now,' said the imagineer, 'I knot a turnip to this end and throw it up through the grille, it loops over one of the bars and I gently lower the turnip down again.'

'Go on then.'

Maxwell had a crack at it. His first throw fell short, and his second. At the third, the turnip dropped off the end.

'Give me the line, fool,' ordered Rushmear. 'I was roping horses when I was four years old.'

'You might have said.'

Rushmear gave a surly snort, re-knotted the turnip, twirled it with surprising dexterity for such a huge man, flung up the line . . . And missed.

Maxwell opened his mouth.

'Don't you dare,' cautioned Rushmear.

Twelve throws later, the line passed through the grille, the turnip passed over a bar and Rushmear carefully lowered it down.

'Now,' said he, 'perform your party piece.'

'Certainly.' Maxwell took MacGuffin's magic pouch from his pocket, placed it on the awful floor and put one leg into it. He sank down with a terrible thud, striking certain tender parts of his anatomy upon the aforementioned awfulness. Rushmear clamped a hand over Maxwell's mouth. 'Get in, fool. *No*, hold up.'

Maxwell with one leg in and the rest of him out, managed a 'What?'

'I don't care for this,' said Rushmear. 'The plan as

you explained it is that you climb into this magic pouch, I tie the pouch to the turnip end of the line then pull on the other. The pouch goes up through the grille, you climb out, release the bolt and open the grille.'

'Yes?' said Maxwell. 'And a fine plan it is too.'

'But how do *I* get out?'

'I lower the pouch back down to you. You climb inside and I haul you up. I don't even need to release the bolt and open the grille.'

'I am not happy with this,' said Rushmear. 'I will climb into the pouch and you will pull me up first.'

'No,' said Maxwell, 'I won't.'

'You will, or I wring your neck.'

Maxwell shook his head. 'A degree of trust must exist between us. I thought up this plan, so I go first. If you refuse to abide by my rules, step into the pouch and see what happens next.'

'What *will* happen next?'

'I will stamp on the pouch,' said Maxwell. 'And escape by another means I have just thought of.'

Rushmear set free a low growl. 'And what if I abide by your rules, and pull you up first? You climb free and run off, leaving me here.'

'Then shout at the top of your voice. No doubt I will soon be recaptured.'

Rushmear made more low grumbling sounds.

'Look,' said Maxwell, 'escaping from this cell is the relatively easy bit. Seeking out Ewavett and wresting her from the Sultan Rameer, then returning to MacGuffin to reclaim our souls will prove far more tricky. I have no wish to form an alliance with you, but together we may succeed. And we may snuff out the egregious MacGuffin. Singly our chances are not too good. Already I am down to twenty-two days. You are down to twenty-one, I believe.'

'Climb into the pouch,' said Rushmear. 'I will pull you up.'

Maxwell stepped smartly into the magic pouch, pulled himself through the opening and crouched down inside the nothingness within. Rushmear attached the pouch to the turnip end of the knotted yarn and pulled upon the other. The pouch travelled up, plopped over the grille bar and would certainly have fallen back into the cell, had not Maxwell hastily thrust out his arm.

He climbed from the magic pouch, onto the grille, drew in great drafts of clean night air, and then he looked furtively about. All seemed quiet and still. The Skaven rat ogres were evidently early bedders. Maxwell lowered the empty pouch back down into the foul hole beneath.

Rushmear climbed hastily inside. Maxwell hauled him up.

Drawing the pouch through the grille, Maxwell held it at arm's length and smiled a wicked smile.

'Let me out,' called a little voice from within.

'Silence.' Maxwell gave the pouch a shake. 'A slight change of plan.'

'Let me out.'

Maxwell drew the draw-string tight. 'Certain doubts assail me,' he explained. 'Certain fears that, should I release you, you might choose to play me false. Possibly even murder me where I stand.'

'I would never think of such a thing!' called the little voice. 'We are as brothers in our quest to reclaim our souls.'

'Nevertheless,' whispered Maxwell, 'I feel it better that you remain in the pouch for now.'

'Traitor! Bastard! Whore son! Wait until I—'

'That's quite enough from you.' Maxwell tucked the pouch into his trouser pocket. Rushmear was no doubt kicking away like a mad man, but Maxwell could feel nothing of it. The magic pouch negated the gravity of anything within and nothing of it could be felt without.

Giving his pocket a little pat for luck, Maxwell slipped quietly from the town of Kakkarta and ran off into the night.

12

Maxwell didn't run far from Kakkarta. He sorely needed to sleep and the prospect of a mad dash into yet another wilderness, with the probability of recapture, when he fell down from exhaustion, was not to his liking.

Maxwell had other ideas. Other thoughts.

Thoughts of an imagineering nature.

The moon was high and by its unromantic light he spied what he was looking for: a little stream that danced along beside the road. Maxwell stamped down the bank, being careful to leave nice big footprints and jumped into the stream. Then he waded back towards Kakkarta.

At a bridge close to the outskirts of the town he removed his boots, knotted the laces together, hung them about his neck and came ashore.

Maxwell sought the Governor's house. It was not hard to find, being substantially larger than all the rest and sporting a flag pole in its garden. With a wary eye out for watchdogs or guards, Maxwell tiptoed across the garden and searched for the convenient vine.

The convenient vine, as everyone who has ever watched an adventure film will recall, is a sturdy affair that clings to the wall of the villain's abode. It offers a series of strong footholds which afford the hero easy access to either a balcony (where the villain can be spied out pacing the floor or shaking a fist at the heroine, who sits defiantly upon a bed with her clothes in disarray) or the roof.

Of course, the convenient vine must not be treated disrespectfully. Somewhere, high up in its branches, is 'the loose bit', which comes away in the hero's hand and nearly has him tumbling to his doom.

Maxwell found the convenient vine at the back of the Governor's house. He put on his substantial boots and shinned up it.

Halfway up he happened upon a balcony, peeping over he spied a lighted bedroom. Within, the Governor paced up and down.

Maxwell climbed on up. He almost came to grief near the top, when a loose bit came away in his hand and threatened to send him tumbling to his doom. But Maxwell clung on by his fingertips and hauled himself onto the flat roof above.

Here he ducked down beneath the parapet, caught his breath and pulled the magic pouch from his trouser pocket.

'Rushmear,' he whispered, 'are you still awake?'

'*Awake?*' roared Rushmear, though his voice came as from a great distance away. 'I'll not sleep until I've put my hand down your throat and torn out your spleen.'

'Spot on,' said Maxwell. 'Now listen, I am going to release the draw-string of the pouch by just a smidgen. When the first ray of sunlight touches you, set up a shout and awaken me, OK?'

There was silence in the pouch department.

Maxwell gave the pouch a violent shake, which evoked bitter wails and curses. 'Should you fail to awaken me and I over-sleep, then most surely will I grind my heel upon you.'

Maxwell loosened the draw-string a weeny bit, not

sufficient for Rushmear to worm a finger through, of course. And set down the pouch upon the roof. 'Good night, Rushmear,' said Maxwell.

Silence.

Maxwell gave the pouch another violent shake.

'Good night, Maxwell,' said Rushmear. 'Sleep well.'

At dawn the sun came up like a big red Coca-Cola sign without the logo. Or a vast flat tomato. Or any one of a dozen other oversized bright red objects, none of which springs immediately to mind.

The air was crisp, there were no clouds. There seemed all the makings of another day that was just like the one that had gone before.

Maxwell awoke to the sounds of cock-crow and profanity.

He yawned, stretched, picked up the pouch. 'Good morning, Rushmear,' he said. 'And how are you today?'

'I need a shit,' said Rushmear.

'If I let you out of the bag to have one, do you promise to get straight back inside afterwards?'

'With all my heart,' said Rushmear.

'Yeah, right.' Maxwell retightened the drawstring and tucked the pouch back into his pocket, further muffling the torrent of abuse that poured from it.

Maxwell climbed over the parapet and shinned back down the convenient vine. He dropped silently onto the balcony of the Governor's bedroom, crept across it and tried the handle of the french windows. Unlocked.

On the tippiest of tippy-toes Maxwell crossed the room to the Governor's bed, glared at the sleeping figure, picked up a weighty earthenware jug that stood on the bedside table and brought this down with immoderate force upon the Governor's head.

A brief period of activity followed, the activity being all of Maxwell's making.

A bucket of water struck the Governor full in the face. He jerked into consciousness. Eyes wide, mouth ready to cry out. It did not cry out. The Governor's teeth chewed upon a gag.

His head jerked about. He tried to rise. He could not. He was bound to a chair by lengths of shredded bed sheet.

The wide eyes grew wider as the Governor took in the figure seated upon his bed. This figure wore the Governor's white suit and panama hat. He was gently flicking the Governor's fly whisk.

'Morning, Blenkinsop,' said Maxwell, gently flicking away. 'Been having a spot of shut-eye, what? Dashed sorry to waken you, old chap, but there's been a bit of a *coup d'état*. Town now under new management, doncha know.'

The Governor's eyes were quite round now, like polo mints with blue smarties stuck in the holes. He wriggled and squirmed but Maxwell had taken great care with the knot-tying.

'Now the thing is,' said Maxwell, adjusting the panama to a rakish angle, 'I need a bit of the old transportation. Have a pressing appointment with the Sultan. Send him your regards, naturally. Posthumous regards if needs be. If you catch my drift, old chap.'

The Governor no doubt did, because he hung his head. In doing so he caught sight of the clothes he now wore: Maxwell's clothes. He renewed his struggle with vigour.

'Don't like the suit?' Maxwell asked. 'S'pose you recall mentioning to me that one white man looks just like another to the natives. By the by, I came across

143

your phrase book. Been committing a few lines to memory. Care to hear them?'

The Governor shook his head fiercely from side to side.

'Still, I'll tell you anyway, what?' Maxwell recited the mouth load of Skaven gibberish he'd been rehearsing. His enunciation was far from perfect but the Governor was able to get the gist, which was, 'Chaps of Kakkarta. Behold, another gift from MacGuffin which fell from the sky in the night and I, the Governor, captured for you. He's a violent one, so don't release his gag. Just cook him at once.'

The Governor hung his shaking head once more. Maxwell got up from the bed, went over and released his gag. 'So,' said he. 'Let us discuss matters in a sensible fashion. I require maps, provisions and transportation. You will furnish me with these. Should you show any signs of hesitation or duplicity, I will have no compunction about dragging you into the town square and performing my recitation. Do I make myself quite clear?'

'Quite clear,' said Governor Blenkinsop.

'Right,' said Maxwell. 'Now, as Governor, I am quite sure the Sultan has supplied you with some marvellous means of transportation. What would this be? Seven-league boots, perhaps, or a magic carpet?'

Governor Blenkinsop shook his head. 'Such wonders are not issued to a humble servant of the Sultan. I have an old ox cart I would be prepared to lend you.'

Maxwell shook *his* head. 'That is sad news. You are being absolutely truthful with me, aren't you?'

'Oh yes,' said the Governor. 'Absolutely. Now look, I do have a raging stonker of a headache. Do you think you might untie me? There's a good fellow.'

'Shortly perhaps,' Maxwell raised a calming hand. 'But before this, let us test out a proposition. It might just be that the blow upon the head has caused some short-term memory loss and that you do, in fact, possess another means of transportation. What say I take a stroll down to the square and call out in the Skaven tongue, "I the Governor require my fastest means of transportation, bring it to me at once"? How do you feel about that?'

'I feel somewhat sick,' said the Governor. 'Might I have a glass of water?'

'Indeed,' Maxwell turned his back upon the Governor, went over to a dresser near the window, decanted water from a glass ewer into a pottery mug. He returned with this, held the Governor's nose up and tipped the contents of the mug straight down his throat.

Blenkinsop coughed, gagged and swallowed.

'Better now?' Maxwell asked.

Blenkinsop spat. 'The water is vile,' said he.

'Your town is vile,' said Maxwell. 'You are vile. Now I have no further time to waste, accede to my demands at once, or it's gag back on and down to the square for you.'

'You'd never get away with it, old chap. These creatures are not complete oafs, they'd see through you in a moment. They might well kill me, but they'll kill you also.'

'All right,' said Maxwell. 'Enough is enough. I have been far more reasonable with you than you deserve. Extreme measures are now called for.'

Maxwell pulled the magic pouch from his pocket and gave it a little shake. 'Rushmear,' he called, 'I have the Governor here.'

Rushmear released a scream of invective.

'My friend Rushmear,' Maxwell explained. 'The big fierce man you captured the day before yesterday. Constrained by magic and eager for release. He has plans for your future. Rushmear,' Maxwell said to the pouch, 'tell the Governor what you wish to do to him.'

Maxwell held the pouch close by the Governor's ear. Rushmear offered explicit details.

'All right,' cried the Governor. 'All right. Enough of such hideousness. By the happiest of coincidences my memory has just now returned to me. I recall that I have a divan, given to me by the Sultan, which moves upon the air when the correct commands are given.'

'And these commands are?'

'They wouldn't work for you,' said the Governor. 'I must speak them.'

'What are these commands?' Maxwell shook the magic pouch before the Governor's face. 'I will give them a try. Should they fail for me, you can have a go.'

'All right. All right. Just shout from the balcony these words, "*Baluda Baluda kocheck camara poo bah hock*".'

'Thank you,' Maxwell strode over to the french windows. Then he paused and returned to the bed, where he picked up the phrase book and leafed through it. 'Oh dear,' said he. 'By a curious coincidence these commands also mean, "Attention, attention, I am the escaped prisoner, come and get me, you scumbags".'

The Governor ground his teeth. Maxwell leaned down and kneed him viciously between the legs. The Governor doubled up in pain.

'That is it,' said Maxwell. 'All niceties are at an end. When you have regained your breath tell me the commands. In the meantime—'

Maxwell rampaged about the room, tearing open drawers, and cupboards, flinging the contents wither and thus. Maps and provisions, of course, are rarely to be found in bedrooms, but as happy chance would have it*, the Governor just happened to have a case of maps he'd been going through the night before and a packed picnic in a hamper. Maxwell availed himself of these.

'Now,' said he. 'No more time-wasting. I am a desperate man. The commands at once or I release Rushmear upon you, and when he has done his worst, I fling you from the balcony.'

'Shout, Horse and Hattock, Blenkinsop's divan,' mumbled Blenkinsop.

'And that's it?'

'Tell it where to go and it will take you.'

'It will respond to *my* voice?' Maxwell tweaked the Governor's ear.

'The natives don't speak our tongue, there was no need for such securative measures. Up until *now*, that is.'

Maxwell kicked the Governor in the ankle. The red rage he had been struggling to hold in check, was all but consuming him once more. 'You really had better be telling me the truth.'

'I am, I really am.'

'Right then.' Maxwell thrust the magic pouch into the trouser pocket of the Governor's white suit, took up the case of maps and the picnic hamper and strode to the french windows, flung them wide, stepped onto the balcony and yelled, 'Horse and Hattock, Blenkinsop's divan.'

Nothing happened. The town lay still all around. The sun, now somewhat higher, cast down its sombre light. Maxwell turned upon the Governor. 'What of this?' he asked.

'Shout louder. Shout *come* also.'

'If you're lying—'

*Oh yeah!

'Just shout it.'

Maxwell turned. 'Horse and Hattock, Blenkinsop's divan, *come*!'

And then a number of things happened. The Governor, who had been worming his hands free for some time, finally broke out of his bonds. And his bed, which he had thoughtlessly neglected to mention to Maxwell was the divan in question, rose from the floor with a rush.

It passed through the french windows at considerable speed, struck Maxwell from behind and tipped him over the balcony rail. The Governor, with the look of one far gone in dementia, leapt onto the divan as it passed him by, yelping in triumph.

'Halt, divan,' he cried, when the bed was some ten yards beyond the balcony. 'Hold still do.' The bed came to rest and hovered in the air.

Scrambling to the edge, the Governor peeped down, hoping to view Maxwell's broken body on the ground beneath and have a good gloat over it. No body, however, was to be seen.

'Come about, divan,' commanded the Governor. The magical bed drifted back towards the balcony.

The Governor peered at the convenient vine. Had Maxwell managed to grab it as he fell? 'Where's the bastard gone?' asked the Governor.

'Horse and Hattock and divan turn upside down.' The cry came from below. The cry came from Maxwell, who was clinging to one of the legs of the bed.

The divan turned smartly upside down. Maxwell, now on top, cried out in triumph. A voice from below screamed, 'Up the other way again.'

The divan, now uncertain quite what to do, turned upon its end. Maxwell clung to one side and Blenkinsop, the other.

'Out of town,' shouted Maxwell. 'Away to Rameer.'

'Stay where you are,' shouted Blenkinsop. 'Stay where you are.'

The divan began to turn in circles. Maxwell clambered onto the upright end. Governor Blenkinsop grabbed hold of his ankle.

'Get off,' bawled Maxwell, lashing out with a substantial boot.

The aerial commotion was now beginning to draw the attention of the townsfolk. Shuttered windows were opening. Nasty black shapes issued into the streets. Voices other than those of Maxwell and Blenkinsop were being raised. The watchman in the tower set to clamouring his bells.

'Get off!' Maxwell kicked with a will, but the Governor held him fast by the ankle. He evidently had considerable strength about him, for now he was climbing up. Maxwell tried to buffet him down, but clinging for that dear life of his to the violently rotating bed left him somewhat at a disadvantage.

The Governor hauled himself onto the upright end of the spinning bed. He saddled himself firmly and dug in his heels.

'You are a man of considerable enterprise,' he told Maxwell. 'Escaping from the hole, capturing me. But all is in vain. *Down, bed*!'

'*Up, bed*!' shouted Maxwell.

The bed continued to spin. And now took to lurching also.

'We seem to have confused the divan,' said the Governor. 'It will return to its senses once one of us is gone.' He drove forward and grabbed Maxwell by the white lapels. 'Off you go, old chap.'

Maxwell clung on. The Governor held him fast with one hand, raised the other, put out two fingers and drove them towards Maxwell's eyes. Maxwell tried to turn his head away, but could not.

'Time to die,' said the Governor.

The fingers moved closer and closer, filled all of Maxwell's vision.

Maxwell closed his eyes. Gritted his teeth.

The probing fingers pressed against his eyelids.

Maxwell prepared himself for the latest in a line of horrible ends.

He really should just have run off into the night. Coming back had not been all that clever.

'Goodbye, cruel world,' said Maxwell. 'Hail Rock 'n' Roll and praise the Goddess.'

The fingers pushed forwards.

Then stopped.

Drew back.

Maxwell opened his eyes.

The Governor was clutching at his stomach. His eyes were rolling. As Maxwell looked on, the shoulders of the zoot suit burst asunder. The arms ripped apart. Buttons popped from the bowling shirt.

The Governor groaned and moaned. 'What is happening?' he burbled.

That evil grin which Maxwell had worn as he drew tight the drawstring on the pouch containing Rushmear appeared once more upon his face. 'I think you're putting on a bit of weight,' he told the Governor. 'While you were unconscious I took the liberty of adding a handful of those blow-gut seeds you feed your prisoners to the ewer of water and giving it a good old stir. Remember how you thought the taste vile?'

'No,' croaked the Governor, swelling like a blimp.

'Yes,' shouted Maxwell. 'Vile bastard that you are. A taste of your own medicine. What, *old chap*!'

The Governor thrashed about, bloating hideously. Maxwell leaned forward and managed to let fly one really decent smack in the teeth. The Governor fell from the rotating bed. Down and down. As sheer chance would have it the bed was gyrating directly above the mountain of broken chairs as he fell. The Governor smashed down onto it, tumbled and bowled, rolled over and over and finally smacked to the ground, an ungodly naked swollen mass of flesh.

The Skaven rat ogres swarming through the gates fell upon him with relish.

Maxwell turned his face away from the horror. 'Horse and Hattock,' he told the divan, 'on at once to Rameer and no more farting around.'

Horror below, red sky above, Maxwell somewhere in between once more. The bed righted itself, Maxwell settled down upon it.

And the last Kakkarta heard of Maxwell was his voice, crying dismally, the words, 'My beautiful zoot suit.'

And then he was gone.

13

The divan flew off towards the north.

It moved at a sedate pace, some thirty feet above the ground, and stubbornly ignored Maxwell's demands for a greater turn of speed and a slight increase in altitude.

The divan simply dawdled along.

Maxwell lay back upon it, hands behind his head, staring bitterly towards the sky. He was *not* in a jubilant mood.

Certainly he had dealt out just deserts to Blenkinsop and escaped from Kakkarta with an enchanted bed to call his own. But. Well. Bloody Hell! He was still on this suicide mission. *And* he was hungry again. *And* he had lost his zoot suit. *And* he couldn't actually be certain that the bed was carrying him in the right direction. Maxwell thought it all too likely that some sneaky spell had been preprogrammed into the divan, that might dump the potential bedknapper into a watery grave or propel him to the heart of the ailing sun. And so it was for this reason that he had not ordered the bed to fly at once to the outskirts of MacGuffin's village, where, Maxwell felt confident, he could conceive a scheme to grab back his soul and punish the murky magician.

So Maxwell stewed, hungry, nervous and not a nice man to know. The red fug of anger and his hatred for

MacGuffin gnawed away at his senses like rats at a leper's foot. Urgh!

He would just have to get himself organized: set down somewhere safe, seek out some breakfast, ask directions, learn whatever might be learned about the city of Rameer and the Sultan who dwelt within.

And he would have to do something about the man in the magic pouch. Maxwell felt that now might well be the time to dissolve his uneasy partnership with the volatile horse trader.

The chances of this partnership ever becoming one of those now-legendary Cisco Kid and the Pancho jobbies, or a Lone Ranger and Tonto, or even an Abbott and Costello or a Sooty and Sweep, seemed somewhat remote. Rushmear and Maxwell did not seem destined to become soul buddies.

Soul-*less* buddies.

Soul-less adversaries.

But soul buddies? Nah!

Maxwell was going to have to 'let Rushmear go'.

Open the pouch and shake it out over the side of the flying bed was probably the best idea. A tad callous perhaps. But there you go. Or rather, there Rushmear went.

But strangely Maxwell felt disinclined to do it. Even though he now lacked for soul and conscience, he did not actually *hate* Rushmear. And although he knew that the horse trader would most certainly try to kill him the moment he was released, Maxwell also knew that it was hardly Rushmear's fault. Rushmear was, like himself, an innocent victim of circumstance.

Troubled times for Maxwell, but decisions had to be made.

And now.

Maxwell pulled the pouch from his trouser pocket. 'Rushmear, my good friend,' he called. 'Are you well?'

'I am hungry,' replied Rushmear in a voice of no small fury. 'And I am also in imminent danger of crapping myself.'

'But otherwise unscathed?'

'*Unscathed?* I have been shaken to buggeration.'

'No more so than I. But you will no doubt be overjoyed to learn that I have once again saved your life. We are free of Kakkarta and flying speedily towards Rameer upon a magic bed that *I* alone am able to command.'

'You are a living saint,' growled Rushmear. 'Please release me, that I may prostrate myself at your feet and offer thanks.'

'Yeah, right. But listen, Rushmear, I am locked in the horns of a terrible dilemma. And I would be grateful to hear your views, as they would colour my thinking in regard to the matter of your release.'

'Speak on,' muttered Rushmear. 'It is always a joy to hear your words.'

'OK. As I have said to you before, the chances of one man alone succeeding in the mission to acquire Ewavett and return to MacGuffin are less than zero. Two men, acting in harmony, sharing the same goal of regaining their souls before their time ticks away, might well achieve this. If one of them is you and the other, me.'

'So where lies your dilemma?' Rushmear asked in a greasy tone. 'Release me and let us set to the task without further delay.'

'My thinking entirely. But the dilemma lies in the matter of your release. I am haunted by the fear, no doubt unfounded, that you might choose to spring from the pouch and kill me, thereby throwing away *your* chances of success and sealing *your* own fate.'

'Ahem,' went Rushmear, greasier yet. 'Put aside your

154

fear, friend Maxwell. I am a bluff fellow, I know, given to the occasional immoderate outburst. I most fervently apologize if I have fostered the erroneous belief that I might seek to cause you harm.'

'Yet I recall you vowing to ram my head up my bottom.'

'In jest, I assure you.'

'Then, if I release you now, I have your promise to let bygones be bygones, at least until we have completed our mission, destroyed MacGuffin and reclaimed our souls? Specific aims, which, and I cannot stress this too strongly, could never *possibly* be achieved if we do not work *together*.'

'Let me out of the pouch,' crooned Rushmear, 'and I will demonstrate the quality of my friendship.'

The ambiguity of that remark was not lost on Maxwell. The trouble was that he, at least, had (for the most part) been telling the truth – the chances of success *were* far greater if the two of them worked together.

Troubled times.

'All right,' said Maxwell. 'I will release you from the pouch.'

'You won't live to regret it,' called Rushmear. 'Not for one minute.'

Maxwell sighed and put his thumbnail to the draw-string knot. 'Climb out very carefully and slowly,' he said. 'Make no sudden moves, or the bed will upend and spill us both to our deaths.'

Maxwell tugged upon the knot.

And then.

SMASH!

Maxwell flew back on the bed. Head over heels. Heels in the air. The bed slewed to one side, turned in a circle, moved forward with a rush and went *SMASH!* once again.

155

'What the . . . Hey!' Maxwell floundered about, pouch in one hand, fistful of mattress in the other.

'What are you doing?' Rushmear shouted. 'Open the pouch. Set me free.'

'Something's happening to the bed.' Maxwell clung on. The bed took another dash forward, struck something, bounced off, struck again.

'Stop!' shouted Maxwell. 'Blenkinsop's divan, stop! Go down, rest upon the ground.'

The bed dropped down, clumped onto grass beneath.

It came to rest in a bit of green and pleasantness. A veritable Arcadian glade, all bulbous trees like giant broccoli, feathered ferns and drowsing dabbled blooms. Very nice.

Very very nice.

'Let me out now,' cried Rushmear.

'In a moment.' Maxwell tucked the pouch back into his pocket, and jumped from the bed. 'What is your trouble?' he asked it. 'Are you broken, or is this some trick?' He took a step backwards, struck something himself and was catapulted from his feet.

Maxwell tumbled in a heap on the grass.

He rose angrily. 'Who did *that*?' he demanded to be told.

'Have a care now. Have a care.'

Maxwell turned. A little man in a great big coat came hurrying up. He was a very little man and his coat, numerous sizes too large, dragged along the ground behind him. He had a big candyfloss of pink hair and a jolly red round face made grave by a look of concern.

'Please don't touch the grid again, sir,' he implored. 'You will come to harm.'

'What?' asked Maxwell. 'Eh?'

'The grid.' The little man gestured towards nothing that could be seen. 'The grid encircles the city of

Rameer. It rejects magic. The Sultan does not allow unauthorized magic to enter his garden.'

'His *garden*? Then the city is not far away?' Maxwell rubbed at a grazed shin.

'A day's march. Less if you were to run. Somewhat more if you were to hop upon one leg, of course.'

'And who might you be?' Maxwell asked.

'I am Phlegster the gridster, southern area 801. And who might you be, sir?'

'Do you know the town of Kakkarta?'

'Well, I've never been there myself, but I've heard it's a very nice place.'

'Quite charming,' said Maxwell. 'And I am its new Governor.'

'I'm very pleased to meet you, sir.' The little man put out a hand and Maxwell shook it.

'Also,' said Maxwell, 'I am one most highly skilled in the magical arts and prepared to blast, upon a whim, any who delay my journey. I command the use of a magical bed, as you can see. And also,' he drew the pouch from his pocket, 'a bag containing a demon, which I must deliver to the Sultan.' Maxwell shook the pouch. Rushmear raised curses. Phlegster stepped back smartly.

'So,' continued Maxwell, 'be a good fellow and disarm the grid so I can pass on my way.'

The little man shook his head. 'I wish I could,' he sighed, 'but it would be more than my job's worth.'

Maxwell sighed also. 'I too have a job to do. Namely, the delivery of this pouch.' Maxwell shook it once again, raised an eyebrow to Rushmear's outcries and returned the pouch to his pocket. 'The Sultan will not be best pleased when I tell him you delayed me.'

'I'm in no doubt,' said Phlegster. 'So, if you will kindly show me your official travel documents, letters of recommendation, pilot's licence, proof of bed-ownership, signatured authority for the inter state transportation of a registered demonic entity, I will stamp these and cause you no further delay.'

Maxwell made a show of patting his pockets. 'Wouldn't you just know it?' he said. 'I've left them all in my other suit.'

Phlegster nodded politely. 'Isn't it always the way? But let us be glad you have discovered this now, rather than at the city gates, where the guards are less charitable than I.'

'*Less* charitable, you say?'

'Far less. For where I see a noble gentleman – the Governor of Kakkarta, who has accidentally mislaid his documents – they might see a potential assassin upon a stolen bed. And, once having slain him most cruelly, they would no doubt send a legion to arrest the gridster who let him slip past. We can count ourselves fortunate men today, sir, can't we?'

'Indeed we can.'

'So,' said Phlegster. 'The way I see it, two options lay open to you: return to Kakkarta and pick up your documents, or leave your magical appurtenances here in my safe keeping and proceed through the grid on foot. If you carry no magic you will pass unshredded and not be challenged at the city gate.'

'Outrageous,' cried Maxwell. 'I do not have the time for this falderal. Surely other options must exist.' He mimed the jingling of coins in his pocket.

Phlegster gave Maxwell a hard looking over. 'None that I know of. Bribery is, of course, out of the question and violence against my person would serve no useful end. I have no power to disarm the grid.'

'If this is the case,' said Maxwell, 'then how would you have arranged for me to pass safely through if all my documentation had proved to be in order?'

The little man shrugged. 'This is a moot point. As

clearly you have no such documentation, it does not warrant further discussion.'

'Hm,' said Maxwell. 'Moot point or not, I have no more time to waste.' And so saying, he jumped forward, grabbed Phlegster by the collar of his over-large coat and hauled him into the air.

'Let me down,' wailed the gridster. 'This is appalling behaviour.'

'Be quiet,' ordred Maxwell, 'and listen to me. We are going to conduct a scientific experiment. I will put forth a theory. You will test it out.'

'I like not the sound of that. Put me down, sir, please.'

'Take off your coat then.'

'My coat? What do you want with my coat?'

'It seems a very large coat, for such a small man.'

'A family heirloom, and I'll trust you to keep your sizist remarks to yourself.'

'Very well.' Maxwell pulled out the pouch once more and dangled it before Phlegster's face. 'Carry this through the grid for me,' he said.

'Impossible,' squeaked Phlegster. 'I would be shredded.'

'I was not shredded. I merely bounced off.'

'I might not be so lucky. The grid is now alert to the presence of magic.'

'My theory, in essence is this,' said Maxwell. 'I do not believe in some vast grid, a day's journey away from the city. It would have to be manned by hundreds, no, thousands of gridsters. I suspect that this is some localized phenomenon, one that you are well acquainted with. One that you exploit to your own ends, by relieving the gullible of their magical items.'

'Nonsense. Stuff and nonsense.'

'Further,' said Maxwell, 'and I agree this is pure guesswork on my part, my theory is that you can transport items of magical power through the grid by means of your coat.'

'Outlandish. Mere speculation.'

'We shall see.' Maxwell tucked the pouch into the pocket of the little man's big coat. 'I will heave you through the grid. We will observe the results.'

'No,' shrieked the little man. 'I mean *yes*. All right. You are correct. The coat is invested with an immunity against the grid's power. Put it on yourself and walk through. But just leave me here. I am not allowed to enter the garden beyond.'

Maxwell shook his head. 'I have become somewhat distrustful of late. Should you pass through unscathed, take off the coat, with the pouch still in the pocket, leave it on the other side and walk back to me. Thus you will have proved that a man wearing the coat can carry magic safely, and a man without the coat, who carried no magic, may also travel safely through. I will be satisfied with this demonstration. I will then step through, put on the coat, step back and drag my bed through. Then you will have seen the last of me.'

'Far too complicated,' complained Phlegster. 'Put on the coat and bugger off. I will say you stole it. Perhaps the Sultan will let me off with a flaying and some minor amputation. Or possibly I will just flee to the south. They say Kakkarta is very nice at this time of year.'

'At its very best,' said Maxwell, hoisting Phlegster higher, swinging him about and freighting him towards the invisible wall of the grid.

'No!' shrieked Phlegster. 'Have mercy.'

Maxwell examined the ground that lay before. There was a clear straight line burned into the grass. It stretched away in either direction, vanishing amongst the giant broccoli trees. It was all that signified the location of the grid's invisible wall.

Maxwell took a step back. Swung a substantial boot, kicked Phlegster in the squirming bottom and propelled him through the grid.

There was a blinding flash. And a most alarming sound. The sort of sound that bluebottles make when they hit the electric wire on those things with the mauve lights that butchers have in their shops.

But hideously amplified.

Maxwell covered his face as Phlegster exploded into a million fragments. Ribbons of big coat trailed away in all directions. Little bits of charred carcass trailed with them. There was a lot of smoke.

Presently it cleared.

Maxwell fanned at his face. 'Oh dear,' he said. 'Well, I suppose I can't be right every time.' He peered beyond the line of burnt grass and was most surprised and somewhat heartened to observe the magic pouch, lying there amongst a smouldering lump or two of Phlegster and looking none the worse for its travel through the grid.

'That's handy,' said Maxwell. 'Now I wonder how the bed might—'

But his wondering was brought to an abrupt end by a stone that bounced off the back of his head.

'Ouch!' cried Maxwell, springing around.

Several small men were approaching. They wore big coats, had pink candyfloss hair and carried stones and stout sticks.

'He has murdered Brother Phlegster,' shouted one.

'Pushed him with magic through the grid,' shouted another.

'Let us put him to a slow death,' shouted a third.

'Just hold on,' yelled Maxwell. 'It was a mistake. I had this theory, you see.'

But the little men did not seem anxious to hear of Maxwell's theory. And as Maxwell looked on, others appeared through the trees, some carrying nets, some long staves with pointy ends. There were shouts regarding the use of a 'maggot box' and red-hot gelding tongs.

'Well, if you're not prepared to listen . . .' Maxwell turned, held his breath, closed his eyes and then leapt through the grid.

14

Maxwell plunged through the grid, rolled over and came to rest on the grass beyond.

Unsinged and intact.

He picked up the pouch and ran.

Shouts and threats and stones and staves followed Maxwell, but the kin of the ill-fated Phlegster did not. They remained on their side of the invisible border, fearful to step across.

Maxwell ran till he could hear their cries no more, then slumped onto a grassy knoll to gather his breath and his wits.

He was quite fed up with this new world. He'd done more running during the past few weeks than ever before in his life – and always for his life. If he ever succeeded in retrieving his soul, Maxwell promised himself, he would pursue some quiet, unrushed occupation, such as mushroom growing or the keeping of a hermitage.

Maxwell flung the pouch to the ground, raising a howl from Rushmear.

'Silence,' Maxwell puffed and coughed, 'ungrateful buffoon. Yet again I have saved your life, while you loaf about in the bag.'

Rushmear's response was a torrent of abuse. And Maxwell, in fury, raised a boot to staunch it for good and for all.

*   *   *

His fine substantial boot cast a fine substantial shadow over the pouch. A fine substantial *black* shadow it was. Crisp at the edges. Clearly defined. Maxwell brought his foot to a halt an inch above the pouch.

He raised it. Examined the shadow. Peered up at the sky.

Up at the sun.

It was no longer red here. It was gold, pure gold.

Maxwell gaped and blinked his eyes. The garden all around was bathed in golden light. It wasn't the light of the old sun he'd known before the time of the great transition. This was rich and mellow, softer. Quite beautiful, in fact.

Maxwell jumped to his feet, narrowly avoiding the accidental stamping flat of Rushmear. He glanced to left and right, espied a suitable tree and, without further ado, clambered up it.

From a high branch he stared off towards the way he had come. The line marked by the grid was most apparent, creating the effect of a clear glass barrier that rose endlessly into the sky. And beyond this: a world of red.

'By the Goddess.' Maxwell shook an awestruck head. 'The Sultan must control the very sun itself. Not a man to be taken lightly. But possibly one who might . . .' A sequence of thoughts moved into his mind.

Maxwell kept these thoughts to himself. They were great thoughts these. His greatest yet, and not thoughts to be bandied about without care. Imagineering thoughts were they.

And *he* the Imagineer.

Maxwell climbed down from the tree, his head abuzz with plans and stratagems. He had twenty days. Surely enough for what he had in mind. First priority was food, and to eat, certain risks must be taken.

Maxwell snatched up the pouch. 'Rushmear,' he said, 'I am going to release you. I have protected you for long enough. Now you must take your share of responsibility.'

Rushmear was speechless.

'I have formulated a plan,' announced Maxwell, untying the pouch, 'and because you enjoy my favour, you will have but a small part to play in its execution. Great wealth will be yours for the taking, so rouse yourself from your comfortable repose and let us be on our way.'

Maxwell turned the pouch upside down and gave it a shake. It was quite a sight to behold, the enormous horse trader pouring from the tiny bag. He thumped to the ground on his great fat arse and sat there rubbing his eyes.

'Now,' said Maxwell, 'first things first. We should eat before we go any further. As you have knowledge regarding what may be safely consumed, hasten to the task of finding us some breakfast.'

'*What?*' Rushmear blinked his eyes, gawped up at the golden sun, glared at the man in the white suit and climbed ponderously to his feet. 'Now just you—' But he said no more. A look of alarm appeared on his face. He clutched at his hind quarters and rushed off into the trees.

Presently he returned, sighing deeply and rebuttoning his trousers.

'I hope you've washed your hands,' said Maxwell.

'I will shortly, to get the blood off.'

'Spare me your threats, Rushmear, we do not have the time.'

'I have nineteen days,' said Rushmear. 'You less than a minute.'

'Such ingratitude. After all I've done for you.'

Rushmear threw himself at Maxwell. Maxwell

ducked nimbly aside, pulled from behind his back the length of branch he had torn from a tree during Rushmear's absence and struck the horse trader a devastating blow to the head with it.

Rushmear collapsed in a groaning heap. Maxwell stepped astride him, branch raised in both hands. 'Swear allegiance to me or I bust out your brains.'

'Never!' Rushmear brought up a knee that caught Maxwell in the cobblers. Maxwell staggered forwards and trod on Rushmear's face. The big man grabbed his ankle. Twisted it. Maxwell fell heavily to the ground. The big man rolled over to claw at Maxwell's throat. Maxwell hit him again with the branch.

Rushmear sank back, holding his head. Maxwell sat gasping, his hands at his groin. 'This is getting us nowhere,' he gasped. 'How many times must you be told? One man alone cannot succeed.'

'I'd rather throw in my lot with the devil himself.'

Maxwell snatched up the branch. 'Then let me send you to him. I have no more time to squander on your welfare.'

'Why, you—' Rushmear launched himself forwards. He swept the branch from Maxwell's hand and fell upon him, pressing down with all his weight.

Maxwell's ribs began to buckle. Rushmear's face leered into his.

Maxwell craned his neck and bit the end off Rushmear's nose.

Rushmear toppled over. He writhed about, legs thrashing the air, clutching his face and moaning with pain. Maxwell crawled to the branch, dragged himself erect and raised it high, preparing to administer the *coup de grâce*.

He spat the tip of Rushmear's nose onto the moaner beneath.

This had all got completely out of control. It was

pure Tobe Hooper stuff. Maxwell would finish it now.

He gripped the branch tightly. 'You're dead, you fu—'

'No, stop.' Rushmear covered his face. 'Stop. Listen.'

'To what? Your pleas for mercy?'

'Sssh. Listen. Can't you hear?'

'Forget it,' said Maxwell. 'It's too late for tricks.'

'Horses,' said Rushmear. 'Many horses.'

And now Maxwell could hear them too. A dull rumble of hoofbeats, rising in volume. Becoming a regular thundering.

'Get down, hide yourself.'

Maxwell hesitated. It would be far better to smash Rushmear's head in while he had the chance and take once more to his heels.

'Get down, fool, they're coming this way. And I know these horses.'

'You do?' Maxwell cast aside his branch and threw himself to the ground.

'Into the cover of those bushes.'

'Lead the way,' whispered Maxwell.

'After you.'

'Bollocks!'

'All right, after me.' Oozing blood from his maimed hooter, Rushmear scuttled into the bushes, Maxwell close behind.

And then the riders were in view.

Maxwell stared out at them and he was lost for words.

Knights they were . . .

Knights in golden armour. The sunlight dazzled about them. Dancing in bright coronas on their polished morions and bucklers. They were romantic. Arthurian. Heroic.

Maxwell whistled softly between his teeth. 'Would

you look at those flashy bastards?' he said, not lost for words for too long.

'Keep your mouth shut, fool.'

The knights steered their horses between the trees. 'Any sign?' called one.

'No,' called another. 'But he'll be close. He entered through the grid a mile south of here.'

'They're searching for *us*,' whispered Maxwell.

'*You*,' whispered Rushmear. 'Only *you*.'

Maxwell chewed upon his bottom lip. 'Then luck is ever with us. This is my plan. First you—'

'No!' Rushmear clamped a ham-hock hand across the mouth of Maxwell. 'Horses I know,' he muttered. 'Wait until the last one passes, then do as I tell you. Understand?'

Maxwell nodded without enthusiasm. Rushmear withdrew his hand.

They watched the riders passing by, fanning out to the left and right. A sword blade swept suddenly through the bush, clearing Maxwell's head by inches. Rushmear dragged him down by the scruff of the neck. Maxwell peeped out.

A knight had dismounted. He stood before the bush. As Maxwell looked on, the knight unbuckled his golden codpiece.

Maxwell chewed upon a knuckle. It was quite clear what the knight meant to do.

And he did it.

Inside the bush Maxwell fumed.

And now steamed also at the shoulders.

Micturition accomplished, the knight rebuckled himself into decency and strode back to his horse. As he mounted, Rushmear thrust his face out of the bush, put his fingers to his lips and blew a most curious whistle.

The knight, expecting his horse to rear, held fast to the reins and dug in his spurs. But the horse dropped its head instead and threw up its hind legs. The knight sailed forward and crashed to the ground.

'Make sure he's unconscious,' Rushmear sprang from the bush. 'I'll deal with the horse.'

'The pleasure's all mine.' Maxwell emerged, a sorry sodden sight. He took off his jacket and flung it to the ground then stalked over to the fallen knight and prepared to put the boot in.

But the knight wasn't moving. His helmet was twisted around the wrong way. His neck was broken.

Though the red fug of fury raged in his head, Maxwell drew the line at kicking a corpse. He turned towards Rushmear. 'He's done for,' he said. 'Hang about . . . What?'

The big man with the gory face sat high upon the horse. He twitched the reins in a professional manner and the beast plodded forward. 'So,' said Rushmear. 'Events adjust themselves.'

'Help me up,' said Maxwell, affecting a chummy grin.

'I think not. We part company here. I ride alone to the city of Rameer.'

'Oh come now,' Maxwell stepped in front of the horse.

'Stand aside, or I order the mare to use its teeth. Have you ever been bit by a horse?'

'No, I—'

'Stand aside then.'

Maxwell stood aside. 'Now, listen,' said he.

'No, *you* listen.' Rushmear put a hand to his ear. 'The riders are returning, so I must be away. Perhaps you can keep up, if you run very fast. I somehow doubt it, though.' He wheeled the horse about, dug in his heels and flicked the reins.

Then he galloped away at the double.

Leaving Maxwell alone with a corpse.

15

When the riders did return, which was half an hour later, Maxwell was nowhere to be seen.

The knights dismounted, examined the tracks made by the galloping horse and gathered about its fallen rider.

Happily this fellow wasn't dead at all. Although his helmet was twisted around and his visor jammed shut, he was only a bit dazed and spoke in a voice of muffled rage concerning the giant with the gory face who had leapt from a bush and startled his horse.

The knights were glad that their comrade had come to no real harm. But being professional soldiers, they recognized the subtle distinction between a gallant hero who is knocked from his charging steed in the thick of bloody battle by fearsome adversary, and a careless oaf who is tipped from his strolling horse, in the still of a country glade, by a loon with a bloody nose.

A good deal of ribaldry then ensued and the poor Sir Knight found himself the butt of much gallant humour which called into question not only his bravery and prowess as a horseman.

'Me thinks me Lord Percy hath a swidgen for a billydock,' quoth one hearty fellow.

'Perhaps next time he swankles, he should dab a moult of grimbah on his trump,' quoth another.

'Surely I discern a swattle in the air,' quoth yet a third, 'which lends me to suppose some clabbing of the strubbart has occurred.'

And further such and so forth.

And to those unschooled in the arcane terms employed by these Knights of New, it might well have been thought that here was something other than the usual crap innuendo and barrack-room smut you get from dickheads in uniform.

But such, of course, wasn't the case and the jibes levelled at the now horseless Lord Percy, were, for the most part, directed towards the manner of his conception and the dimensions of his willy.

The unseated knight took it like the man he was. Possibly because he knew that if you cry when other knights are taking the piss out of you, it is considered a sign of weakness. But more likely (as those astute enough to reason things out will already have guessed) because the man now wearing Lord Percy's armour was not Lord Percy at all.

Maxwell peeped out through the 'jammed' visor of the late lord's helmet and said nothing as he was unceremoniously hauled from the ground and dumped upon the back of another knight's horse.

'Hold tight to me, Perce,' called the gallant chap up front. 'I'd be fair saddened should you slip from my steed and blabber your thubs upon a rock.'

'Lord Percy's thubs might do better for a wistering of thark,' quoth the hearty fellow who had got a laugh earlier with the gag about Lord Percy having a swidgen for a billydock.

'Prettily put, Lord Archer,' quoth the chap who'd done the one about the swattle in the air that presupposed a degree of strubbart clabbing. 'A double wistering and heavy on the mingewort.'

'Get a move on, you twerps,' whispered Maxwell, as

the knights chortled with mirth. 'Follow Rushmear's tracks and let's get to the city.'

The horsemen moved off with a glitter of gold, a chinking of chainmail, a haughtiness of hauberks, a proudery of pickelhaubes and no doubt a veritable defustication of dortwonglers also.

Maxwell clung to the fellow at the reins. He had a right sweat on and was in considerable discomfort, the armour, although extremely light, chaffed beneath the armpits and the codpiece played havoc with his tender goolies*.

They galloped over hill and dale the way that knights will do, but they soon lost Rushmear's trail, which came as a great disappointment, what with the knights considering themselves to be expert trackers and on home territory and everything.

Maxwell sighed as they circled hopelessly around, and paid a grudging homage to the equestrian talents of the resourceful Rushmear, who had no doubt ordered his horse to walk backwards on its hind legs or trip daintily along the tops of the drystone walls.

'The varlet said he was going to slay the Sultan,' Maxwell shouted gruffly, when he could stand no more of the dithering.

'What?' cried the knights. 'What? What? What?'

'Going to slay the Sultan,' Maxwell said once more.

'No not that bit,' said the fellow who'd done the dabbing-a-moult-of-grimbah joke, 'the first bit.'

'Eh?' said Maxwell.

'Varlet?' asked Lord Archer. 'What does *varlet* mean?'

'Well, it's the same as blackguard, or rapscallion, isn't it?'

'Come again?'

---

*Or thubs.

'Oh you know, scallywag, spalpeen, scapegrace. Caitiff, there's a good'n. Whelp, roughneck. Tergiversator, although that's more like a quisling really.' Maxwell stared out at the knights, who were now staring somewhat intently at him.*

'Does he mean *bullygarve?*' someone asked.

'No,' said Lord Archer. 'He didn't mean *bullygarve*. Did you, Lord Percy?'

'I might have,' mumbled Maxwell. 'Do you think it matters?'

'Matters?' Lord Archer drew himself erect in his saddle. '*Matters?* Did we spend five years at the University studying the subtle nuances of the chivalrous vernacular for nothing? Toiling into the long evenings sorting the irregular inflection from the modifying noun?'

'Those were the days,' said Maxwell.

'Ha!' Lord Archer gave Maxwell a hearty slap on the back that rattled Maxwell's teeth. 'Those *were* the days. Where do the good times go?'

'Search me.'

'Come again once more?'

'Oh let's get going,' growled Maxwell. 'This, er, person, means to assassinate the Sultan.'

'Ha!' Lord Archer laughed again. And the other knights laughed with him.

Maxwell shook his helmet. This bunch of golden clowns went in for more jollity and thigh-slapping than the cast of a *Robin Hood* remake.

'Ha!' Lord Archer gave Maxwell another hearty tooth-rattler. 'If the scrumian rides to his doom, let's not waste our time in pursuit.'

'Scrumian,' said Maxwell, 'that's the word I was

---

*They had their visors up. He still had his down, of course.

looking for. But, no, hold on, not waste our time? We must get after him. Er, get my horse back. Warn the Sultan.'

'Ha!' Lord Archer took another swing at Maxwell's back. But this time Maxwell ducked aside. Lord Archer lost balance and fell from his horse.

'Ooooh!' went the other knights, reining back their mounts. 'That's torn it.'

As is often the case when you fall in the country, Lord Archer now sat in a cowpat. He looked up at Maxwell, and no hint of jocularity remained upon his face. 'By crumble,' he roared, 'thou hast unseated thy superior, Percy. Know what thou must do?'

'Write a formal letter of apology?' Maxwell suggested. 'Penned in knightish patois and expressing great remorse?'

'Engage in mortal combat,' quoth Lord Archer (as no-one had 'quoth' for a while).

'Couldn't we just hug and make up?' Maxwell asked. 'Go in for a bit of male-bonding?'

'You'll taste my blade, sir.'

'Well, I wasn't thinking of taking it that far.'

Several knights groaned at this, which was hardly surprising really.

'Down from the steed, knave. Lord Grade,' called Lord Archer to the knight at the reins, 'toss Lord Percy off.'

'It's knob gags again,' said Maxwell. 'Why is it always knob gags?'

'Down!' cried Lord Grade, heaving Maxwell from the horse.

'No, hold on. Aaaagh!' Maxwell crashed to the ground. 'Now look,' he mumbled, trying to right himself. 'Do you know what kind of a day I've had so far? I don't need any of this.'

'Stand up and fight, are you man or mousaka?'

'I'm mousaka, all right? I'm hungry and I've got a headache. Take me to the city where I can recuperate for a couple of days. Then I'll beat the shit out of you.'

'Ooooh!' went the knights. 'Naughty word.'

'Naughty word?' Maxwell struggled to his feet. 'You're barking mad, the lot of you. Prancing about on your horses, talking a load of old twaddle. Get a life, why don't you?'

'Fight me, you blumpit.'

'Blumpit?' asked Maxwell. 'Is that the same as, bullygarve?'

'It's worse,' said Lord Grade. 'Much worse.'

'Right,' said Maxwell, who had been controlling his red fug quite well up till now. 'No-one calls me a blumpit and gets away with it. Someone hand me a sword.'

'Use your own,' said Lord Archer, drawing his and whirling it about.

'I haven't got mine, it must have been on my horse.'

'Well, you're not having mine,' said Lord Grade. 'I only polished it this morning. I used two quadroons of pilch on the hebbereen alone.'

'No more of that. Come on, someone, give me a sword.'

'Oooh. No. No. No.' The knights all backed away, tucking their swords out of sight.

'Right, I'll use a bloody stick then.' Maxwell sought a fallen branch.

'You can't use a stick,' said Lord Archer.

'Well, have *you* got a spare sword I could borrow?'

'I've got one at home. But it's my best one, you can't use that.'

'I could fetch it,' said Lord Grade. 'Then Lord Percy could use the one you have here.'

'He might break it.' Lord Archer examined the blade of his sword. 'And I only polished it this morning, I used a full quart of—'

Maxwell stepped forward and biffed Lord Archer in the chin.

'Oh my!' shrieked the knight, falling down in a heap.

'Come on,' said Maxwell, doing the Prince Naseem shuffle. 'On your feet, let's see what you're made of.'

'You beastly man. I'm wounded. Wounded.'

Knights rushed forward. But not at Maxwell. They flustered about Lord Archer, making soothing noises and patting his wrists.

'You pack of pansies.' Maxwell kicked the nearest in the seat of his golden armour.

'Lord Percy is bereft,' this fellow cried. 'Flee before he does us mischief.'

'I'm not Lord Percy, you idiots.' Maxwell lifted his visor and grinned at the knights, exciting them to shrieks of terror and sending them scurrying.

'Come on.' Maxwell stood, making fists with his golden gauntlets. 'Come on, you sissy boys. I'll take on the lot of you. Who's first?'

The knights were hopping back towards their horses. There was much bumping into one another, and putting feet into the wrong stirrups and falling off and that kind of thing.

Maxwell danced amongst the scampering warriors, shaking his fists and making the kind of remarks that would not have endeared him to the readers of *Gay News*.

Lord Archer was back on his horse.

'Oh no you don't,' Maxwell cried, grabbing the knight by the leg. 'I'm not walking any more. I'll have your horse.'

'Not my bonny Black Bess. Save me, someone.'

But Lord Archer's bold companions were digging in their spurs and having it away upon the hoof.

'Down!' shouted Maxwell. 'Or I'll twist your ankle.'

'No, please, I'm getting down.' Lord Archer climbed

from his bonny Black Bess. 'Good girl,' he said. 'Easy now.'

'You're a bloody disgrace.' Maxwell cuffed Lord Archer across the helmet. 'Call yourself a knight? You're not fit to wear the armour.'

'We're mostly a showpiece,' whimpered his lordship. 'Mostly ceremonial, we don't go in for any of the, you know—' He mimed a feeble sword thrust.

'Never mind,' Maxwell went to pat the knight's shoulder, but the knight flinched away. 'You certainly look the part. Splendid get up.'

'I've got cowpat all over my grieves.'

'It'll wash off. Use plenty of pilch, that would be my advice.'

'Yes, thanks, I'll do that.'

'I'm going to take your horse,' said Maxwell. 'It's nothing personal, but I'm in a hurry. Which way is it to the City of Rameer?'

'Over yonder hill. You can't miss it.'

'I'll leave your horse at the city gate. Don't worry, I won't race it or anything.'

'Thanks. There's sugar in the saddle-bag.'

'Any food?' Maxwell asked.

'My sandwiches – they're in the saddle-bag too.'

'Splendid. I'll take those too if you don't mind.'

'Well, I . . . er, no. Please do.'

'My thanks. Would you mind helping me up? I've never ridden a horse before.'

'Who are you?' asked Archer, hastening to oblige.

'I am Max Carrion, Imagineer.' Maxwell seated himself in the saddle. 'She's not rough this horse, is she?'

'No, she's sweet as a lamb.'

'Right. Then I'll bid you farewell. Give my regards to the other knights. Say sorry for me that I frightened them.'

'Thank you, they'll appreciate that.'

'Farewell, then.'

'Farewell.'

Maxwell said, 'Giddy up,' and the horse clip-clopped forward.

He'd actually done all right this time. A horse to ride on and sandwiches in the saddle-bag. Maxwell dipped in a gauntlet and drew them out. Cheese. Fine. Maxwell set into munching.

Over the hill and off to the City of Rameer.

Dressed as a knight, he'd get in OK.

This was it. Almost there.

All set to put into operation the mighty plan he had conceived earlier, the plan that would set everything to right.

He was scoring points.

It was time to move in for the big K.O.

Maxwell laughed between munchings. 'Rock 'n' Roll.' he shouted. 'Rock 'n' Roll.'

16

So out rode brave Sir Maxwell on his noble snow-white steed (Black Bess). He cut a pretty dashing figure: tall and proud in the saddle, sun a glitter on the suit of golden armour, bit of a designer stubble about the chiselled chin, lots of breadcrumbs round the mouth.

Maxwell dug deeply into the saddle-bag once more. He found a bottle of blueberry cordial to wash down the sandwiches, a cream cake for afters and a bag of boiled sweets. When all these were done, he ate the horse's sugar lumps.

Maxwell grinned. Things weren't turning out too badly at all, considering his dire circumstances. The armour wasn't too uncomfortable and the codpiece no longer pained him, now that he'd slipped MacGuffin's magic pouch over his lunchbox. The horse clip-clopped beneath him at an easy pace, birdies twittered in the hedgerows, the sun beamed golden blessings.

Up the hill he rode, the very picture of all things chivalrous. The fact that he wore a dead man's armour and sat astride a stolen horse did not enter into it. Oh no. He was rocking now and no mistake.

At the top of the hill Maxwell drew Black Bess to a halt and gazed towards the City of Rameer.

There was *no* City of Rameer.

'Eh?' Maxwell gave the vista a severe looking over. A green and pleasant valley lay before, with a track that wound down through grassy meadows towards a line of distant hills.

Maxwell swung about in the saddle, but Lord Archer was well beyond sight. 'Stupid sod,' said Maxwell. 'I suppose he must have meant the next hill.'

So Maxwell rode on. Down into the valley he went, along the meandering track. It was all terribly picturesque, very John Constable. At length he approached the next hill.

And here Maxwell espied an old woman. She hobbled down the track, dragging a small boy by the arm. The small boy, upon sighting Maxwell, whispered something and the old woman bopped him on the head.

As they drew near, Maxwell reined in Black Bess.

'Good woman,' said he, affecting a knightly manner. 'Good woman, whither lies the City of Rameer?'

The old woman gestured past her shoulder with a sinewy mitt. 'Over yonder hill,' she said.

'Ah, thank you very much.'

The small boy whispered something more to the old woman and she clubbed him over the head again.

'Good woman,' said Maxwell.

'Yeah? Wotcha want now?'

'Good woman, 'why clubbest thou the lad?'

'Because he's stupid,' the old dame replied.

'That's hardly a reason for clouting him.'

'I've always found it sufficient.'

'Fair enough.' Maxwell shrugged in his armour. It was none of his business, after all. He had a pressing appointment with the Sultan. 'Good day to you,' he said, 'and farewell.'

And on once more rode Maxwell. This hill was more substantial than the last and though Maxwell was eager to get to the top, Black Bess stopped to chomp grass and drink from a stream.

'Come on,' said Maxwell, clicking the reins. 'Giddy up.'

The horse plodded up the winding track and finally crested the hill. Maxwell took a deep breath and gazed down towards the City of Rameer.

There was *no* City of Rameer.

'*What?*' Maxwell shook his head, glanced down the track. Of old woman and child there was no sign. 'Stupid crone,' muttered Maxwell. 'I suppose she must have meant the *next* hill. After all she was walking down this one. Good grief.'

And Maxwell rode on.

Down into the new valley he went. It was much like the last.

Possibly a bit more Gainsborough than Constable, but there wasn't a lot in it. The next hill along the track was a good way off, though, and Black Bess's pace was slowing.

At considerable length Maxwell finally approached the next hill and here saw an old woman descending. She dragged a small boy by the arm.

Maxwell squinted and sighed. It was *not* the same old woman, although there were similarities. Maxwell halted his horse and hailed the woman thusly. 'Good woman,' he hailed, 'whither lies the City of Rameer?'

'Over yonder hill,' replied the old woman, thumbing over her shoulder.

'Are you absolutely certain of that?'

'Course I am.'

'OK, fine.'

The lad whispered something to the old woman and the old woman clouted him across the skull.

'Good woman,' said Maxwell, 'why cloutest thou the child?'

'Because he's stupid.'

'I see. Tell me, is it the regular practice in these parts to clout stupid children?'

The old woman shrugged. 'I wouldn't know,' she said. 'I'm not from around here. But I could ask, if you want.'

'Have a nice day,' said Maxwell, riding on.

It was late in the afternoon when Maxwell reached the top of the next hill. *This* next hill was not the next hill which the old woman to whom Maxwell had said 'have a nice day' had told him was the one beyond which lay the City of Rameer.

Nor, in fact, was it the one after that, which an old woman, who was smiting a child when Maxwell met her, assured him would be the very one he sought.

This hill was the hill that the old woman whom Maxwell found sitting sorrowfully beside the track, weeping bitterly for the fact that her daughter had never married and borne any boy children for her to clout, told him, with utter conviction, was the *very* hill beyond which lay the City of Rameer.

Maxwell now stood upon the top of *this* hill. And it has to be said, there was not the vaguest hint of surprise to be found in the expression on his face for the fact that absolutely no City of Rameer whatsoever dwelt in the valley below.

There was, however, an expression of such black fury, as would be better left without closer description.

As the golden sun sank slowly in the west, Maxwell trudged bitterly up yet another hill. He was on foot once more – Black Bess had thrown a shoe – and no longer did he cut the dashing figure that he had cut earlier in the day. Maxwell's head was down. His fine substantial boots, which he had been carrying in the magic pouch, were now back on his feet. The suit of golden armour was stashed in the magic pouch. The pouch was in Maxwell's trouser pocket.

Maxwell swore and grumbled as he toiled up the rugged track, finally to reach the hilltop and gaze over the darkening landscape that lay before.

The last light of the day touched down upon rooftops, chimneys, danced upon gables, a weather-vane.

The City of Rameer!

It was *not* the City of Rameer.

It was a coaching inn.

Maxwell marched down the hillside, followed by the limping horse. Now seething with fury, Maxwell determined that he had done with all hills for the day. Tonight he would enjoy the comforts of the inn. He had discovered a purse full of gold coins in one of the saddle-bags, and now, he felt, was the time to squander them upon whatever luxuries this inn had to offer. Good ale. Good food. A good hot bath. A cozy bed. A barmaid with a thing about knights, perhaps?

Maxwell marched down the track and presently reached the inn yard.

A number of horses were tethered there. A welcoming glow showed through bottle glass windows, set beneath low eaves. The inn sign was illuminated by lighted lanthorns. It read, THE PROSPECT OF RAMEER.

'Yes!' said Maxwell. 'Praise the Goddess.'

Now shivering in his shirtsleeves, he tethered the horse, gave her an encouraging pat, then strode across the yard and entered the inn.

If rustic Tudoresque without, the inn was not so within.

It had more the look of some elegant twentieth-century wine bar.

The floor was tiled in travertine, the tables topped in teak. Some framed architectural prints hung upon walls stencilled with lilac lattice over peachy pink. A number of folk, neatly dressed in colourful attire, were arranged in pleasing compositions, chatting, sipping drinks. Some discoursed at tables, others at the bar counter, which was of polished slate and behind which stood the innkeeper.

A thin man was he, with narrow shoulders, an overlarge head and a jutting brow, black hair in a centre parting and a tiny black moustache. His get-up was informal: white shirt, knitted cardy, grey slacks. He raised an eyebrow as Maxwell approached, but looked otherwise jolly enough.

'Good evening, sir,' said the innkeeper. 'How exactly may I help you?'

'I require four things,' said Maxwell politely.

'Four,' the barman nodded. 'The cardinal number which is the sum of three and one. Four I like, please go ahead.'

'Thank you. Firstly I require someone to tend my horse which has thrown a shoe.'

'Absolutely no problem at all, I will send my groom to deal with it. Secondly?'

'Secondly I require a bed for the night.'

'It will be a pleasure to accommodate you, I will have the maid prepare our finest room.'

'Thirdly', said Maxwell, 'I need to know the precise whereabouts of a place I believe to be near by.'

'I have lived here all my life,' said the barman, 'and am acquainted with the terrain for many miles about.'

'Splendid. And fourthly I would like some ale.'

'Ah,' the innkeeper paused. '*Which* ale would that be, *exactly*?'

'I don't mind,' said Maxwell. 'Any ale you have.'

The innkeeper shook his head. 'I take great pride in my work, sir,' said he, 'and I consider it my bounden duty to serve the weary traveller with *exactly* what he, or she requires.;'

'Nice sentiment,' said Maxwell.

'Thank you, sir. There are those who consider that the degree of exactitude I employ is over pedantic. But as I always say, if a job's worth doing, it's worth doing well.'

'I do so agree.'

'So, sir, do you like a very strong ale or a very weak one?'

'Something in between,' said Maxwell.

The innkeeper fingered his tiny moustache. 'Very dark or very light?'

'Don't mind,' said Maxwell. 'Which would you recommend?'

'That's hardly for me to say, sir. I do not wish to impose my preferences upon you.'

'How about something in between, then?' said Maxwell.

'Still as pond water or fizzy as sherbet?'

'In between once more,' said Maxwell.

The innkeeper nodded his head approvingly. 'Now,' said he. 'A pint or a half-pint?'

'Tell me,' said Maxwell, 'how close do you think I am to actually getting served?'

'Close, sir, very close. Did you say a pint or a half-pint?'

'A pint,' said Maxwell. 'Definitely a pint.'

'Fine. If we were out of pint pots would you object strongly to taking your ale in two half-pint glasses?'

'Not at all,' said Maxwell.

'Some would,' said the innkeeper.

'Perhaps they would not be so desperate for an ale as I.' Maxwell frowned hard at the innkeeper.

The innkeeper nodded once more. 'So, let us summarize. You require an ale which is neither too strong nor too weak, neither very dark nor very light, neither still as pond water nor fizzy as sherbet. And you don't mind whether you have it in a pint pot or two half-pint glasses.'

'Sounds *exactly* what I'm after,' said Maxwell.

'Fine, fine, fine.' The innkeeper clapped his hands. 'Jack,' he called to the potman, 'pint of ale over here for this gentleman.'

Maxwell looked from the potman, who was now pulling a pint, back to the innkeeper who was smiling upon him.

'You didn't tell him *which* ale I wanted,' said Maxwell.

'We only do the one, sir.'

'But what if I'd wanted a very strong one?'

'You didn't.'

'Or a very dark one.'

'You didn't.'

'Or . . . Oh, forget it.'

The potman served Maxwell's ale in a pint pot.

'Aha!' cried Maxwell in a voice of triumph. 'I thought you said two half-pint glasses.'

'No, sir. I said, if you recall, would you object strongly to taking your ale in two half-pint glasses. That was nothing to do with the other questions which were aimed specifically at identifying the exact sort of ale you required. *That* was for a private survey I'm doing. I hope to go into the hotel business eventually and what I always say is, he who never questions, never learns.'

'Do you indeed?' Maxwell pulled Percy's purse from his pocket and paid for his pint in pennies.

'Perfect,' said the innkeeper. 'Enjoy your ale.'

Maxwell took a swig. It tasted pretty good. *Really* good, in fact. But then, of course, it was *exactly* what he'd asked for. Maxwell tried to recall the last time he'd actually drunk a pint of beer. It had to have been in The Shrunken Head on the day of the Great Transition, when the old aeon became the new. And that was nearly one hundred years ago.

Maxwell knocked back his pint and ordered another. He'd been taking abstinence to a quite unreasonable extreme.

'Now,' said he, when his new pint was presented. 'I wonder if you can help me regarding the *exact* location of the destination towards which I'm bound upon most urgent business.'

'You can rely on me, sir. Cartography is a hobby of mine, the study of lands both near and distant. As a man needs to know his place in the universal scheme of things, so too is it essential that he should know exactly *where* he is when he's doing the knowing. I have a fascination for exactitudes. Some might say an obsession.'

'Not me,' said Maxwell. 'I always say, a man must have a hobby.'

'No, sir, it's a *boy* must have a hobby. A man must do what a man must do.'

'Right,' said Maxwell. 'Now what I wish to know, and this is where your fascination for exactitudes is really going to pay big dividends, is this: where is the City of Rameer?'

The innkeeper laughed. 'No problem there, sir. The City of Rameer lies over yonder hill.'

'No!' Maxwell slammed down his pint pot. 'All afternoon I have heard that. Over yonder hill! I have been over every bloody yonder hill for miles. I want to know *exactly* where it is.'

'It's over yonder hill,' said the innkeeper.

'*Which* yonder hill?'

'*The* yonder hill.'

'Ale please,' called a fellow at the end of the bar.

'Excuse me, sir, I have to serve a customer.' The

innkeeper sauntered away from the now fuming Maxwell. 'Exactly which ale would you like, sir?' he asked.

'Don't fuck about with me, Tom,' said the fellow. 'I'm a regular here.'

'Sorry, Frank.'

Maxwell turned to the fellow called Frank. 'Good evening to you,' he said.

'I've known better,' said Frank. 'There was the summer of eighty-nine. We had some evenings then, I remember. One in particular I recall was—'

'Yes,' said Maxwell. 'Now, no doubt you overheard the conversation I've been having with the innkeeper here.'

The innkeeper nodded politely.

Frank nodded also. 'I think you've been doing very well,' he said. 'I've seen grown men tear their hair out trying to get a bacon sandwich. There was this sales rep from the brewery once who—'

'Do *you* know where the City of Rameer is?' Maxwell asked.

'Of course I do. Everyone around here does.'

'So, *where* is it?'

'It's over yonder hill.'

Maxwell swung a fist, chinned Frank and knocked him to the floor.

The patrons of the inn looked up from their conversations and clicked disapproving tongues.

'I'll have to ask you to desist from that kind of behaviour, sir,' said the innkeeper. 'We have no truck with bullygarves or blumpits here.'

'All right,' said Maxwell, putting up his hands. 'I'm sorry. It was the heat of the moment.' He helped Frank from the floor. 'I've had a rough day,' he explained. 'Allow me to pay for your pint.'

'Rough day?' said Frank, testing for loose teeth.

'Don't talk to me about rough days. I remember back in seventy-three, it was a Wednesday I recall and—'

'Twenty-seven pence,' said the innkeeper, presenting Frank with his pint.

'But you charged *me* thirty,' said Maxwell.

'So I did, sir. Then thirty it is.'

Maxwell shook his head. 'Now listen,' he said to Frank, 'I will ask you politely, just one more time. Where is the City of Rameer?'

'It's over—'

'No,' Maxwell clamped his hand over Frank's mouth. '*Exactly* where?' He opened his fingers.

'—yonder—'

'No. One more time.'

'—hill,' said Frank.

Maxwell raised a fist.

Frank took to flinching. 'Don't hit me again. You asked where it is and I've told you.'

'It hasn't helped,' said Maxwell.

'Well, it's a stupid question. Like, how high is the sky, or which way will the wind blow tomorrow.'

'It's north,' said the innkeeper.

'What?' said Maxwell. 'The City of Rameer is north?'

'No, the wind. The wind will blow north tomorrow.'

'I bet it won't,' said Frank. 'I bet it will blow north-east, it always does at this time of year. Except for the big blow of sixty-eight. I recall—'

'Frank,' said Maxwell, 'if you don't tell me exactly where the City of Rameer is, right now, I will kill you where you stand.'

Frank looked hopelessly at Tom the innkeeper.

And Tom looked hopelessly at Frank.

Then they both looked hopelessly at Maxwell.

'Look,' said Frank, 'there is no other answer to your question. It's just a saying. The City of Rameer lies over yonder hill, means, well, that something you really really want in life is always just beyond your reach.'

'Like a bird in the hand won't get the baby bathed,' said the innkeeper.

'No not like that at all,' said Frank. 'You know what it means.'

'Oh yes, I know what it means. I was just saying that, a bird in the hand won't get the baby bathed, is a saying as well.'

'Oh, yeah, right. It's a saying as well. But it doesn't mean the same as, the City of Rameer lies over yonder hill.'

'Well, I know *that*,' said the innkeeper. 'Do you think I'm stupid, or something?'

'Shut up!' Maxwell shouted, as the red mist filled his head. He glared at the innkeeper. 'What is the name of this inn?' he asked.

'The Prospect of Rameer.'

'And do travellers pass this way seeking the city?'

'It has been known,' said Frank. 'One time in eighty-three a whole charabanc load of monks—'

'I'm talking to the innkeeper,' said Maxwell. 'Do people seek the city?'

'They do.'

'And what do you tell them?'

'That it's—'

'Over yonder hill.' Maxwell threw up his hands. 'Right,' said he, swinging about and spreading his glare over the gathered patrons. 'Has anyone here ever been to the City of Rameer?'

Heads shook.

'Does anyone here know where it is?'

Heads nodded.

'Would someone care to tell me?'

Heads shook again.

'Why?' demanded Maxwell.

'Because you'll hit them,' said Frank. 'They'll tell you it lies over yonder hill and you'll hit them.'

'Not until after I've hit you. Perhaps the demonstration will inspire them to exactitude.'

'It won't. It won't. How can I make you understand? There *is* no City of Rameer. It's a fable. A fairy-tale place. Like the Isles of the Blessed, or Atlantis—'

'Or Cardiff,' said the innkeeper.

'Or Cardiff,' said Frank. 'There is no such place as the City of Rameer.'

'There is too! I met some knights today from there.'

'Golden knights?' asked the innkeeper.

'Very,' said Maxwell.

'Hah,' Frank laughed. The folk about the bar laughed, somewhat nervously though. 'Knights of the Golden Grommet,' said Frank. 'They're not from Rameer, they come from Grayson. They just ride around the grid making a bloody nuisance of themselves.'

'Ah!' said Maxwell. 'Yes! The grid! That encircles the City of Rameer, raised by the Sultan. Deny that if you will.'

'You can't deny the grid,' said Frank.

'I wasn't going to,' said the innkeeper. 'But whoever said that the Sultan raised the grid?'

'A gridster,' said Maxwell. 'He told me he works, er, *worked*, for the Sultan.'

'The gridsters are all mad.' Frank twirled his finger at his forehead. 'A generation ago they were big fellows. But look at them now, shrinking away. That's what too much contact with the grid does for you.' He looked hard at Maxwell. 'Do *you* live close to the grid?' he asked.

'No I don't. But the existence of the grid proves the existence of the Sultan.'

'It does nothing of the sort. It merely marks

the boundary between our world and the one next door.'

'I'm missing something vital here,' said Maxwell.

'You don't know much about cosmology, do you?' the innkeeper asked.

'Apparently not,' said Maxwell, draining his pint.

'Right, well you know when the four worlds banged together?'

'What?'

'At the time of the great transition.'

'Oh, that, yes. What four worlds?'

The innkeeper sighed and pulled Maxwell another pint. 'Thirty-five,' he said.

'What?'

'Never mind, you can pay me later. Now, what was I saying?'

'About four worlds.'

'Right,' said the innkeeper. 'According to accepted scientific doctrine, the earth was once all alone in its particular orbit around the sun. Then one day, out of the blue, or black, three extra planets arrived. They caught up with the earth and shunted into it. All four worlds amalgamated to form a single planet, which is now the shape of a sausage. A cylinder with a hemisphere at each end. Are you following this?'

'I think so,' said Maxwell.

'Good, so now there is our world, the red world next door, bashed up against it, the silver world beyond that and the blue beyond that.'

'And all forming the shape of a sausage?'

'Or a cigar,' said Frank. 'You can prove it for yourself. If you walked along the edge of the grid, then many months later you would find yourself back where you started.'

'But the grid is kept in place by the Sultan,' said Maxwell.

'Cobblers,' said Frank. 'The grid is the boundary between our world and the red one. Their natural laws are not our natural laws. Magic flourishes there. No-one knows exactly what the grid is, but it keeps out magic, so let's be grateful for that.'

The innkeeper nodded. 'They say the women in the red world have got three tits and two—'

'Don't talk silly,' said Maxwell.

'—handbags each,' continued the innkeeper. 'But then they probably believe that about our women.'

'I wouldn't fancy a woman with three tits,' said Frank.

'Nor me,' said the barman. 'I'm a four-tit man. Always have been, always will be.'

'Stop!' shouted Maxwell. 'Do you realize what you're saying?'

'You don't like them with three then, do you?'

'No! I mean about the folk in the red world. What they might believe about this one. That they might believe in a Sultan Rameer. A powerful ruler who has a great city.'

'They might,' said the innkeeper. 'But they'd be mad if they did. There is no city and no Sultan.'

'But that's terrible. Terrible.' Maxwell clutched at his head.

'You know,' said Frank, 'three tits wouldn't be *that* terrible. One for each hand and one for your mo—'

'No!' said Maxwell. 'There *has* to be a city. There *has* to be.'

'There isn't,' said the innkeeper. 'Take our word for it. Perhaps there was one, long ago. But there isn't any more.'

'There *has* to be.' Maxwell raised his fists. 'You don't realize what this means to me. I *must* find the city and the Sultan. I must. I must.'

A traveller now entered the inn. He was tall and

grave and bore the look of one who had seen much and knew of more. He approached the bar. 'Someone seeking a city?' he asked.

Maxwell turned upon him. 'I am.'

'And what city might that be?'

With pounding temples and the red mist in his eyes, Maxwell said slowly, 'The City of Rameer. Do *you* know where it is?'

'I do,' said the traveller.

'You do?' said Frank and the innkeeper and many patrons too.

'You do?' asked Maxwell, knotting his fists.

'The City of Rameer lies—'

17

It took at least six strong men to throw Maxwell from the inn. There was quite a lot of unpleasantness, furniture was broken and pictures knocked from the walls.

Maxwell slept the night in the stable with Black Bess.

He awoke to the sound of a crowing cock and the smell of horse dung. He had a hangover, a blackened eye and numerous cuts and abrasions. He was not in the best of spirits.

He sat in the straw and set once again to the gathering of his scattered wits. What was he to do now? According to the innkeeper, he had entered a different world, passed from an angry red planet, with its magicians and man-eating rat ogres, into a golden world of namby-pamby knights and old women who struck small boys on the head.

And if there really was no city and no Sultan, there was probably no Ewavett either. Everything he'd gone through, all the privations he'd suffered, had been for nothing. The whole affair was pointless, ludicrous, plain stupid.

'Stupid!' Maxwell punched himself in the head. 'Stupid!' He punched himself again. 'Stupid! Stupid! Stupid!' Maxwell stopped punching himself. Well, it *was* stupid, punching yourself like that.

Maxwell groaned. He'd been rightly stitched up. What was he going to do now?

Go forward?

Go back?

He *could* go back through the grid, hope to find the flying bed and order it to fly to MacGuffin. If the bed knew where MacGuffin was, of course. And if he could escape the attentions of the gridsters who would be waiting, eager to toast his testicles with gelding tongs or stuff him in the maggot box.

And if he just sneaked out and walked . . .

To where? Through Kakkarta? Then swim the ocean?

'Aw shit!' said Maxwell. 'Shit. Shit. Shit.' He was doomed. Nineteen days to live and no hope of either succeeding in his mission or returning in time. Not good.

Maxwell sat in the straw with his head in his hands and gave things a good thinking through. Perhaps things were not as black as they appeared. Perhaps he was *not* limited to nineteen days. Not *here*. Perhaps if what the innkeeper had said was actually true, he was in a different world, which obeyed different natural laws, a world without magic. Perhaps MacGuffin's magic couldn't touch him here. Couldn't reach through the grid and get at him.

'Yeah,' said Maxwell. 'Perhaps it doesn't matter. Perhaps I won't die at all. Let him keep my soul. I can learn to live without it. If I tried really really hard, I bet I could keep my temper and not keep wanting to kill people. Yeah, stuff MacGuffin. Stuff him.'

Maxwell raised two fingers towards the oak timbers above. 'Stuff you!' he shouted. 'Stuff you!'

The pain that hit him was unlike any he had known before. It came from every direction at once. Maxwell had read in a book by George Ryley Scott about the torture of one John Clarke by the Dutch at Amboyna in 1662. Church candles had been lit beneath his feet, which periodically went out due to the quantity of human fat dripping onto them. The very thought of this had caused Maxwell to run to the bathroom and throw up. The pain that tore through him now, was such an agony as had been poor John Clarke's.

Maxwell rolled about, and through his screams he heard the voice.

'I hope he *is* working,' it said.

The voice of MacGuffin.

'No,' shrieked Maxwell. 'Leave my soul alone.'

The pain subsided and he lay in a wretched heap.

There was no escape. MacGuffin had him. He had shaken the crystal globe containing Maxwell's soul, no doubt to impress his next victim. The next man for the night flight to Kakkarta.

Maxwell rolled himself into a ball and passed from consciousness.

He awoke from a horrid dream about Dutchmen in clogs to find the innkeeper standing over him.

'Time to settle your account,' said this man.

'Oh yes?' said Maxwell, with no interest whatsoever.

'Indeed.' The innkeeper produced a scroll of paper and began to unroll it. 'I don't know how you slept,' he said, 'but I've been up all night with an abacus working this lot out. I pride myself that I have calculated the exactitude of your owings with a preciseness which leaves error without a peg to hang his hat upon. It covers the ale you consumed; the room you booked, but chose not to occupy; the groom's charges for tending to your horse and shoeing him while you slept, and the damage caused to fixtures and fittings, which occurred during your unprovoked attack on the travelling cleric and the subsequent mêlée which concluded with your forcible eviction from the premises.

'Now, my real problem lay in calculating the exact

value of the fixtures and fittings. Opinions varied as to the trend in current market prices. Some said they were up, and others down. But I poured oil upon the troubled waters of commercial debate by declaring my philosophy, that the cost of a replacement item does not necessarily equate with the value the owner puts upon the original. For instance, let us take the stool you hit Frank over the head with. I asked Frank what he thought it was worth and, possibly as the result of rage or concussion, he declared that you should be made to pay twenty gold pieces for a new one. Twenty gold pieces, I ask you. "Frank," I said, "Frank, the stool was not new, it had a wobbly leg and I paid less than five gold pieces when I bought it." Yet, and here is a curious thing, yet I value that particular stool at one hundred gold pieces, a staggering sum some might think. But if you think that staggering, just listen to how I value some of the other fixtures. Wait now! Unhand me! What are you doing?'

Maxwell rode north. He met a trader and purchased some bread and some fruit. Maxwell asked the trader if he knew where the City of Rameer was. The trader told him and Maxwell punched the trader . . .

And rode on.

The landscape was more of the same: each valley like the one before and not unlike the next. The golden sun moved up the sky, the grass was green, the horse was white and Maxwell's rage was red and raw and no nice man was he.

He rode a bit and walked a bit, lay down at times, kicked stones at times and counted little old ladies that clouted little boys.

Noon found him sitting under an oak tree munching an apple, effing and blinding between each bite. It was his helplessness that really got to him; the fact that he could do *nothing*. If the city had existed he just knew he could have found a way in. And if he'd met the Sultan he just knew he'd have come up with some scheme to win Ewavett away from him. And if he'd got back to MacGuffin, he'd have dealt with him as well. He *would* have. Maxwell just knew that he would have. He was the Imagineer, after all. The man with the plan. The sport with the thought. The tactician with the vision. Maxwell could think of a hundred more such epithets (which was more than any author could!).

He was doomed. Doomed to ride across valleys until his nineteen days were up. Then kaput.

Maxwell bit a final chunk from his apple and flung the core into the air.

'Ouch!' said a small voice.

Maxwell leapt up and made fists. 'Who is that? Come out.'

'I'm not doing anything, mister.'

Maxwell looked up into the tree. A small ragged-looking boy clung to a branch. 'Come down,' said Maxwell.

'You won't hit me, will you?'

'Possibly not.'

The small boy climbed down and stood looking worried. His face was unwashed and his knees were good and dirty. He wore a grey jacket, short trousers and what had once been a white shirt. He had that Just William look to him.

'What is your name?' Maxwell asked.

'It's William, Mister. Just William.'

'And what are you doing up the tree, William?'

'Hiding from my gran.'

'Well,' said Maxwell. 'I think that puts you beyond the category of *stupid* boy.'

'Oh, I'm stupid enough in my way.'

'Do you want an apple?' Maxwell asked.

199

'Oh, yes please.'

Maxwell handed him an apple and the boy tucked into it.

'Tell me,' said Maxwell. 'Out of interest. All these old women who I keep meeting, who clout small boys. Where do they all come from?'

The small boy looked puzzled. 'Don't you know *that*?'

'If I knew, I wouldn't be asking.'

'Well,' the small boy tittered, 'they come from the same place everybody comes from.'

'And where is that?'

'Out of their mummies' tummies.'

Maxwell clouted William in the head.

William rubbed at his head. 'I was sure I was right that time,' he said. 'I must be even more stupid than I thought.'

'No, you're not. I'm sorry I hit you.'

'Oh, don't be. If I never got smacked round the head, I'd never learn anything, would I?'

'Well, there are other methods of teaching.'

'Oh yes,' said William. 'But not round here. Round here the elders subscribe to the principle of "beat some sense into them". It works well enough.'

'Well, I've never actually witnessed the tuition side of it. I've only seen the clouting on the head.'

William looked puzzled once more. 'But I thought that the clouting on the head *was* the tuition side of it. There's nothing more involved.'

'You mean they don't actually teach you anything? They just keep clouting you on the head?'

'That's the way they do it,' said William. 'That's how my father was taught and his before him. You can learn a lot from a clout round the head.'

'Have you tried learning how to duck?'

'I tried that once, but I got a clout round the head for it.'

'Well,' said Maxwell, 'I have learned, and partly through having most other parts of me clouted, to keep my nose out of matters that do not concern me. If that's the way things are done around here, so be it.'

William tucked into his apple.

'Why were you hiding from your gran, then?' Maxwell asked.

'I have become sated with education,' William said. 'The old one beats my head with such enthusiasm that I have learned more than it is good for a boy of my years to learn.'

Maxwell smiled, something he hadn't done for some time.

'Only yesterday', William continued, 'she knocked into my skull certain branches of advanced mathematics. Do you know of the quantum theory?'

'No,' said Maxwell, scratching his head, something else he hadn't done for a while.

'It's a theory concerning the behaviour of physical systems based on the idea that they can only possess certain qualities, such as energy and angular movements, in discrete amounts. It's been developed into several mathematical forms, all of which I am now conversant with.'

'Good grief,' said Maxwell. 'That's incredible.'

'Precisely,' said William. 'In fact, I don't credit it at all. Any theory based on the behaviour of physical systems would need to encompass an almost infinite number of variables. How can you judge the qualities that a single system possesses, without first being certain that it interacts with the next only within a three-dimensional framework?'

'I have absolutely no idea,' said Maxwell. 'And you learned all this simply by being struck repeatedly on the head?'

'I suspect there is a knack to the striking,' said

William. 'I learned absolutely nothing when you hit me just now. It is still my firm conviction that everyone comes out of their mummy's tummy.'

'But this knowledge.' Maxwell shook a head that he now felt might do well for a skilful striking. 'This knowledge you have. It's awesome. What do you intend to do with it? What do you want to be when you grow up?'

'An innkeeper,' said William.

Maxwell gave his head a shake. 'I am frankly amazed by this educational system. Have you had anything beaten into your head which might offer an inkling into how it actually works?'

'Percussive perlocution,' said William. 'The theory is, as I understand it, that a man's thoughts are not wholly his personal property. A man draws his thoughts from a common pool, a common consciousness, comprised of racial memory implanted within his genetic code; experience, which is to say observation and the assimilation of ideas through the vocal structure we call language; and intuitive reasoning, which enables him to envisage the predictable outcome of a certain course of action. But also, and here we step tentatively into the world of metaphysics, by attunement to universal awareness. The head beating induces a morphic resonance within the brain of the beatee which clears the synapses and allows a through-put of knowledge drawn from the common pool. Of course you will ask, what *is* this common pool—'

'Of course,' said Maxwell, re-shaking his head.

'And there I must answer that nobody knows. Perhaps the universe itself is sentient. Perhaps the planet speaks to us. Perhaps it is God or Goddess.'

'Phew,' Maxwell whistled. 'I am now more amazed than ever I was.'

William looked Maxwell up and down. 'Can I

assume that you were not educated in these parts?'

'You can.' Maxwell climbed to his feet. 'Well, it's been an, er, education, talking to you. But I must be on my way. To somewhere.'

'May I ask where you're riding to?' William gave his nose a pick and examined the yield.

'You *may* ask,' said Maxwell. 'Let *me* ask you this: if I told you that the answer was, "it lies over yonder hill", what do you suppose the question might be?'

William flicked away his bogey. 'An interesting conundrum,' said he. 'And one that presents again an almost infinite number of variables. However, if we assume that there actually exists one question more likely than all the rest, I would have to answer that the question would be, "Where is the City of Rameer?" '

'You are correct, of course,' said Maxwell.

'Only in principle,' said William. 'For here we enter the realms of sylogistics. I have identified the correct question, but the answer is clearly at fault. Because the City of Rameer does *not* lie over yonder hill.'

'Something I have learned to my cost,' said Maxwell.

'The City of Rameer lies *under* yonder hill,' said William.

'Do *what*?'

'Beneath our very feet. It is a subterranean city.'

'Good grief,' said Maxwell. 'But have you actually seen it?'

'I know where the entrance is. But obviously I have not been inside.'

'Why, *obviously*?'

'Because I would not be discussing it with you now if I had.'

'You mean whoever enters does not return?'

'On the contrary. But it is a curious business and one which has played its part in my decision to have done with education. Do you wish me to explain?'

'Please do.'

'Then it's like this. I am nine years of age and on my tenth birthday I must enter the City of Rameer to take my examinations. The curiosity is this, children enter the city, their heads crammed with knowledge, take their examinations, then emerge as men.'

'Some kind of rite of passage?'

'Something of the sort. Yet when they emerge, they no longer appear knowledgeable. In fact, they seem to have completely forgotten the greater part of their learning. And when asked about the city, they just stare blankly and say, "The City of Rameer lies over yonder hill." I am at a loss to explain this. Can you enlighten me at all?'

Maxwell made a thoughtful face. 'A sinister explanation springs immediately to mind. The knowledge is somehow extracted from the children and then their memories erased. How this is done, I dread to think. But listen, if adults have no memory of the city, who takes you there on your tenth birthday?'

'On the night of my brother's tenth birthday I pretended to be asleep. I watched as a stranger came and took him. When my brother returned four days later, he had become a man and spoke of the city as a fairy-tale.'

'The stranger who took your brother. How was he dressed?'

'He wore golden armour and he rode a horse such as yours.'

'Rock 'n' Roll,' said Maxwell.

'That is the name of your horse?'

'No it's not. Now listen, one other thing. If adults no longer know of the city, how do *you* know of it? How do you know where the entrance is?'

'The knowledge was knocked into my head along with all the rest.'

'As likely an explanation as any other, I suppose. William, how would you feel about showing me the entrance?'

'I am confused by your request. Surely, as an adult, you do not believe a single word I've told you.'

'I believe everything you've told me. Although much of it I did not understand. Will you take me to the entrance?'

'I have no wish to go inside. I want to hold on to my knowledge.'

'You're a very bright boy. Perhaps if I succeed in my mission, this land will see its children grow to adulthood with all their knowledge intact.'

A crowd of thoughts now bustled into Maxwell's head: the rise of a new age of science, precipitated by the fall of the Sultan, and guided by William the philosopher PM; do-it-yourself courses in head banging; the disbanding of a certain regiment of knights; success for Maxwell. Many, many more.

'How far is it to the entrance, William? And please don't tell me it lies over yonder hill.'

'Why should *I* tell you that? My brother was gone four days. I don't know how long he spent within the city itself, but the entrance must surely be within two days' ride of here.'

'But you said you knew where the entrance was.'

'I have a very clear mental impression. I believe I could find it without difficulty.'

'Praise the Goddess.' Maxwell clapped his hands together. 'Then you will take me to it?'

'Take you to it?' William laughed uproariously. 'Leave it out, mister, I'm not even supposed to speak to strange men.'

18

The clout William took to the head increased the sum of his knowledge, only by teaching him that Maxwell was not a man to be dealt with in a flippant manner.

Maxwell spoke at length to William, telling him of his misadventures, of MacGuffin and the stolen soul and the flying chair and the rat ogres of Kakkarta. And of the Governor and of the grid and dah-de-dah-de-dah.

William listened with great interest, asking questions here and there. He made it clear to Maxwell that in his opinion it was impossible for one man to take another's soul. Yet he conceded that his knowledge of magic was scant and that 'weird shit happens'. He *did* ask Maxwell why he had lost his faith in the existence of the city, when the Governor of Kakkarta had told him that he was a personal friend of the Sultan.

Maxwell asked William whether he had ever heard of such a thing as a continuity error. William said he had not.

The talk of Ewavett and Aodhamm inspired much wonder in the lad, who explained that recently some knowledge had been knocked into him regarding cyborgs and artificial intelligence, but that he had been at a loss to make any sense of it at the time.

When Maxwell had done with the telling of his tale, William mulled it all over and then agreed without

206

reservation to direct Maxwell at once to the City of Rameer.

'But you must understand', he stressed, 'that technically you lay yourself open to the charge of kidnap. Should the men of my village catch up with us, they will not deal leniently. Your pleas that you seek the City of Rameer will hold less water than a bucket with no bottom.'

'That is a crap metaphor,' said Maxwell, 'but I take your point.'

'I think you'll find it's a simile,' said William, 'but I'm glad you do.'

'So shall we be off?'

'Let's go.'

'Which way?' Maxwell asked.

William pointed. 'Over yonder hill,' he said.

The day passed on to afternoon, to evening, then to night. William proved himself to be a boy of considerable resource. Skilled not only in the arts of scrumping fruit, stealing cow's milk, snaring, killing, skinning and cooking rabbits, but also in woodcraft.

Having no sleeping-bag or cloak, Maxwell was grateful for the shelter of the bush-branch bender he constructed. Also for the meal. They talked not long into the night as they agreed it best to douse the fire and make an early start in the morning.

Maxwell lay awhile gazing up through the canopy of leaves towards the star-strung sky. What was it all about, eh? What did it all mean? Maxwell shrugged, Black Bess farted and that was the end of the day.

The night passed without incident. No villagers with flaming torches. No wolves, nor snakes, nor creeping things. Neither William nor Maxwell were abducted by aliens. There was no earthquake.

At dawn, a tall grey-haired man with iron-framed spectacles came to enquire why Maxwell and William were camped in his front garden, and could Maxwell do something about his horse, because it was eating the flowers in the man's window-box.

Maxwell apologized profusely. The man said he thought it, 'A diabolical liberty.' Maxwell said he was sorry once again. The man claimed that the world was going to the Devil and such things shouldn't be allowed. Maxwell punched the man's lights out.

And off they rode once more.

It was *really* boring.

There is always that bit when nothing very much happens. Sometimes it's relieved by a little humorous anecdote, or a descriptive passage that's part of a running gag, or some conversation with a lot of long words in it that implies there's a lot more *depth* than there actually is. But sometimes – *rarely!* – but sometimes . . .

There's nothing!

'What is *that*?' William asked, pointing excitedly.

Maxwell stared off into the distance. 'It's nothing,' he said.

And it was.

So they rode on.

'I'm getting bored with this riding,' said William. 'Don't you know some humorous anecdote you could tell me?'

'No,' said Maxwell.

'How would you describe this countryside?'

'I wouldn't,' said Maxwell.

'Isn't that a parsnip over there?'

'No,' said Maxwell.

'Did I tell you my thoughts on the quantum theory?'

'Yes,' said Maxwell.

*   *   *

And so they rode on.

'I once saw a man who was only one inch tall,' said William.

'Did you?'

'No, not really. He turned out to be just very far away. *Ouch!*'

They rode on.

After more of the same for several hours, William suddenly said, 'Look up ahead.'

Maxwell looked. 'Ah!' said he. 'Splendid.'

A knight rode before them. He wore golden armour, a child clung on behind him.

'Look back,' said William. 'There's another one coming after us.'

'Simply splendid.'

'What do you plan to do when we reach the entrance to the city, Maxwell.'

'I plan to go inside, of course.'

'What about me?'

'I plan to take you in too.'

'Oh no,' said William. 'Oh no. Not me.'

'Listen,' Maxwell gave the lad an encouraging pat on the shoulder. 'I have a magic pouch in my pocket. It contains a suit of golden armour. I will put the armour on and we will enter the city with the other knights. It will appear that I am delivering you for your examination.'

'I suspected you had something like that in mind.'

'I'll see you come to no harm. I promise.'

'Promises are easier made than kept.'

'You have all the makings of a fine innkeeper, William. Perhaps we will acquire some of the Sultan's wealth. You could buy your own inn. Conduct affairs of state from there, once you're elected Prime Minister.'

'That statement might carry a bit more weight were it not prefixed by the word *perhaps*.'

'Yes, you're right.' Maxwell drew Black Bess to a halt. 'I may be a soul-less, angry, violent bastard with only eighteen more days to live, but I won't be instrumental in letting any harm come to a child. Get down from the horse. You can either wait here until I return, as I surely will, or go your way. Not that I think it a good idea for a boy of your age to be wandering about on his own.'

William remained in the saddle. 'Just testing,' he said. 'Let's go.'

'You'll trust me, then?'

'Don't you think I want to know what's inside the city?'

'Rock 'n' Roll,' said Maxwell. 'Rock 'n' Roll.'

'You'll have to explain to me just what that means,' said William.

The landscape had begun to change. Rocky outcrops showed through the grassy meadows. The trees were autumn-leafed. The setting sun saw Maxwell, once more in the golden armour, but it didn't see the worried face he wore beneath the visor.

'The track's going down, isn't it?' William said.

'It has been for some time. Are we nearly there, do you think?'

'Oh yes. I feel as if I know this place. We're very close now.'

The path grew steeper and as the moon rose up it cast its light upon a scene of such surpassing strangeness that Maxwell had to pull up the horse short and just stare at it in disbelief.

It appeared that they had entered the crater of some vast extinct volcano. The track spiralled down the inner rim, down and down into a great black void. Knights rode slowly on before, diminishing away to tiny golden dots on the track below.

'You don't suppose', said Maxwell, 'that the term, The City of Rameer, is in fact a euphemism for Hell?'

'I knew this is what it looked like,' said William. 'I just didn't want to put you off by mentioning it.'

'Thanks very much.'

'Don't mention it.'

And as it had been the order of the day . . .

They rode on.

Down and down and down. And down. And down and down. And down.

And down.

'I see light,' said William.

'Me too,' said Maxwell.

And they did see light. Ahead. Like a thin line of dawn.

'Do you get the feeling that we're not going down any more?' William asked.

'I get the feeling that we're going up. But I don't see how we can be.'

But they were. After a fashion.

The light grew before them. And then rose *above* them.

'The sun's coming up,' said William.

'That's impossible,' said Maxwell.

And then they rode out. Upon grass.

Maxwell stared. And William stared.

'William,' said Maxwell, 'do you realize what we're doing?'

William nodded. 'We would appear to be riding upside down on the inner skin of the planet's outer shell. Clearly in defiance of at least one law of physics.'

'Then that sun we see above us—'

'Would appear to be the molten core of the planet.'

'I'm very impressed,' said Maxwell. 'I don't believe it, but I'm very impressed, none the less.'

'An entire world, upside down. Look, you can see, there's no horizon, it curves up and out and away. We're like flies walking on a ceiling.'

'I feel dizzy,' said Maxwell. 'The blood must be rushing to my head.'

'Don't be silly. If it was doing that, we'd fall, well, *up* I suppose, into the heart of the molten core.'

'It's just like the world above. Grass and flowers and trees. And look, way ahead. What is that?'

'Do you mean over yonder hill?'

'I do.'

'The City of Rameer,' said William. 'Definitely.'

And this time it really was.

'Let me tell you', said Maxwell, 'what I mean by Rock 'n' Roll.'

19

Maxwell was not really sure just how he'd imagined the City of Rameer might look. Naturally he'd thought that a city ruled over by a Sultan would probably have an Arabian Nights flavour to it: a bit of old Baghdad, with plenty of domes and cupolas and minarets; a high city wall with tall Moorish gates, manned by fierce-looking guards with turbans and scimitars. Things of that nature.

He had *not* expected it to look like Milton Keynes.

So he wasn't surprised when it didn't.

He was quite surprised by what it did look like, though. And it really didn't look like a city. It was big, which is to say there was a lot of it about. Tall buildings, elegant, in pale brick.

Neo-Gothic, Palladian style. Horizontal skylines broken at intervals by triangular pediments atop Doric colonnades. Heavy on classical influences. A great many of these. Graeco-Roman, Spanish, high baroque, Renaissance, reflected through Wren and Hawksmoor, Adam and Inigo Jones.

To Maxwell, whio knew sweet damn all about Hawksmoor and Inigo Jones, and who might have guessed that a Doric colonnade was a kind of Morris dance, it was none the less pretty impressive, if something of a jumble. Here was an architectural folly on a scale to dwarf the work of the now legendary,

Sir Clough Williams-Ellis himself.

Surrounding all were beautiful gardens, tended lawns, rose arbors, marble statuary.

'We're going the wrong way,' said William. 'The knights are turning off, see they're going towards those buildings over there.'

'I think it's time for us to drop out of the procession,' said Maxwell. 'Come on.' He steered the horse to the shelter of a spreading chestnut tree, removed the golden armour, slipped it into the magic pouch and returned the pouch to his trouser pocket.

'It's clever how it does that, isn't it?' said William. 'I suppose a state must exist within the pouch where the quotient of fundamental physical properties possessed by the object placed inside no longer conforms to the accepted three-dimensional paradigm on which much of the quantum theory depends for its veracity. You forgot to take your substantial boots out, by the way.'

'Thank you, William,' said Maxwell.

'What do we do now?'

'First we try and blend,' said Maxwell, 'check out what the locals are wearing and nick some clothes. As you possess a natural flair for petty thievery, this will be your job.'

'And then?'

'Well, I've got this far so I don't mean to blow it all by doing something rash. I intend to find out everything I can about the Sultan before I put my grand scheme into operation.'

'You haven't explained to me about your grand scheme.'

'You're right there,' said Maxwell. 'I haven't.'

They crept from the cover of the spreading chestnut tree, skulked from bush to bush, sidled down hedge-bounded avenues and finally approached a grand-looking archway, beyond which lay all the main buildings that composed the City of Rameer.

Maxwell stared up. The arch was wrought in cast iron, an intricate tracery of metal rose and briar. Across its top ran an arc of gilded lettering. Maxwell read the words aloud.

'The University of Life,' he read.

'What does that mean?' William asked.

Maxwell scratched his head. 'It doesn't mean anything. It's like the School of Hard Knocks. It's just a saying.'

'Like, the City of Rameer lies—'

'*City*,' said Maxwell. 'Yes. Univer*sity*. It's not the *City* of Rameer, it's the *University*.'

'It says, the University of *Life*, not Rameer. We've come to the wrong place.'

'No,' Maxwell shook the head he had previously scratched. 'Think about it. A University used to be a place where the young came to be educated. A place of learning. In this arse-about-face world, it's a place where the young come to be de-educated. To have their learning removed.'

'But, why?'

'Well, if I knew that then— Sssh, what was that sound?'

'I didn't—'

A cheer went up and much applause.

'It's over yonder hedge,' said William. 'Shall we take a look?'

'Indeed.' They scuttled over to the hedge and Maxwell took a peep over. He blinked. And blinked. Then blinked again and then ducked down beside William.

'What is it?' the lad asked.

'It's – a – a . . .' Maxwell gave his head another

shake, then rose once more to take another look. 'It's a cricket match,' he whispered.

And it was.

But not like any cricket match he'd ever seen before. No, siree.

Upon a lawn, so pure and flat as if it were of velvet, two teams were in play. With the batsmen and their fellows, who looked on from the pavilion end, Maxwell found no fault. Elegant young chaps were these in dapper cricket whites, striped ties knotted through trouser-belt loops, club caps, rolled sleeves. In every inch they looked the part, decked out for the summer game.

The fault lay with the bowler and the fielders of the opposing team.

And the fault was this: none of these was human.

They were animals.

Now, Maxwell knew, as every Englishman knows, that his national team has always had problems with 'animals': Jamaican fast bowlers, Australian body-liners, Pakistani ball-tamperers. The British touring side never *ever* lost abroad due to lack of skill. Oh no, after all, we invented the game, didn't we? It was always down to the dirty doings of the opposition. Animals they were.

Bloody animals.

But here, however, the 'animals' weren't men. They really *were* animals.

The bowler was an elephant, big and glossy black, though togged up in cricket whites. He walked upon his hind legs and though slow upon the run up, bowled the ball with an awesome force.

The batsman took a mighty swing, but *crack* went the centre wicket.

The crowd in the stand, consisting of numerous small boys in grey uniforms, clapped politely. The elephant raised his trunk in triumph and his team-mates surrounded him, congratulating heartily.

Maxwell spied out a tiger, a wolf, a panther, all walking upon two legs and clad in cricketer's kit.

Maxwell looked on with his jaw hanging slack.

A heavy hand fell upon his shoulder.

'What are you skulking about there for, boy?' asked the owner of the hand. 'Why aren't you padded up?'

Maxwell jerked around and found himself staring into the face of a tall distinguished-looking gent. Maxwell took in a magnificent handlebar moustache, a mortar board perched upon the head, a gown draped about the shoulders.

'Ah,' said Maxwell.

'Ah, *what*, lad?'

'Ah, *sir*?' Maxwell suggested.

'Ah sir, yes, sir. Where are your pads?'

'My pads?' Maxwell looked down at himself. He was still wearing the Governor's white shirt and matching strides. Though these were now somewhat grubby, there was no doubt that they did allow him to pass for a cricketer. 'My pads, I've—'

'Left them in your locker, I'll be bound.'

'That's probably it,' said Maxwell.

'Are you in the first team? I don't recognize your face.'

'I'm a reserve,' said Maxwell.

'What's your name?'

Maxwell was about to say, Ian Botham, but felt he could do better than that. 'Flashman, sir,' he said. 'Harry Flashman, and this is my fag, Tom Brown.'

'Your kit's in an appalling state, Flashman, and it looks as if your fag's been up a chimney.'

'I locked him in the boot hole', said Maxwell, 'for not cleaning my kit.'

217

'That's the ticket. Well, get over to the pavilion and get padded up. Jennings took a ball to the left eye in the first over. Cleaved his skull open. The umpire gave him not out and the captain's been barking for a reserve for half an hour.'

'But I've no pads, sir,' said Maxwell, who knew as much about cricket as he did about architecture, and didn't fancy losing an eye for sport.

'Get someone to lend you a pair, tell them Mr Pederast gave you permission.'

'But sir, I—'

'Cut along,' said Mr Pederast. 'Or I'll take you up to my study and you know what that means.'

'I think I could hazard a guess,' said Maxwell.

'Off on your way then.'

Maxwell weighed up the pros and cons. He could easily just chin Mr Pederast and don the mortar board and gown. But then he did cut a far more convincing figure as a cricketer. If he went over to the pavilion he could probably talk his way out of actually playing and he might be able to learn a few things also.

'Come on, Brown,' said Maxwell. 'The honour of the school's to play for.'

William hurried after Maxwell. Beyond the earshot of Mr Pederast, he asked, 'Maxwell, why did you call that man sir? What's a cricket match? What are pads? What does a reserve do? Who is Flashman? Why did you refer to me as Brown? What's a fag? What's a boot hole? What—'

'William,' said Maxwell, 'shut up.'

They passed through a gap in the hedge and strode out towards the pavilion. And here young William caught his first sight of the game in play and the players, er, playing.

He made a kind of strangled gasping sound and fell to his hands and knees.

'What *are* you doing?' Maxwell asked.

'It is the Pantheon, prostrate yourself.'

'Certainly not. William, get up at once.'

'The Pantheon.' William began to babble away in words Maxwell took to be Latin.

'Get up, before somebody sees you.'

'Get *down* before they see *you*.'

Maxwell rolled his eyes and sat down beside William. 'What are you going on about?' he asked.

'The Pantheon. The gods beneath.'

'The animals?' Maxwell, having put two and two together and come up with a number substantially in excess of the approved *four*, had by now convinced himself that the clothed animals were those of the trained and performing circus variety and that this was some kind of entertainment. He did worry about Jennings having his skull cleaved open, of course, but accidents *will* happen. Ask Aspinell. 'Gods?' asked Maxwell. 'Are you serious?'

William pointed a trembly finger towards the bowler. 'Papa Legba,' he whispered. 'The tiger is Ju Ju Hand. The panther, Ouanga. There is Jephthah and Papa Nebo and Dr Poo-Pah-Doo. The bull is Unkosibomvu.' And so on and so forth, until he had named all of the visiting side.

'And the gods played cricket?' whispered Maxwell to himself. 'I wonder if that's a lost Jimi Hendrix track.'

'What?'

'Nothing. William, I never had you down for a superstitious lad. Surely that doesn't conform to your scientific outlook on the world.'

'Up until now I considered myself an atheist.'

'Yes, but *gods*? That's pushing things a tad.'

Papa Legba, if such was he, bowled a serious googly, but the new batsman managed to catch it before the off stump and push it out past the silly mid on for a leg by.*

Ju Ju Hand leapt up to take the catch, but fumbled his Ju Ju hands and the ball caught him squarely between the eyes, felling him to the ground.

'Beware the thunderbolt,' cried William, assuming the foetal position.

Maxwell looked on, as the team-mates of Ju Ju Hand gathered about the fallen fumbler, who was presently stretchered away from the field of play.

'I don't think they're gods,' said Maxwell. 'I don't know what they are, but I don't think they're gods.'

'You don't think so, really?'

'Nope.' Maxwell shook his head. 'Not gods.'

William climbed to his feet. 'Please forgive me for that unseemly lapse. We get a lot of religious dogma drummed into our heads.'

'So what's new?' Maxwell helped the lad to his feet. 'Let's get over to the pavilion. There might be some tea and cucumber sandwiches.'

As they approached the pavilion, Maxwell counselled William to hold his peace. 'Just shut up and leave all the talking to me,' he said.

The pavilion was everything a cricket pavilion should be. All painted white, little clock tower jobbie with weather-vane. Steps up. Veranda, Lloyd loom chairs. Posts to lean against. That certain smell that only cricket pavilions have, the one which is impossible to describe.

Maxwell swaggered up the steps, wearing a foolish grin.

'You there,' called a chap in whites, who was lounging against one of the posts-to-lean-against and

*No. I don't know what that means either.

cradling a glass of what seemed to be Pimm's in a languid hand. 'Who are you there then?'

'Are you talking to me – there?' Maxwell asked.

'Yes, you there, you.'

'Flashman,' said Maxwell. 'Harry Flashman, and this is my fag, Brown.'

William tugged upon his forelock.

'I don't think I know any Flashman.'

'I don't think I know *you*,' said Maxwell. 'What's *your* name?'

'Archer. Lord Edgar Archer. I'm the side's captain.'

'*Archer?* Do you have a brother in service as a knight?'

'My elder brother Jeffrey. Do you know him?'

'Like a brother,' said Maxwell. 'He recently loaned me his horse, Black Bess.'

'Damn me for a bullygarve,' quoth Archer minor. 'He won't even let me take her for a canter round the paddock.

'Brotherly love, eh?' said Maxwell.

'We never did,' said Archer minor, reddening at the cheeks. 'He never told you *that*, did he?'

'We're very close,' said Maxwell, making a knowing face.

'Swipe me. Well, I mean, care for a tot of something?'

'A drink would be nice, and a sandwich. Come on, Brown.'

'Hold on there a moment.' Archer made a grave face. 'Something's not right here.'

'What?' asked Maxwell, making a fist behind his back.

'Can't have fags in the long room.'

'Quite so,' said Maxwell. 'Wait here, Brown. I'll bring you something out.'

William shook his head, shrugged and sat down on

the pavilion steps. Maxwell followed Archer inside.

'Welly-well-well,' said Lord Archer, pouring Maxwell a drink. 'Fancy you, er, knowing the brother.'

'Fancy that,' Maxwell accepted his drink and took a swig. 'Have you been at the University long?'

'Nearly three years. Another two and I'll be ready to mount up and join the golden knights.'

'Once you've learned all the subtle nuances of knight-speak though. Must know your plumpit from your bullygarve.'

'Too true. But what are you doing here?'

'In the pavilion, do you mean? Mr Pederast sent me over to stand in as a reserve, since poor Jennings took a spill. I don't normally play, but, you know how it is.'

Archer nodded as if he did. But he didn't.

'Tell me,' said Maxwell, 'chum to chum, as it were. I've only been here for a week or so and I don't know the form. How would one go about getting to see the Sultan?'

'Walk in, clip him about the ear, sit yourself down and make your demands known.'

'Ah,' said Maxwell, and to make a change from scratching his head, this time he pulled upon the lobe of his left ear. 'That sounds a rather cavalier attitude to take. Shouldn't one make an appointment? Go through certain channels?'

'What? To see the silly Sultan?'

'*Silly* Sultan?'

'Daft old geezer. Deaf as a dumblat.'

'Dumblat?'

'Keevle, swimpit, purgler.'

'Purgler,' said Maxwell. 'Right, yes.'

'Shout,' said Archer. 'Tell him exactly what you want. Say, *Just trim the sides, you old Purgler. None off the top!*'

'None off the top?' Maxwell reverted to head

scratching. '*None off the top?* I am rightly confused. Am I not correct in thinking that the Sultan Sergio Rameer controls this entire University?'

'Controls the University?' Archer spat Pimm's over Maxwell and fell about in a fit of hysterical laughter. 'Sergio Rameer, control the University? That's a good'n. I must tell the chaps. Someone's been pulling your chain, old fellow, cos you're a new-bug.'

'Let me get this straight.' Maxwell flicked Pimm's from his shoulders. 'The Sultan Sergio Rameer does *not* control the University?'

'No, sorry, sorry.' Archer fought to keep his hilarity in check. 'You've not started on Latin yet?'

'No,' Maxwell shook his head, spraying droplets of Pimm's, hither and thus.

'So you don't know what Sultan means?'

'Apparently not. Please enlighten me.'

'It's Latin, old fellow. *Solum tonsor. Solum* Tonsor. *Sol-ton,* Sultan.'

'I'm no better off for this explanation.'

Archer sighed. '*Solum* means the bottom, the bottom of anything, beneath. *Tonsor* means barber. So the *Solum Tonsor,* The Soltan, means barber below everything. The barber here, at the bottom of the world. The Sultan is the University barber.'

'*What?*' went Maxwell. 'What? What? What?'

'And as for Sergio Rameer. Your pronunciation is all to fault. It's not Ser-gio-Rameer. It's Sir John Rimmer. *Sir John Rimmer.*'

20

'*Sir John Rimmer?*' Maxwell took a step back. His brain took a giant leap. Sir John Rimmer? He of the Hidden Tower? He who'd done the dirty on Maxwell and somehow bucketed him forward a hundred years to land up in the mess he had landed up in. So to speak.

That Sir John Rimmer?*

Well, it was unlikely to be another.

And *Sultan* really meant *barber*?

'One thing,' Maxwell stood swaying, waving a finger in the air. 'One thing. If Sir John Rimmer is the Sultan.'

'*Solum tonsor*,' said Archer.

'*Solum tonsor*, yes. If Sir John Rimmer is *Solum tonsor*, who controls this university?'

'The principal of course.'

'And the principal's name is?'

'Count Waldeck,' said Archer. 'Count Otto Waldeck.'†

As if at the name, a cheer went up outside. Archer loped over to the door. 'Damn and buggery!' he swore. 'Fudger run out, that leaves you as last man in.'

'Last man in?' Maxwell's brain had turned to soup. His thoughts waded about, knee deep in Brown Windsor. How could *they* be here? One hundred years

---

*A quick flip back to Chapter 2 would probably be a very good idea at about this time. †Told you!

224

after the great transition. Sir John Rimmer as a barber and Count Waldeck, whom Maxwell was certain he had shot dead, as principal?

'It's ludicrous,' said Maxwell. 'It just can't be.'

'Fraid it is. Damn Fudger, out for a duck.'

'Duck?' Maxwell slumped into a Lloyd loom chair. 'I'm losing this. I can't make any sense out of this at all.'

'You'll be fine.' Archer was at Maxwell's legs. 'Let me help you.'

'What are you doing?' Maxwell didn't really care.

'Getting you padded up. You're our last hope, Flashman. Have to beat the visitors.'

'Visitors?' Maxwell shook his head this way and that.

'Visiting side,' said Archer. 'Bloody animals, they are.' He thrust a cricket bat into Maxwell's hand. 'Honour of the school, Flashman, all down to you now.'

'Honour?' mumbled Maxwell. 'Honour?'

'Slay 'em,' said Archer. 'Slay 'em.'

Somewhere, deep down in the Brown Windsor soup of Maxwell's brain a certain molecular transformation occurred. Whether it was the old ribonucleic acid,* or one of those cellular lads, affecting a metamorphosis, was difficult to say. But the Brown Windsor began to bubble, change from muddy brown to bloody red – to Campbell's cream of Tomato – and then began to boil.

The steam filled Maxwell's head with what he had come to know, but not to love, as the dreaded RED MIST itself.

---

*It is interesting to note that the abbreviation for ribonucleic acid, RNA, occupies a place in the *Collins English Dictionary* up at an angle of precisely 23° from the definition of Rock and Roll on the opposite page.

'Slay 'em,' said Archer, squeezing Maxwell's fist about the handle of the cricket bat. 'Slay 'em. We only need six runs to win.'

'Yeah! Slay 'em!' Maxwell rose with a jerk (Archer, but that's not particularly funny), and lurched to the door of the pavilion. As he stepped out into the light of the inner sun, a great cheer went up from the boys in grey who crammed the stand and the loungers in white who leaned upon posts.

Red eyed and breathing deeply through his nose, Maxwell strode across the veranda and down the steps.

Had cameras been rolling, there would have been a close-up on his eyes. Another on the hand as it gripped the bat, carried like an axe across the shoulder. One, from beneath the steps, viewing a long shot of the playing field, suddenly filled by the heel of a substantial boot. Then cut to the elephant bowler, dabbing his wrinkled black brow with an oversized red gingham handkerchief. Then cut to William looking worried. Archer wringing his hands. Faces of the lads in the stand. Faces of the visiting side.

Back to the red eyes of Maxwell.

Then one of those high crane shots, tracking down to follow the mighty wielder of the bat as he marched across the pitch.

Cinematography?

Piece of cake.

Over the velvet field marched Maxwell, bat across his shoulder, fire behind his eyes. The wicket-keeper, a black panther who possibly answered to the name of Ouanga, archdemon to the voodoo pantheon of Gris Gris Chang Ba in the third bed-sitting-room of Hell, viewed Maxwell's approach with a black-lipped sneer and a grin of sharkist teeth.

'Come eat red leather, white boy,' he chuckled in a manner which might have put the wind up some.

Not Maxwell. He glared the panther bloody knives and positioned himself in the crease. With slow deliberation he did that tapping-at-the-turf thing cricketers do with the edge of the bat, prior to taking up the stance. It's a bit like that blowing-on-the-fingertips-and-turning-the-racket-round thing tennis players do. No-one knows why they do it. Tradition possibly, or an old charter, or something. But do it they do, none the less.

Maxwell dug in his heels, wiggled his bum and raised his willow ball-basher as you would a baseball bat.

Tension in the crowd. Just six runs to take the match.

The bowler turned away, rubbing the cricket ball up and down his crutch (and we all know why they do *that*).

A low rumbling growl escaped from between Maxwell's clenched teeth.

Fearing it a bottom burp, the wicket-keeper shifted back a pace.

As further tension creaked amongst the crowd, the bowler slowly turned and the umpire chewed upon a brand of gum containing civet, ambergris and musk, which has no relevance here.

Tension.

The bowler drew in a mighty breath, his chest barrelling out, his proud tusks, polished yellow scythes, dancing with light from the underworld sun.

Further tension.

As Leviathan himself, the bowler took the slow run up. Great ground-shaking foot falls. Like amplified heartbeats, echoing Bah-doomp Bah-doomp. Bahdoomp. Gathering speed. Bah-doomp-bah-doomp-bah-doomp. All eyes upon the bowler as he prepared to bowl the ball.

And tension. Solid tension. Ear-popping. Nose-bleeding. Sphincter-tightening. Gut-twisting. Trouser-wetting. TENSION!

Six runs to take the match.

To win the day.

For glory.

For honour.

The huge arm swings. The ball let free. Maxwell, red-eyed, knuckle-white. Soar ball. Red ball. Red eyes. Red ball. Breath held.

Bat swing. Blur of willow.

CRACK!

Crack! Yes, can it be? The willow on the leather? Crack. The ball bent out of shape, soaring, soaring. UP. Over the pitch. Up into the inner sky. High. Over the pavilion roof and on and on and on – A six—

'HOWZAT!'

'You're out!'

A gasp. A cry. A lad faints in the stand.

The ball at Maxwell's feet. A red graze of its leather imprinted on his right leg pad. Disaster. Calamity.

'LBW, you're out.' The umpire raised the finger of doom.

'Not out!' Maxwell turned upon the umpire. 'That was never out. My leg was nowhere near the stumps. You *cannot* be serious.'

'Out, sir,' said the umpire.

'Rubbish! I'm not having *that*.'

'You're out, white boy,' smirked the wicket-keeper. 'You better keep your legs crossed in the shower.'

'Shut your face,' warned Maxwell. 'That was never LBW.' He swung about to glare at the stand. 'Was that out? I ask you.'

Heads shook doubtfully. Shoulders shrugged. Three more lads fainted. William said to Archer, 'Was that good or bad?'

'Off,' said the umpire.

'No.'

The animal team was leaping about, tossing their caps into the air, punching the sky. As there was little chance of carrying the elephant shoulder-high from the field of their triumph, they clamoured about him, cheering, congratulating.

'It was *not* out,' Maxwell stamped his feet, turned once more upon the umpire and kicked the stumps from the ground.

'You're definitely out now, white boy,' purred Ouanga.

Maxwell stared at the creature, red eye to his yellow. Then he swung his bat.

No man but one had ever swung a bat with such a force as Maxwell now swung his. And that man was, as those who know such things will know, the now legendary wielder of Clikki Ba himself, The Wolf of Kabul (applause).

The bat struck Ouanga a murderous blow. The panther went down amidst a hailstorm of fractured teeth. Maxwell leapt forwards to finish the job, but Ouanga was out for the count.

A drawing in of breath.

And a terrible hush.

Boggle-eyed, the umpire backed away. Maxwell turned to face the winning team who gaped at him in horror. And then, with roar and howl and snort, they rushed forward in attack.

Though the Wolf of Kabul might have taken them on, and probably triumphed to boot, Maxwell shouted a curse, kept tight hold of his bat and ran like a hare for the stand.

The stand was clearing fast. Small boys, clad all in grey, with faces now to match, ran shrieking, this way, that and t'other. The chaps at the pavilion just looked on, aghast.

Maxwell fled and the beasts bounded after him, all semblance of human mimicry gone. Snarling, a-growling, thirsty for his blood.

Up the stand ran Maxwell, leaping from one row of seats to the next. A tiger sprang and Maxwell ducked, then hit it hard across the head. The tiger fell and Maxwell ran some more.

Along the topmost row he ran, wildly swinging the bat around his head. The creatures swarmed after, ripping up the seats, cruel claws drawn to kill. Amongst them now, the bowler, trumpeting and mashing seats aside.

At the end of the row Maxwell came to a shuddering halt. He had run out of places to run. He raised his bat and made a most menacing face. But his menace was lost on his pursuers. Creeping forward, heads down, wild eyes glittering, they stalked their cornered prey and prepared to move in for the kill.

'Now, lads,' said Maxwell. 'Let's not do anything we all might regret.'

The creatures growled, black lips drawn back to show those razor teeth, haunch muscles tense for the final spring.

For the ripping and devouring.

Maxwell held his breath. He had the terrible feeling that this time there really was no way out, this time he had pushed things that little bit too far. He hadn't thought things through.

He'd been a tad too hasty.

This time was the last time. It was the end.

Forward now they came, all low growls and terrible fangs. Closer and closer. Bestial and dreadful drool.

Closer.

And closer.

Then—

CRACK!

It wasn't Maxwell's bat.

It wasn't Maxwell's nerve, though it might well have been.

It wasn't anything to do with Maxwell at all, in fact.

CRACK! Once again, it went and *CRACK!*

Maxwell gawped. The animals froze.

CRACK.

The animals turned their heads.

The elephant stood, looking down at his feet. Beneath him the wooden boards of the stand were going *CRACK!*

'Aw shit!' said the elephant, as beneath his mighty weight the boards gave way and with a *CRACK!* surpassing all *CRACK*s past, the stand collapsed. Down went the bowler, down went rows of seats and splintered wood. Down went the animals and down too came the roof.

Maxwell found himself clinging to an upright roof support which now, having nothing left to support, became no longer upright and angled away from the falling stand, taking Maxwell with it.

'Oooooh!' went Maxwell.

The support arced down like a pole-vault pole, with Maxwell Ooooohing, as it fell. Much ground rushed up. And with it, the pavilion.

Maxwell struck the roof of the veranda, passed through this and was cushioned from concussion by chaps in white below.

He landed upon Archer and the younger brother of Lord Grade, staggered to his feet and called out for William.

'I'm here,' the lad replied. 'Under the steps.'

'Then come out, quick.'

'Are you kidding or what?'

'Come on, hurry.'

William struggled out and Maxwell grabbed him by the wrist. 'You do know how to run fast, don't you?'

William nodded.

'Then just do what I do.' And Maxwell did what he had done so many times before.

In William's company this time, he took to his heels and fled.

21

Maxwell ran and William ran.
Away from the cricket ground they ran.
At a fair old lick and a light-foot dance.
Without so much as a backwards glance.

And bells rang out from high stone towers,
And folk poured forth from inner bowers.
Men in gowns and lads in grey,
Hurrying, scurrying, every way.

There were cracks and groans and growls
    and roars,
And fearsome fangs and cruel claws,
And in the pavilion none was spared,
From curling lip and white tooth bared.

It was 'orrible, as a lion's den.
The floor ran red with the blood of men.
The beasts devoured all those in sight,
'Cos all men look the same in white.

And mangled limbs and shredded hearts,
And ripped-out guts and private parts.
And—

'Hold on,' cried Maxwell, raising a hand.

'What is it?' William skidded to a halt.

'Poetry,' said Maxwell. 'Quite appalling poetry.'

'I didn't hear anything.'

Maxwell cocked an ear, then shrugged. 'Must have imagined it. Come on, this way.'

'Where are we going?'

'Into the University buildings. There's something I have to do.'

'I hope it's hide.'

'That too. Come on.'

They slipped into the shadow of an arch, passed through an open doorway, and found themselves in a long narrow passage.

'I don't suppose that by some happy chance you just happened to have had the floor plan for this establishment knocked into your head?' Maxwell asked.

'Funny you should say that.'

'Then you have?'

'Of course I haven't. That really would be pushing credibility, wouldn't it?'

Maxwell clouted William in the ear. 'You're right,' he said. 'It's never wise to push credibility. I wonder what's through here.' And Maxwell pushed open a door.

The room beyond was long and low and miserable and mean.

A single tallow candle, guttering in a wall sconce, illuminated a mirror beneath and two down-at-heel leather pedestal chairs. These were bolted to a floor of pitted linoleum. Before them and below the mirror, stood a table. On this were a number of cutthroat razors and a pair of antique hair clippers.

'Well,' said Maxwell. 'Fancy that.'

'Who is there?' Something moved in a far corner of the room. It was a very frail something. It rose upon creaking joints and tottered into the uncertain light. It

234

was a tall something also, though stooped. It supported itself upon a lacquered cane.

Maxwell stared at the apparition. It was a man. Of sorts. An ancient man, his bald head dappled with liver spots. A thousand wrinkled lines and crusted folds composed his face. A long white beard shivered as he spoke. 'Have you come for a shave or a short back and sides? You'll have to speak up, I'm a trifle deaf.'

'Sir John?' Maxwell took a step forward. The old man flinched at the sudden movement, swayed upon his cane as if a gust of wind might waft him from his feet.

'Sir John, is it *really* you?'

Maxwell stared at the trembling figure. It had been his sworn intention that if he ever met up with Sir John Rimmer again he would wreak a terrible vengeance.

But seeing him, here, now.

In this state.

'Do you know him?' William asked.

'A little boy.' The ancient stretched a shaky withered claw to tousle William's hair. 'I have some sweeties somewhere for little boys.'

'No thanks,' said William. 'Sugar causes a build up of plaque, which can lead to tooth decay and gum disease. However, regular brushing will—'

Maxwell clouted William once more in the ear.

'Ouch,' said William.

'Don't cuff the little boy. I expect he's a good little boy. *Are* you a good little boy?'

William nodded. 'Let's get,' he whispered. 'The old buffer is clearly suffering from advanced senile dementia and a chronic disorder of the central nervous system, characterized by impaired muscular coordination and tremor.'

'That would be your diagnosis, would it?'

'Yes,' said William.

Maxwell took him firmly by the clouted earhole and hoisted him through the doorway. 'Wait outside,' he said, returning to the room and slamming the door behind him.

'He's a naughty little boy then, is he?' The ancient nodded his withered old head.

'*Sir John*,' Maxwell peered into the rheumy eyes. 'It *is* you, isn't it? *Sir John*.'

'Surgeon? No, I'm not a surgeon. I'm the barber. Short back and sides, was it? Or a shave? I'll have to strop the razor, it's terribly rusty.'

'Sir John, it's *you*.' Maxwell reached out to shake the trembling shoulders, but didn't for fear that the old man might fall apart. 'How can you be here, after all this time? What happened to you? How did Waldeck—'

'*Waldeck? Waldeck?*' The ancient made an alarmed face and began to parry about with his cane. He sank with a thud and a cloud of dust into one of the leather chairs.

'You remember *him*, don't you? Do you remember *me*?'

'You?' The old man nodded. 'Yes, I remember you.'

'You do?'

'Archer, isn't it? Did you win the match? Did you beat those bastards, did you?'

'I'm not Archer. I'm Maxwell. *Maxwell*. Remember? Max Carrion, Imagineer.'

'Mick Scallion, engineer? I didn't call for an engineer.'

Maxwell's brain began to fog. He made a fist and then unmade it, thrust his hands into his trouser pockets. His right hand closed about the magic pouch.

'Magic,' said Maxwell. 'You remember magic, your magic. You had powerful magic.'

'Magic?' The old man coughed. 'No magic here. None comes through the grid. No magic here at all.

Did *I* have magic? Can't remember. Must have lost it if I did.'

'You don't remember anything? About me? About who you are?'

'I'm the barber. Do you want a short back and sides, did you say?'

Maxwell stared once more into the red-rimmed eyes. '*He* did this to you, didn't he? He took away your memory, like he takes the memories from the kids. Sucks out the knowledge. He took everything from you. This University was yours, wasn't it? The City of Sergio Romeer. The University of Sir John Rimmer. He took it all from you and twisted it about.'

'The University?' the old man's eyelids fluttered. 'Am I still in my University? So very long ago. I forget things. Hearing's not too good. You'll have to speak up and tell me how you want your hair cutting.'

'I don't want my hair cutting,' shouted Maxwell. 'I just want to get even. I will kill Waldeck and get you back your memory and your knowledge.'

'Knowledge?' The old man rocked to and fro on his chair. 'It's in the air, floating all around us. You have to know how to pluck it out.' The old man chuckled hideously. 'Tap it, that's the secret. To tap it you have to tap it. Tap the head, just so. Or was it trim the head? Or shave the head? Something to do with heads. I'm the barber, you know.'

Maxwell glanced about the terrible room. 'I need a change of clothes. A disguise. They'll be looking for the mystery cricketer. I need to dress up in something else.'

'You should have an overall, if you're an engineer.'

'I'm not an engineer. I'm the *Imagineer*.'

'Imagineer. Imagineer? You don't look like an imagineer. Not dressed like that. You look like a cricketer. Did we win?'

Maxwell threw up his hands.

'Wardrobe,' said the old man.

'Wardrobe? Where?'

'Over there in the corner. Did I say wardrobe? Why did I say wardrobe?'

'Never mind.' The wardrobe stood in a shadowy corner. Maxwell stalked over to it and flung wide the doors.

Then he took a step back and simply stared.

The light of the guttering candle fell upon a suit of clothes.

And such a suit of clothes.

A waistcoat of rich brocade, a cravat of dark material, a pair of corduroy trousers and a pair of riding boots.

From a hook hung belts that holstered pistols, daggers and a samurai sword in a polished scabbard.

From another hung a simply splendid coat of night-black leather.

Maxwell set a whistle free. 'Rock 'n' Roll,' he said.

The barber hobbled over to stand at Maxwell's shoulder. 'Was I keeping those for someone?'

'You were keeping them for me.'

Sounds of commotion came from the passage. William ducked into the room, closed the door quietly behind him and turned the key in the lock. 'They're coming this way,' he said. 'Horrid big things. They're searching the rooms.'

'Then we'd best be gone.' Maxwell reached into the wardrobe and brought out the suit of clothes.

William gave a whistle. 'What a simply splendid coat,' he said.

'Is there a back door?' Maxwell asked the barber.

'Yes, of course.'

'Where is it then?'

'You came in through it.'

'Go on,' said William. 'Hit him. You know you want to.'

'I don't.'

'You do too. I can see it in your eyes.'

'I *don't*! Where is the *front* door, Sir John?'

'The *front* door? Oh I see, the front door. Yes.' Sir John thought about this. 'Go out the way you came in, along the passage, right at the end, into the foyer, pass the gift shop and you're there.'

'You needn't hit him hard,' said William. 'Just a little tap would do.'

Bang. Bang. Bang. Went someone, bang-bang-banging on the back door.

'There has to be another way out.' Maxwell squinted all around the shadowed room in search of one.

Crash. Crash. Crash and, 'Open up in there.'

'Secret passage,' said Sir John.

'What?' said Maxwell.

'Secret passage.'

'Where?'

'If I told you that, it wouldn't be a secret.' Sir John titttered.

Crash!

William stared down at the now unconscious barber. 'I think you've killed him,' he said.

Maxwell examined his right fist. 'It was only a little tap. And he *was* asking for it, after all.'

Crash! at the door, and smash! also.

'Follow me,' said Maxwell.

'Where?' asked William.

'Here,' said Maxwell.

Big crash! at the door now. Then the door bursting from its hinges.

Two awful-looking beings stormed into the room. Great distorted heads with crests of quill. Light-bulb eyes and snapping jaws. Massive shoulders heaving out from leather harnessing. Mighty fists that swung from lengthy muscled arms.

They raged about, ripping the chairs from the floor, smashing the mirror, overturning the table. They dragged down the wardrobe and kicked it to pieces. When finally satisfied that the room lacked for any other entrance, especially a hidden door that led to a secret passage, they sniffed at the unconscious barber, swore great oaths and shambled from the room.

When all was once more silent, William said, 'I didn't like the look of them at all.'

'Two of Count Waldeck's personal body guards.'

'Who's Count Waldeck?'

'The ruler of the city, the University.'

'I thought that was Sergio Rameer.'

'No, Sergio Rameer is really Sir John Rimmer, the barber I just knocked out.'

'What? But if—'

'I'll explain it all as we go along,' said Maxwell. 'Give me a hand with this simply splendid coat.'

'Just one more question before we go,' said William. 'Where exactly are we?'

'Hiding inside the magic pouch in the corner of the room,' said Maxwell. 'I thought that would have been bloody obvious.'

Maxwell marched along the passage in full Max Carrion regalia. The simply splendid leather coat billowed out behind him. The riding boots click-clacked on the marble floor, the armoury chinked and rattled.

Maxwell looked the business.

And he *was* the business.

It was heading for that showdown time and Maxwell knew it. That time of epic confrontation, when loose ends are deftly tied, villains get their just deserts and the hero bravely triumphs.

As Maxwell marched, dark thoughts stirred in his head. The great imagineering plan he'd planned a while before now lay all in broken wreckage. Much of it relied upon the element of surprise, the fact that the Sultan of Rameer wouldn't know who Maxwell really was or what he was really after.

However, all was far from lost and as Maxwell marched, certain new thoughts came to him. One by one. But all at once.

And by the time Maxwell had reached the end of the corridor it was all sorted out in his head. Which was just the way it should be.

'Stop!' ordered Maxwell, jerking to a halt.

'What?' said William, tripping over Maxwell's heels.

'I have a plan.' Maxwell helped the lad to his feet. 'I will explain it to you in outline and I want you to do exactly what I tell you to do, *without question*. Do you understand?'

William made a doubtful grubby face. 'Are you certain you wouldn't welcome the occasional question, if it was pertinent to the success of the plan and beautifully articulated?'

'Absolutely certain.'

'Pity,' said William, 'as much of my characterization apparently depends on me spilling out complicated sentences with lots of long words in them. To great comic effect, I might add.'

'I've never found them particularly comic myself,' said Maxwell. 'Most appear to be direct cribs from the dictionary. It's a laugh for a bit. But it soon wears thin.'

'Oh right,' said William. 'Perhaps I should "take to my heels and flee" more often. Or say "Rock 'n' Roll", or make reference to my "substantial boots".'

'That's hardly fair,' said Maxwell. 'There's a lot more to being the hero than a few running gags.'

'Oh yeah, I forgot the punching people. If stuck for a punch line, punch someone's lights out. Very original.'

Maxwell looked hard at William.

And William looked hard at Maxwell.

'Do you get the feeling', said William, 'that we shouldn't have said any of that?'

'Let's just pretend we didn't, and pass on.'

'OK. Where were we?'

'I have a plan.' Maxwell helped the lad to his feet. 'I will explain it to you in outline and I want you to do exactly what I tell you to do. *Without question*. Do you understand?'

'Absolutely,' said William.

And Maxwell spoke to William of his plan. He explained it all down to the finest detail and when he had done so, he asked what William thought.

'I think it's a blinder of a plan, Maxwell, and I will be happy to play my part in it.'

'Rock 'n' Roll,' said Maxwell. 'Now let's get it done.

Alone marched Maxwell, down the last bit of the passage. He turned right at the end, marched into the foyer, passed the gift shop and marched on towards the reception desk.

It was a bit hard to get all the makings of the University together. There was a lot of the old public school here, and in this foyer there was a great deal of the commercial enterprise also. T-shirts hung in the window of the gift shop. They had mottoes like 'schooled at the University of Life' on the front, and 'Bullygarves do it backwards'.

Maxwell marched up to the reception desk. A most

attractive young woman sat behind it. She had golden ringlets, golden eyes and that look which says, 'I know you'd love to, but you can't.'

'Good day,' said Maxwell.

The young woman sniffed. 'I've got a cold,' she said. 'So I can't breath through my nose.'

'Sorry to hear that,' said Maxwell.

'Why should *you* be sorry?' the young woman asked. 'You weren't going to get any oral sex.'

'I never asked for any,' said Maxwell, somewhat bemused.

'No, but it's obvious that's what you were hoping for.'

'I never was.'

'Of course you were. But you can't have any. And that's that.'

'I want to see Count Waldeck,' said Maxwell, squaring his shoulders.

'He won't give you any oral sex.'

'I don't want any oral sex. What is all this talk of oral sex?'

'You started it.'

'I didn't. All I said was, good day.'

'Yes, but that's not what you meant.'

'It was. I just said, good day. That's all.'

'So you *don't* want any oral sex?'

'No,' said Maxwell.

'Why not?' asked the receptionist. 'Give me a good reason why a man wouldn't want oral sex.'

Maxwell scratched his head. 'I can't,' he said.

'So you *do* want it.'

'Well. I *like* it.'

'Well, you can't have it. My nose is blocked up.'

'Look,' said Maxwell, 'you are a very attractive woman. And were you to offer me oral sex, I would not refuse it. But that isn't why I'm talking to you. I want to see Count Waldeck now. At this minute. Oral sex does not enter into it at all.'

'Count Waldeck likes oral sex.'

'I'm sure he does. Perhaps he and I will discuss it, at length.'

'Well, leave me out of the discussion. I hate oral sex.'

'So why do you keep talking about it?'

'Well, it's a comic device, isn't it? You march up to the reception desk, bound upon some heroic mission, and you get side-tracked into a lot of old hooey about oral sex.'

'Ah,' said Maxwell, 'I went through something similar to this a moment ago. I hope it doesn't mean what I think it means.'

'How may I help you, sir?' asked the receptionist, suddenly prim, proper and correct.

'I have an appointment to see Count Waldeck,' said Maxwell. 'Please direct me to his office.'

'I'm sorry, sir, but I can't do that.'

'It is most urgent,' said Maxwell. 'I have something to deliver to the count. He will not be pleased to be kept waiting.'

'You cannot see him, sir, and that is that.'

'Send a messenger,' said Maxwell. 'Tell the count that MacGuffin the magician is here and that he has brought Aodhamm with him.'

'Impossible,' said the receptionist.

'It's not impossible,' said Maxwell. 'It's vital. Just do it.'

'I can't, sir.'

'And why can't you?'

'Because Count Waldeck is not here, sir. He has gone on his holidays.'

'*What?*' went Maxwell. 'Gone on his holidays?'

'His holidays, sir.' The receptionist leafed through her desk diary. 'I can fit you in for an appointment when he gets back. Which will be . . . She flicked pages forward. 'In precisely *nineteen* days' time.'

'*Nineteen days?*' Maxwell took one step back. Then took another.

'Nineteen days,' said the receptionist. 'Do you want me to pencil you in?'

22

'Nineteen days?' Maxwell dithered. That couldn't be right. He hadn't come this far just to find that the man he sought had *gone on his holidays*. That wasn't the way things were done, with the epic confrontation due at any time.

And everything.

'Check the appointments diary again,' said Maxwell. 'You've made a mistake.'

'A mistake about what?' asked the young man behind the reception desk. Young *man*?

Maxwell blinked at him. 'Where did you come from?' he asked. 'What happened to the young woman I was just talking to?'

The young man put a finger to his lips, then gestured to an area beneath the level of the counter (and that of his own waist). He offered Maxwell a knowing wink.

'She's *not*, is she?' Maxwell leaned over the counter to view what was on the go beneath. 'Good grief,' he said, springing back. 'I mean, well, good grief.'

'How may I help you, sir?' asked the young man, his eyes beginning to glaze.

'I have an appointment to see Count Waldeck,' said Maxwell. 'I'm Mick Scallion, the engineer. It's an emergency. Which way to the count's office?'

'You can't see the count, he's—'

'*Not* gone on his holidays,' said Maxwell. 'I'm not having that.'

'He's *dead*,' said the young man. 'Died last Tuesday. Tragic business. We're still trying to get over the shock.'

Maxwell stared at the idiot grin the young man now wore. 'You seem to be bearing up rather well,' he said. 'However, I don't believe that either. Which way is it to the count's office?'

'Over the hills and a great way off,' said the fish.

'You have turned into a fish,' said Maxwell. 'Why?'

'I'll have to ask you to move to the other side of the safety cordon,' said the policeman.

Maxwell took a step backwards and found himself amongst a crowd. A crowd in twentieth-century costume.

Outside. In the street.

In *his* street.

It was all there: the houses, the cars. The smell. The people. His neighbours. Friends. Duck-Barry Ryan and Jack the Hat. Maxwell was home.

'Hello, Maxwell,' said Sandy, the landlord from The Shrunken Head. 'I'm glad I caught up with you, you dropped this in the bar.'

'I . . . what?'

'This scroll.' Sandy handed Maxwell the Queen's Award for Industry Award award of what now seemed a very very long time ago.

'What's this?' Maxwell shook his head. 'What is going on?'

'It's a reality fracture, sir,' said the policeman. 'Scientists are working on it. The house over there is where it started.'

'That's my house.'

'You'd better get away before anyone finds out,' said the policeman. 'Go to Patagonia. That's my advice.'

'No,' said Maxwell. 'I'm *not* having this. This isn't real.'

'Are you all right, dear?' asked Maxwell's wife.

'The dear one.' Maxwell made those gagging sounds he sometimes made. 'I'm back with *you*? I don't want to be back with *you*. I don't want to be here.'

'You've been working too hard, dear. Much too hard.'

'I never worked,' said Maxwell. 'What are you talking about?'

'You won the award, dear, for your services to publishing. But you've been too engrossed in your work. Twenty-three John Rimmer novels. You've been living more in the books you write, than in the real world.'

'The books *I* write?'

'The doctor says it's stress. You've had a breakdown. Believing that the characters in your books are out to get you.'

'No,' Maxwell shook his head fiercely. 'No. No. No. I'm not real here. I was never real here. I was nobody here. I'm not this person any more. I'm the Imagineer.'

'It's true, Dad.'

'*Dad?*' Maxwell looked down.

William looked up at him. 'Do what Mum says. Go along with the doctor. He's got a special drug that can make you better.'

'I'll just bet he has.' Maxwell pushed his way past the safety cordon. He closed his eyes and took a giant leap.

'How may I help you, sir?' asked the golden-haired receptionist.

'I have to see Count Waldeck *now*.' Maxwell smashed down his fists on the reception desk. 'No more nonsense. No more—'

The golden eyes stared deeply into his.

Maxwell dragged his gaze away. 'Great eyes,' he said, 'very hypnotic. But it won't work twice. Where is Count Waldeck?'

'I'm afraid Count Waldeck has gone on his holidays, sir.'

'No,' Maxwell reached over the reception desk to grab hold of the young woman. His hand passed right through her.

'You'll have to make an appointment,' she continued, turning the pages of her appointments diary.

Maxwell patted the diary. His hand passed through this also and he was patting the desk.

'Perhaps I can pencil you in?'

Maxwell shinned over the reception desk and dropped down behind it. Here he spied upon the floor an intricate-looking device with several lenses projecting light.

Maxwell stooped and ran a hand over the lenses. The young woman's image fluttered and shook.

'A hologram,' said Maxwell. 'It's a bloody hologram. How can that be, here?' Maxwell picked up the projection device. The young woman's image rose with it, until she stood in mid air above the reception desk, still turning the pages of her appointments diary. 'Nineteen days' time,' she said.

Maxwell found the off button, pressed it. The young woman vanished away. Maxwell brought out the magic pouch, slipped the device into it and returned the pouch to the pocket of his simply splendid coat. Then he ducked down beneath the reception desk and rootled about amongst the shelves and drawers. There had to be something here: floor plan, map of the building. Something.

The sound of approaching footsteps kept Maxwell's head well down.

'He said his name was Flashman.' The voice

belonged to Lord Archer. 'He said he knew my brother.'

'Do we have a Flashman here? I don't know of any Flashman.' Maxwell cocked an ear.* This voice he also knew. This voice was that of Count Waldeck himself. 'Where's the receptionist?' this voice went on.

'Gone to powder her nose, perhaps.'

Maxwell heard a smacking sound, which he rightly supposed to be that of Count Waldeck's hand striking the side of Lord Archer's head.

'Lean over the counter and give the holoscope a thump, you craven buffoon.'

'Yes, Your Countship.'

Maxwell heard the young man's steps grow closer. And then his face loomed above. Lord Archer stared down at Maxwell. And Maxwell smiled up at Lord Archer.

Had William been present, there is no doubt that he could have predicted with uncanny accuracy, precisely what Maxwell would do next.

Lord Archer toppled backwards and fell to the floor, well and truly out for the count. (Out for the *count*, geddit? Please yourselves then.)

'Whatever is the matter?' asked Count Waldeck. 'Have you fainted or something?'

'Or something.' Maxwell rose from behind the reception desk, pistol drawn and red sparks flickering in his eyes.

The count took in the figure in the simply splendid coat. 'Who are you?' he asked. 'You're not the receptionist.'

Maxwell took in the count. He hadn't changed, not one evil jot. Same great horrid-looking bastard. Big and bulky, bald and bad. Not at all unlike Joss Ackland in

*Something better seen than described.

Bill and Ted's Bogus Journey. He always plays a good villain does Joss Ackland. The count wore a kind of full-length black monk's habit with a mysterioso motif in silver on the chest.

'Who am *I*?' Maxwell flexed his shoulders, leapt up onto the reception desk and stood with the old legs akimbo. 'I am Max Carrion, Imagineer.'

'Never heard of you,' said the count. 'Are you standing in for the receptionist? Has the machine broken down again?'

'I am Max Carrion,' said Max, 'your nemesis.'

'I don't recall ordering a nemesis. Would you care to explain yourself?'

'It's *me*.' Max jumped down and swaggered over to the count. 'Me, Max. I killed you. Remember?'

The count shook his big bald head. 'If you'd killed me, I'm sure I would remember. I don't feel very dead. Have you been smoking something, young man?'

Maxwell looked the count up and down. It definitely was the right man. And Sir John Rimmer *was* in the barber's shop. There was no mistake.'

'Don't mess with me,' snarled Max, brandishing his pistol. 'I have come for Ewavett. Take me to her at once.'

The count shook his head once more. 'I'm frightfully sorry,' he said, 'but you now have me rightly bewildered. Who is Ewavett?'

'The metal woman. The mate of Aodhamm.'

'Now let me see if I have this straight. You are Mick Scallion—'

'Max Carrion,' said Max.

'Max Carrion, sorry. You are Max Carrion, Imagineer, who killed *me*. And you've come for a metal woman.'

'Correct,' said Max, who was almost having *his* doubts.

'You wouldn't also be this "Flashman", would you?'

'That's me,' said Max.

'I see.' The count chewed upon the thumbnail of a big fat thumb. 'Whose form are you in?'

'I'm not in anybody's form. I have travelled across two worlds to get here. I demand Ewavett at once. And certain other things besides, but we can get to those one at a time.'

The count glanced around the foyer. There was no-one about. The count glanced at his wristwatch. Maxwell also glanced at this. It was a *digital* wristwatch.

'School is going to be turning out in a moment,' said the count. 'Would you like to come up to my study and talk about this?' He dug a big hand into a habit pocket.

'No tricks,' said Maxwell, cocking his pistol.*

'Just finding my keys.' The count produced a big bunch. 'Follow me, if you will.'

'I will, don't worry.'

The count led the way up a broad sweep of marble stairs. The marvellous architectural style and the elaborate décor of the staircase walls mirrored that of the foyer, which was a shame, as the foyer had received no description whatsoever.

Along a pillared gallery they went, up another flight of stairs, through rooms decorated in many colours, all of which began with the letter *G*, across an open courtyard high upon an upper level.

Through a chapel. Past several laboratories. In through one door of a deserted refectory and out through another. Across a landing. Down a flight of steps . . .

And back into the foyer.

'We are back in the foyer,' said Maxwell.

*Something better described than seen up close.

'My office is behind the reception desk,' said the count. 'Follow me.'

Maxwell followed. The count unlocked a big pine door. 'After you,' he said.

'Bollocks,' said Max.

'After me then.' Count Waldeck lead the way.

Maxwell stepped into the room. 'Aha!' he cried. 'Aha!'

'Aha?' asked Count Waldeck, settling himself behind a desk.

'Aha! This room.' Maxwell looked all about this room. It was long and wide, yet low of ceiling, and a full and precise description of it can be found on page 24.* 'Sir John Rimmer's room.' Maxwell gestured thus and whither. 'This is his room. And *shit*, that's my armchair.'

Maxwell stalked over to the armchair in question. '*My* armchair, that my wife sold to a gypsy who sold it to Sandy at The Shrunken Head.'

'It's a Dalbatto,' said the Count. 'Very valuable.'

'Then you admit that this is Sir John Rimmer's room?'

'Indeed.' The count flipped open a silver cigarette case, took out a ciggy and lit it from a table lighter the shape of the World Cup.

'Oily?' said he.

'Pardon?'

'Oily rag. Fag.'

'No thanks,' said Maxwell. 'I evidently gave it up.'

'Now, let me see,' the count puffed upon his cigarette. 'You were saying that this was Sir John Rimmer's room.'

*As will be well known to those who followed the advice offered in the footnote of the start of Chapter 20 and flipped back.

'I was,' said Maxwell, seating himself in his favourite armchair.

'Do you really have to sit there? It is most valuable.'

'I do.'

'Then, as you wish. Now, yes. This *was* Sir John Rimmer's room. Sir John was the Dean of the faculty. In fact, he was the founder of the University. It was once known as the University of Rimmer.'

'City of Rameer,' said Maxwell.

'Knight-speak,' said the count. 'They twist things all about. But Sir John founded it. Sad. Sad.'

'Why sad?'

The count twirled a plump finger against his forehead. 'The strain. Old age. He is retired now. A great man. Quite mad. Thinks he's a barber. We look after him. Very sad.'

'No. NO. No.' Maxwell shook his no-ing head. '*You* took the University from him. *You* took his memory. Like *you* take the memories of the boys who come here on their tenth birthdays.'

'Take their memories? Wherever did you get that idea?'

'They come here with knowledge which you steal from them. They return to the outerworld with all memories of this place wiped away, saying, "The City of Rameer lies over yonder hill." That's what *you* do to them.'

'I think you have it slightly wrong,' said the count. 'Sir John Rimmer perfected the Percussive Perlocution technique for drawing knowledge from the ether. At the age of ten the boys are brought here. They are given the choice, remain here, further their education and join the Knights of the Golden Grommet to patrol the borders of the grid as an extra degree of protection against the denizens of the red world. Or return to their parents.'

'Without their knowledge,' said Maxwell.

'They still have all their knowledge, but they take an oath of allegiance not to reveal the whereabouts of the University. And they're very loyal. They understand the importance of this institution for the future of this world. You won't find an adult out there who'll give you directions to this University. How did *you* find your way here, by the by?'

'A child of nine told me,' said Maxwell.

'That shouldn't have happened. The boys are supposed to be kept under the guidance of their grandmothers, who are trained in the art of Percussive Perlocution. Is the child here with you?'

'No,' lied Maxwell. 'I came here on my own.'

The count raised a hairless eyebrow. 'I think, maychance, that you speak an untruth.'

'If it's a lie, then it's in good company. Because I think that all you've just told me is a pack of bullshit.'

'Indeed?' The count puffed once more on his cigarette. 'Well, your opinions are no business of mine. I'm afraid I will have to ask you to leave now. Something most important has come up and requires my full attention.'

'I'm not leaving without Ewavett,' said Maxwell. 'I *cannot* leave without Ewavett.'

'Well, you're welcome to look all around the University,' said the Count. 'If you can find this Ewavett, then please take her. I would gladly help you search, but the important something will not keep.'

'And what important something is this?'

The count sighed and stubbed out his cigarette. 'For several days now strange events have occurred at the University. Pockets of non-causality in the corridors. Bad poetry springing from nowhere. Hallucinatory episodes. Then today, something that if you are this "Flashman" you witnessed with your own eyes: an entire boys' cricket team metamorphosed into a pagan pantheon of animal gods. The only explanation for these curious circumstances that I can think of is one of such far-reaching implication that the very thought sends shudders through me.'

'And what is that?' Maxwell asked.

'That somehow the unthinkable has occurred and someone has smuggled magic through the grid.'

Maxwell's hand strayed towards his simply splendid coat pocket, wherein lay MacGuffin's pouch. 'And this would be a bad thing, would it?'

'Disastrous. The natural laws of the red world are not our natural laws. Live magic here could trigger a chain reaction, destroy everyone and everything.'

'That's a slight exaggeration, surely?'

'A room full of gun powder is as safe as milk, until you add a single spark.'

'And a single spark of magic could—' Maxwell mimed an explosion with his non-gun-toting hand.

'Chaos. Natural laws overturned. Death and destruction.'

'Good grief,' said Maxwell. 'Are you really serious?'

'Never more so,' said the count. 'I am having the University thoroughly searched. If the magic accoutrement is here, then possibly it can be neutralized in some way to spare millions from a horrifying death.'

'A horrifying death?'

'Horrifying. So you understand the urgency of the situation?'

'I do,' said Maxwell, nodding his head.

'Listen,' said the count. 'This Ewavett of yours. You say she is a metal woman.'

'MacGuffin says she is an automaton. But I believe she is something much more.'

'And who is MacGuffin?'

'A magician in the red world.'

'Heavens above. You have *met* a magician?'

'More than met. MacGuffin has taken my soul. He will not return it to me unless I bring him Ewavett.'

'Taken your soul? Can such a thing be possible?'

Maxwell nodded gloomily.

'Horrifying,' said the count. 'All magic is horrifying.'

'It is,' said Maxwell. 'I can vouch for that.'

'Tell you what.' The count drummed his fingers on the desk top. 'A thought occurs to me. Sir John had a very large collection of bizarre items. I believe that several automata were numbered amongst this. His collection is now boxed up in the basement. There is a list somewhere.'

'There is?' said Maxwell. 'Where?'

'In the cupboard over there I think.'

Maxwell leapt from his seat. 'Do you mind if I take a look?'

'Please help yourself. If this Ewavett is amongst the collection you are welcome to take her. Sir John has no further use for any such thing.'

'Splendid.' Maxwell tucked his gun into one of his belts. He crossed the room and flung open the cupboard door.

There was a click and a whirring sound. Bands of metal sprung out from the cupboard, secured Maxwell's hands to his sides, clamped his legs, fastened about his throat.

Held him good and fast.

'Ever been had?' asked Count Waldeck.

23

'You bastard!' Maxwell raged and struggled, but all to no avail. The count strolled over to the cupboard and turned a little handle on the side. Cogs engaged and Maxwell swivelled around to face the grinning villain.

'You bastard!' he continued. 'You lied to me.'

'I never lied to you at all. Well, *hardly*, at all. I did lie when I said that I didn't know who you were. And I did neglect to mention that the boys swear allegiance because I demonstrate to them the extent of *my* magic and what will happen should they defy me.'

'Let me free,' raged Maxwell. 'Let me free this instant.'

'Don't be absurd. I must say that I'm impressed with you though. You're the first of MacGuffin's minions ever to reach here. Tell me, does the fool still sport a ring through his nose?'

Maxwell nodded.

'I put it there. Fecund as a bull, that MacGuffin.'

Maxwell continued with the fruitless straining. 'Would I be correct', he asked, 'in supposing that you also lied to me about Ewavett?'

'Yeah, well, perhaps.'

'And the matter of Sir John's senility?'

'Yes, that too.'

'And that magic coming through the grid would bring this world to an end?'

'I'm a villain,' said the count. 'I lie about all sorts of stuff. Do you think I look a bit like Joss Ackland?'

'No,' said Maxwell.

'So,' said the count, 'the big question is, what should I do with you now?'

'You could set me free,' Maxwell suggested.

'That features rather low on the list of alternatives. Right at the very bottom, in fact.'

'And what is at the top?'

'Pulling this little lever on the side of the cupboard and having the steel bands crush the life out of you.'

'Hm,' said Maxwell. 'What's next on the list?'

'Perhaps I might employ you.'

'That is a fine idea. Release the bands at once.'

'I could dispatch you to MacGuffin, have you bring Aodhamm here to me.'

Maxwell groaned. 'MacGuffin holds my soul,' he said.

'Oh yes. I've taken that into consideration. I'd have to remove something else from you. Something that would encourage a speedy return on your part.'

'I have nothing left for anyone to take.'

'Not altogether true. I have magic at my disposal. I know of a spell that could remove your genitalia.'

'What?' Maxwell made that gagging sound again.

'Snatch off your old John Thomas. I'd keep it safe for you, pickled in a jar beneath my bed.'

'No!' said Maxwell. 'No. No. No!'

'Oh well, it was only a thought.'

'What else do you have on the list?' Maxwell asked.

'Just the pulling-the-lever alternative, I'm afraid.'

'I'm sure we could think of something else, if we both put our minds to it.'

'Where is the magical accoutrement MacGuffin gave you?'

'I lost it,' said Maxwell.

'Really? And yet when I spoke to you of the terrible consequences of magic being brought into this world, I'll swear your hand strayed towards your coat pocket. *This* coat pocket.' The count dug his hand in and removed the magic pouch. '*My* pouch!' he declared. 'I wondered where that had gone.'

Maxwell grinned a foolish face.

'Now let's see what we have inside.'

'It's empty,' said Maxwell.

'Really, once more. And yet I'm prepared to bet it contains one small boy.' The count opened the pouch, turned it upside down and gave it a shake. Out tumbled Maxwell's substantial boots, the suit of golden armour and the hologram projector. No small boy, however.

'Bit of a magpie, aren't you?' said the count, peering into the open neck of the pouch. 'Anyone hiding in there? Speak now before the pouch is thrown onto the fire.'

'I'm coming out,' called the voice of William.

'Good boy.' The count shook the pouch once more. William fell onto the floor.

'William,' said the count, 'what are you doing here?'

'Hello, Grandad,' said William.

'*Grandad?*' Maxwell groaned once more.

'This bullygarve captured me,' said William, picking himself up from the floor. 'He forced me to bring him here. He made me get inside the pouch.'

'You lying little shit!'

'Silence, Carrion. William, go and find my guards. Tell them to come here at once. There's a piece of rubbish that needs taking out.'

'Right away, Grandad.' William scurried from the room, slamming the door behind him.

'Naughty little boy that,' said Count Waldeck. 'Completely untrustworthy.'

'So it would appear.' Maxwell sank into further dismal groanings.

'Do you have anything to say before I pull the lever?'

'Yeah,' said Maxwell. 'Lots and lots and lots.'

'I'll bet you do. However—' The count reached out a hand.

'No,' implored Maxwell. 'Not just yet please. Not without telling me.'

'Telling you what?'

'Well, everything really. How you came to be here. What actually happened between you and Sir John. About Ewavett and Aodhamm.'

'Nah. It's not all that interesting. Better I just pull the lever.'

'I'd be really really interested, honest.'

'You're sure?'

'Sure as it's possible to be.'

'All right.' The count took himself over to Maxwell's favourite armchair and sat down upon it. 'As you know,' said he, 'at the time of the great transition the age of technology suddenly ceased and the new age of magic and myth began. This occurred with the collision of the four worlds. The reality fracture spread across the planet. It started in your back garden.'

'My back garden?'

'Well, it had to start somewhere. By happy chance it started in your back garden. You were a writer, you see.'

'I wasn't a writer. I wasn't anybody. I didn't write the Sir John Rimmer books, I used to get them out of the library.'

'You *did* write them, Maxwell. You had a breakdown. You lost your memory.'

'How can *you* know that?'

'Because, Maxwell, I used to be your doctor.'

'This is getting whackier by the moment,' said Maxwell.

'You had this persecution complex. Believed that the characters in your books were real. That they were out to get you. You believed that *I* was Count Waldeck.'

'But you are.'

'Yes, but I wasn't before the great transition. I was your doctor. When reality fractured the world became the very sort of place you used to write about. I metamorphosed into Count Waldeck, you into Max Carrion, Imagineer.'

'Sounds rather far-fetched,' said Maxwell.

'I thought it sounded like a loose end being neatly tied up, myself.'

'OK. So how did I get projected into the future?'

'That was my idea.'

'How could it have been your idea? I shot you dead inside Sir John's Hidden Tower. In this very room, in fact.'

'*Inside* the Hidden Tower, yes. It was a *Hidden Tower*, it's location known to no-one but Sir John and his cronies. In your books you never mentioned where it was. It could have been anywhere. So once you had been thrown out of it, you didn't know where you were, did you?'

'Still don't,' said Maxwell. 'It was somewhere in the red world.'

'The point was, that as soon as you were outside the tower, whatever influence you had over Sir John and myself ended. He was born of your imagination, I of your paranoia. We were both alive. And I was no longer dead once you were outside.'

'This doesn't explain how I got projected into the future.'

'I told you. I did that. I couldn't escape from the tower with you hanging around outside. I wasn't certain what you'd be capable of doing. But I didn't dare kill you either, in case I simply ceased to exist once you were dead. So I cast a spell to send you off to where you could do me no harm. Into the far future. I wasn't expecting to live for as long as I have.'

'And how come you have lived so long and not aged like Sir John?'

'You really do want *everything* explained, don't you?'

'Not just *me*,' said Maxwell. 'But go on.'

'Oh, all right. There was a bit of a punch-up in the Hidden Tower, I escaped shortly after having dispatched you into the future. I remained in the red world, perfecting my skills in magic. Sir John Rimmer left the red world, came here and founded the University.

'I had an apprentice. MacGuffin. We worked together on a magical project the like of which had never been attempted before: the creation of two perfect beings.'

'Aodhamm and Ewavett.'

'Exactly. You fathomed out the meaning of the names of course.'

'Of course,' said Maxwell. 'From a world without electricity. Remove *Ohm* from Aodhamm and *Watt* from Ewavett. You have Adam and Eve, of course.'

'Of course. We succeeded in our quest. But I had underestimated MacGuffin. He was powerful in spells and hungry to possess Ewavett and Aodhamm for his own purposes. A magical battle ensued. I flung magic at him and he at me. I succeeded in putting a ring through his nose and confining him to his village. He cannot pass beyond the circle of columns. However, he lofted me on a chair and threw me across the world. I held hard to Ewavett, but lost all my magic passing through the grid.'

'Who put the grid up? Sir John?'

'No, the grid is a natural barrier between the worlds.'

'So how did you beat Sir John? And why is he old and you still young?'

'Sir John had turned his back on magic. He sought natural knowledge. He perfected Percussive Perlocution. It took me a long time to find him, but when I did I threw myself at his feet, told him I was a reformed character.'

'And he trusted you.'

'I'm afraid he did. I learned the art of P.P., tuned into the frequency of magic and knocked it into my own head. I caught Sir John unawares one night and ZAP!'

'So magic keeps you young?'

'That's it. And that's about everything really. So it's lever-pulling time, I think.'

'Oh, not yet. Not yet.'

'There's nothing more to tell,' said the count.

'There's a bit,' said Maxwell. 'Like the matter of your digital watch and the hologram machine. How did you acquire such technology?'

'No technology involved. Only magic. Within the watch two small demons count minutes at my command. The hologram machine contains a captured sylph. The receptionist is a projection of her personality, an astral double. Anything else I can help you with?'

'Could you scratch my head for me, I can't reach.'

The count gave Maxwell's head a scratch. 'Well?' he said.

'Hm, I think I've run out.'

The count reached for the lever.

'Oh, I've thought of one more. Where *is* Ewavett?'

'I told you the truth there. She is stored in the basement. She's in a very fragile condition now. She pines for Aodhamm. I intend to reunite them *very* soon.'

'How?' Maxwell asked, grateful for the opportunity to get one more question in.

'I am going to blast MacGuffin out of existence. I cannot take my magic through the grid. But I have a surprise for him. On the roof above is an airship – steam-powered, fully piloted, ready to fly. You were lucky to catch me, Maxwell. I was just going off on my holidays.'

'To the village of MacGuffin?'

'Correct. I shall bomb MacGuffin from high above.'

'Won't Aodhamm come to harm?'

'No, Maxwell, he won't. Now I am utterly sick and tired of answering your questions. It is time to pull the lever.'

'If you kill me, you will cease to exist.'

'No, Maxwell, my existence is no longer tied to yours.'

'I wouldn't take the risk if I were you.'

Count Waldeck's hand was on the lever. 'Maxwell,' he said, 'let me explain something to you. I control this world. But this is not enough. Soon I shall have control over the world of the red sun also. Then the next world and the next. Ultimately all will be mine. My playground, Maxwell. My garden of unearthly delights. A new Eden for Aodhamm and Ewavett to populate.'

'With you as God?'

'That's about the shape of it.'

'You are an evil bastard, Waldeck.'

'I know. And unless you can think of one really good reason for me not to snuff you out, I'm afraid it's goodbye to you.'

'Er—'

A big knock came at the door.

'The cavalry,' cried Maxwell. 'I am saved.'

'It's not the cavalry, Maxwell. It's my guards. *Come.*'

The door swung open and a big shambling figure entered the room.

The count didn't bother to offer it a glance. 'I have some rubbish for you to take out,' he said, pressing down upon the lever.

24

Click. Click. Click, went the iron bands, slowly tightening up. 'Aaaaagh!' went Maxwell, as they slowly began to crush him to death.

The count stepped back to view his handiwork. 'It takes a few minutes. Hideously painful way to go, I'll bet.'

'I'll bet it is,' chuckled the shambling figure.

The count turned smiling, but the smile fled his face of an instant. 'Who are . . . ?' *You*, was the word he didn't manage. The shambling figure flung out a great hand, grasped him about the throat, flung out another and twisted Waldeck's head around backwards. There was a really sickening crunching sound. Count Waldeck fell dead on the floor.

Further such sounds were issuing from Maxwell's chest. The shambling figure reached out, yanked up the lever and pressed a button.

The bands unlocked and Maxwell collapsed to the floor.

He awoke seconds later to a violent shaking. Opening his eyes, he cried, 'Rushmear, it's you.'

'It's me,' said the horse trader.

'But how?' Maxwell's eyes flashed round the room, flashed upon the body of the count, not two feet away.

'Aaaagh!' Maxwell struggled to his feet. 'How did you—'

William peeped out from behind a Rushmear trouser leg. 'I went to get help,' he said. 'I found this man in the foyer. He said he knew you.'

'Good lad, William. But how did you get here?' Maxwell asked the saviour of his life.

'I never left you, Maxwell. I figured that if anyone could find their way here, it would be you. So when I rode away on the dead knight's horse, I just circled around and hid. I saw you put on the armour. I've been following you ever since, never more than a few hundred yards behind. First time ever I lost you was outside in the foyer. That bastard', Rushmear gestured to the dead count, 'led you all around the building, obviously to lose anyone who might have been following.'

'Even the tiniest loose ends get tied up,' said Maxwell. 'Brilliant. That makes us *almost* even for the number of times I saved *your* life.'

'I shall bear that in mind,' said Rushmear, 'once our souls are back in our bodies and I'm pummelling you to death.'

'Quite so. Ah, excuse me, *William*?'

'Er, yes?' said the lad.

'A small matter, regarding this dead man here. This dead man who was *your grandad*.'

'Not a close-knit family,' said William.

'But you knew who was in charge of the University all along.'

'Yes, but if I'd told you right off, it wouldn't have been nearly so dramatic as having you find out for yourself.'

Maxwell threw up his hands.

'Where is Ewavett?' Rushmear asked.

'Boxed up in the basement.'

'Then let us fetch her.'

'Not quite so fast. I have a plan.'

'A pox on your plans,' said Rushmear.

Maxwell picked up the magic pouch and tucked it into his coat pocket. 'MacGuffin may have got a number of things wrong about this place. He thought, for instance, that Sir John Rimmer had Ewavett—'

'Sergio Rameer,' William explained. 'It's a bit complicated. I wouldn't worry about it.'

'Then I won't,' said Rushmear.

Maxwell continued, 'But MacGuffin was right about one thing. A means exists to transport us back. An airship on the roof. That's a *flying craft*, before you ask.'

'Then let us fetch Ewavett and get on board.'

'You know how to fly such a craft?'

'No,' said Rushmear.

'But there is a pilot who does. Now what I propose we do is this . . .'

A short while later, Rushmear, Maxwell and William left the study of the now defunct Count Waldeck. At Maxwell's prompting, Rushmear had donned the count's black habit, with the hood pulled well down to cover his face. Maxwell was once again wearing the suit of golden armour, and William, although he had protested that he too should be disguised as something, went as William.

Of course he *did* know the way to the basement. And a short while after the short while later, they arrived at its very door.

Rushmear pulled out the count's ring of keys.

'Open up the door then,' said Maxwell, taking a step back.

Rushmear hesitated. 'It is possible', said he, 'that some trap might lie within.'

'I hadn't thought of that,' said Maxwell, who certainly had. 'Best open it carefully then.'

'*I* will not open it at all.' Rushmear thrust the keys at Maxwell. '*You* will open it.'

'Me? Must I forever pander to your timidity? When will you learn to behave like a man?'

'What?' roared Rushmear, going as ever for the throat.

'Clunk!' went a golden gauntlet on his still so tender nose.

'Stop it, you two.' William stepped up and pushed open the door. 'It's never locked.'

'See,' said Maxwell.

'Huh,' said Rushmear.

The light from a few small windows fell upon crates and packing cases, rusty suits of armour, dilapidated mechanisms and cardboard boxes containing those *Top of the Pops* compilation albums that you never saw in the shops but which are always there by the dozen at bootsales. Rushmear began to crash and smash amongst the crates and cases.

'Have a care,' said Maxwell. 'We don't want to damage Ewavett.'

'I don't give a damn, as it happens.'

Maxwell sighed and began to search.

William said, 'I think you'll find she's over here.'

Maxwell sighed once more and followed William.

The crate was long and coffin-shaped. It was a coffin, in fact.

'Let's have the lid off,' said Rushmear, pushing forward.

Maxwell tried to hold him back. 'MacGuffin will hardly part with our souls if we bring her to him in pieces.'

'All right.' The big man applied his strength to the

coffin lid. He strained and groaned and inch by inch it came away to fall with a bang to the floor.

Maxwell peeped into the coffin and gasped. 'By the Goddess,' he whispered. 'It *is* the Goddess.'

William peeped in and gave a wolf whistle.

'Let me see,' Rushmear looked in and he too gave a gasp. 'So beautiful,' said he.

And beautiful she was. So beautiful to look at that it hurt. A golden goddess, naked, on a cushion of black velvet. Her slender hands crossed between her perfect breasts. Her lovely face, composed as if in sleep, bore an expression of such sadness, Maxwell felt a lump come to his throat and had to turn his face away.

'Put back the coffin lid,' he said.

Rushmear reached in a hand to touch the golden sleeping beauty.

'No,' cried Maxwell. 'Don't.'

'Why not?'

'It isn't right. It just isn't.'

'Huh!' Rushmear took up the coffin lid. 'She's only a toy.'

'She's much more than that. Fasten the lid, we will put the entire coffin into MacGuffin's pouch.'

Rushmear beat the lid down with a mighty fist, then with Maxwell's help, slid the coffin into the magic pouch.

'I'll take this,' said Rushmear, snatching the pouch from Maxwell's hands.

'All right,' Maxwell said. 'You take it.'

'*All right?* You give up the pouch without a struggle?'

'I'm sure it will be safe with you.'

'Have no fear for that. I'll guard it with my life until we return to MacGuffin.'

'Then you'll die so doing,' said Maxwell.

'Aha,' Rushmear sprang back. 'You mean to kill me for it.'

'Nothing of the kind. If you attempt to carry the pouch back through the grid you will be shredded. We only need it to transport the coffin as far as the airship. Once the coffin is unloaded on board we would do well to fling the pouch over the side. It will have served its purpose.'

'Hmph,' went Rushmear. 'But, of course, this was *my* intention all along.'

'I'm so pleased to hear it. So, shall we depart?'

'Yes indeed.'

The journey from the basement to the roof was quite uneventful. Clearly none of the students knew yet of Count Waldeck's demise, and as Rushmear stomped along with his hood well down, they saluted him and wished him good day.

Maxwell's nerves were somewhat on edge. There was the matter of the count's guards. But it was probable that with the count deceased, his magic had died with him and his guards dissolved away.

There was also, of course, the matter of those rampaging animals. What exactly had become of them?

Maxwell hurried along behind Rushmear. William hurried along behind Maxwell.

Up a final staircase they went, through a small door and onto the uppermost roof of the University.

And here they found the airship.

Maxwell whistled through his visor. A thing of wonder it truly was. And an air*ship* was truly the word. For there stood a vast cigar-shaped blimp secured by many ropes to what appeared to be the hull of a Spanish galleon. From the stern of this projected a number of long metal shafts with fan blades on the ends.

A dull throb of pistons issued from the craft. Smoke rose from a variety of funnels that poked through the foredeck. Anchoring lines held fast to metal rings bolted to the roof.

'And that will *fly*?' Rushmear asked.

Maxwell scratched his helmet. 'I agree it does look somewhat unlikely.'

'Let's get on board,' said William.

Maxwell looked down at the lad. 'Ah,' said he.

'Ah?' William asked.

Maxwell lifted his visor. 'You're not coming with us,' he said.

'I'm *not*? What do you mean?'

'I mean, I want you to stay here until I get back.'

'And what if you *don't* get back?'

'Exactly. Things are likely to become rather unpleasant when we meet up with MacGuffin again. I don't want any harm to come to you.'

'Things could become rather unpleasant here also.'

'Sorry,' said Maxwell. 'But there it is.'

'You heartless bastard.'

'*Soul*-less bastard. I'm sorry, William,' Maxwell reached out a gauntletted hand, the lad took his shoulder beyond its reach.

'Stuff you then,' said William.

'Oh don't be like that. I can't take you. It's too dangerous.'

'Let's go,' muttered Rushmear.

'Yes. All right.'

Maxwell followed the big man up the gang plank. At the top he turned back to offer a wave. But William had gone.

'Damn it,' said Maxwell.

'Welcome aboard, My Lord Count,' said a chap in a seaman's uniform. 'And good day to you too, Sir Knight.'

'Good day,' said Maxwell, lowering his visor.

'Take us to the village of MacGuffin as fast as you can,' ordered Rushmear.

'You're voice sounds terrible gruff,' said the seaman (skyman?).

'I've a sore throat, now get a damn move on.'

'Yes, sir.' The skyman (yes, that's it) blew a whistle. Other skymen scurried onto the deck and began busying themselves at the ropes which held down the airship.

'Let's have the coffin out,' said Rushmear.

'Right.'

They slid the coffin out onto the deck.

'Prepare for lift-off,' called the skyman, blowing his whistle once more.

'Sling the pouch over the side,' said Rushmear.

'Right.'

'Lift off,' called the skyman, as the airship began to rise.

'Oh, Maxwell,' said Rushmear.

'Yes?'

'Just this,' Rushmear leapt forwards and pushed Maxwell over the ship's rail. 'As with the pouch, you have served your purpose,' he called to the falling figure. 'I will send your regards to MacGuffin. Farewell.'

25

They say that anger begins with folly and ends with repentance.

They also say that if you put bigger wheels on the back of your car you will save on petrol because you're always going down hill.

It's funny what they say.

Though perhaps not *that* funny.

Maxwell didn't think it funny. But then Maxwell was angry. He was *very* angry. And his anger, which had indeed begun with folly, did not look like ending with repentance.

A heart attack possibly, but *not* repentance.

The fall had knocked the breath from him, but he was otherwise unscathed. Now he raged about the rooftop like a madman. He tore off items of golden armour, flung them down and kicked them all around. He came upon MacGuffin's pouch and stamped on it again and again and again.

Then he realized that he had stamped the Max Carrion outfit to oblivion, having thoughtlessly neglected to remove it from the pouch before he did the even more thoughtless flinging of the pouch from the airship.

This raised Maxwell to even greater heights of anger and fury.

He shook his fists and fired off volleys of abuse

towards the receding airship. As a berserker he gnashed his teeth and growled and scowled and screamed.

Bilious, he was. Wrathful, stung, incensed. Fuming, boiling, rampageous.

Cross.

Very cross.

Very angry. *Very* cross.

Maxwell threw himself down on the rooftop, thrashed his legs and drummed his fists. And howled and howled and howled.

It was all too much, it really was. He'd got this far just to lose the lot. And to a horse trader. A bloody horse trader! He, Max Carrion, Imagineer, bested by a bloody horse trader!

Maxwell ceased his wrathful thrashings. *He, the Imagineer!* What a fine joke *that* was. He with his high thoughts and his grand schemes. He'd achieved nothing. He *was* nothing. Since he'd been dumped onto this future world, what had he done? Caused a lot of grief and misery and chaos, that's what.

Maxwell groaned and moaned, now bitter with remorse and regret.

Still, they do say that anger begins with folly and ends with repentance, don't they?

'I shall kill myself,' declared Maxwell. 'I am a useless no-mark. I shall end it all.'

He sprang to his feet, kicked off his remaining armour, stalked over to the parapet of the roof and climbed on to it. 'Goodbye, cruel worlds,' he said, preparing to take the ultimate plunge.

And he would have done it too.

But a mighty cheer rose up to greet him.

Maxwell tottered and gazed down. Below, in the quadrangle, stood hundreds of people: little lads in grey, big lads in grey, chaps in cricket whites, masters in gowns and mortar boards, knights in golden armour. They waved their hands at him and cheered again.

'Max-well,' they went. 'Max-well.'

Maxwell gawped. 'What?'

'Three cheers for our deliverer,' cried someone.

'Hip hoorah. Hip hip hoorah. Hip hip hip—'

'Deliverer?' asked Maxwell, shaking a bewildered head.

'Hoorah.'

'Deliverer!' Maxwell swayed on the parapet. '*Deliverer!*' He rather liked the sound of that.

'Speech,' cried someone else. 'Speech from the slayer of the evil count.'

'Ah.' Maxwell's brain went, Click-click-click. Slayer of the evil count. They were cheering *him* as the hero. *He*, Max Carrion, count-slayer and heroic deliverer. *Yes!*

Now, of course Maxwell knew full well that he hadn't *really* slain the evil count. It was Rushmear who had done the actual slaying. But then, Rushmear *had* done the dirty on Maxwell and flown off with Ewavett. So Rushmear wasn't here to take any of the credit. And, after all, if Maxwell hadn't found his way to the University, then Rushmear could never have followed him here and slain the evil count. So Maxwell could really be considered to be the slayer of the evil count. By proxy.

So it wouldn't really be wrong if he took *all* the credit.

Would it?

'My dear friends,' called Maxwell, all thoughts of suicide forgotten. 'My dear friends, I—' And then he lost his footing and fell off the roof.

'Aaaaaaaaaagh!' went Maxwell, like you do. 'Not fair . . . I . . . oh!'

A firm hand shot out from a window he was passing

by at speed and caught him by the ankle. Gripped it tight. Drew him to safety.

'Oh,' went Maxwell. 'Oh,' and 'Oww.'

And then he was dropped on a carpeted floor.

'Ouch,' he said, then, 'by the—'

'Goddess?' asked Sir John Rimmer, beaming down at him.

'Goddess,' agreed Maxwell, wondering up.

The ancient barber was no longer ancient. And barber no longer was he. Sir John wore his suit of bottle green velvet. His hornrimmed spectacles were perched on his hatchet nose. The beard of wispy white was rich and red and marvellous to view.

'You are young,' croaked Maxwell.

'Not as young as once I was, but all the better now the spell that kept me old and daft is dead.'

'I'll try to work that one out,' said Maxwell. 'Thank you for saving my life.'

'Thanks for restoring mine. But come now, you have much to do.'

'I do?'

'You do.' Sir John helped Maxwell to his feet. 'They'll probably want to carry you shoulder-high about the quad. Then there's bound to be a feast and you'll have to make a proper speech. Then there'll be the awarding of some honorific title and swearing you in as a life-long fellow of the University. Then—'

'Er, Sir John,' Maxwell made a guilty face, 'there's something I think you ought to know.'

'Do you mean like the fact that it was really Rushmear who killed Count Waldeck?'

'Yes. But how did you—'

'I told him.' William's face appeared, from behind a green velvet trouser leg this time. 'But then, as I explained to Sir John, if you hadn't found your way here to the University, then Rushmear could never have

278

followed you and done the actual slaying of the count. Logically, in the absence of Rushmear, you are the slayer by proxy.'

'I'm touched,' said Maxwell. 'Naturally I wouldn't have considered taking the credit, but as you put it like that.'

'I do,' said William.

'He does,' said Sir John. 'So we will overlook the fact that as it was actually William who led you here, then he should take all the credit and be slayer by proxy.'

'That's fine with me,' said Maxwll.

'And anyway,' Sir John continued, 'William is going to be the new Vice-Principal of the University. He is going to help me restore it to the great seat of learning it was originally intended to be. Together he and I will spread knowledge and wisdom across this world.'

'We certainly shall,' said William.

'Well,' said Maxwell, 'what a happy ever after. Things have turned out well after all. No, *hang about*. They haven't for ME.'

'I'm sure they will,' said Sir John. 'But for now, let's Rock 'n' Roll.'

And Rock 'n' Roll they did. Maxwell *was* carried shoulder-high about the quadrangle. There *was* a feast and he *did* make a speech (though not a very good one). He *was* awarded an honorific title, that of Imagineer in Residence, and he *was* sworn in and everything.

Toasts were made and drinks were drunk and grub was scoffed a-plenty. And at the end of it all, Maxwell, who now calculated that it was at least two days since he'd last had a sleep, was carried once more shoulder-high, but this time pissed as a pudding, and laid to rest on the dead count's cosy bed.

One tiny piece of unpleasantness later occurred when Maxwell booted with some violence an amorous Lord Archer from this very bed, but other than for this, he had to conclude, most drunkenly, that the day had really been a great success.

And then he slept the sleep of the just. By proxy, of course, but most well.

He awoke next morning with a blinder of a hangover, staggered to the refectory and joined Sir John and William for breakfast at the high table.

Sir John tucked into a fry-up of Herculean proportions. Maxwell sipped coffee and dipped bread soldiers into a boiled egg.

'William has told me everything,' said Sir John, scooping sausage into his mouth. 'It appears that you're really up shit creek in a smegma canoe.'

Maxwell sipped further coffee and grunted a 'yes'.

'If I arranged transportation to MacGuffin, would that help?'

'Magical transportation?'

'In any form you choose, within reason.'

'Then it wouldn't help, as magic will not pass through the grid.'

'*My* magic will pass through the grid, Maxwell.'

'It will?'

'It will.' Sir John stuffed fried bread into his face. 'But don't ask how, because I won't tell you.'

'So you are strong once more in spells?'

'Never more so.'

'Well, Rock 'n'—'

'Please don't,' said William.

'Sorry. But this is marvellous news. Then all I shall require is a cloak of invisibility, an amulet of unlimited power that wards off vicious magic, a spell of demobilization and another to inflict a slow and agonizing death. Perhaps, too, an enchanted sword that cuts through steel and a charm to make me irresistable to women.'

'Why the last one?' Sir John Rimmer asked.

'Because I haven't had a shag in nearly a century.'

'That's fair enough.'

'*All right!* Then let's get casting spells.'

'Ah, no.' Sir John rammed an entire bread roll into his mouth and chewed noisily. 'What I meant by, fair enough, was that it *was* fair enough you should ask for such a charm. I can't let you have one though.'

'Why not?'

'Because you are not a magician, Maxwell. I think we have had this conversation before. I can offer you one-way transportation and anything *reasonable* that you think you might need. But you must rely on your skills as an imagineer. Skills that you have not as yet used to their fullest potential. I have every confidence you will succeed.'

'How about just the cloak of invisibility?'

'No! You can take MacGuffin's pouch. I will arrange that it passes through the grid. But that is all you get.'

'Well, thanks a lot,' moaned Maxwell, scratching on a stubbly chin.

'But there is one thing you really must take.'

'And that is?'

'A bath,' said Sir John. 'You really pong.'

So Maxwell took a bath. And as he bathed he pondered. And as he pondered he thought. And as he thought he schemed. And so on and so forth.

It wasn't really all that bad. He'd only have the pouch, but that was all he'd ever expected he'd have. He'd have the transport. And he'd have the element of surprise. He'd beat the foul MacGuffin. Yes he would. Beat him and snatch back his soul. Beat him and liberate Aodhamm and Ewavett. Beat him and liberate the villagers too. He would do the right thing. Oh yes.

There'd be glory in this for him. And serious shoulder-high carrying too.

And there were women in MacGuffin's village.

'Yeah.' Maxwell lay back amongst the soapsuds. He *would* triumph. He just knew that he would.

And a great plan entered Maxwell's head and he began to smile.

26

The cricket pavilion rose into the air.

Maxwell waved down to the well-wishers gathered below.

There weren't very many of them.

Apparently word had got about that Maxwell was not really the slayer of Count Waldeck after all. That it was, in fact, a chap called Rushmear who'd done the actual slaying, and Maxwell was only slayer by proxy. A petition was being passed around with a view to stripping Maxwell of his honorific title. Someone had even thrown a stone at him in the quadrangle.

Maxwell didn't care. 'Stuff 'em,' he said, as he waved from the veranda to William and Sir John. And Lord Archer. And that was about all.

Maxwell went inside and closed the door. The cricket pavilion had a new smell now: one of fresh paint. It had been tastefully redecorated. The veranda roof mended. Bloodstains scrubbed from the floor. Certain structural alterations made, to provide first-class sleeping accommodation, storage space for provisions, an extensive wardrobe of clothes, certain specific items Maxwell had requested from Sir John and a stable for Black Bess.

The journey was expected to last at least five days. But time can pass pretty quickly when you're on that final stretch of undiverted road, bound for the epic confrontation, when the villain gets his just deserts and the hero bravely triumphs.

Pretty quickly indeed.

The pavilion dropped down towards the village of MacGuffin. Maxwell sat in a Lloyd loom chair, drinking a Buck's Fizz and smoking a small cigar. As the village swelled up to greet him, he leaned an arm upon the veranda rail and tried very very hard to remain cool, calm and calculating. It was not going to be easy.

The pavilion settled onto a grassy meadow, Maxwell finished his drink, rose and stretched. Not fifty yards distant stood Count Waldeck's airship. Though 'stood' was perhaps not the word. 'Wallowed' maybe, or 'lay wrecked', which was two words, but an accurate description.

Clearly the landing had not gone as smoothly as the take-off. The galleon lay with its keel arse-up'rds and its prop shafts bent and banjoed. The gas bag sagged like a wounded willy. The airship's airshipping days were done.

Maxwell shrugged, stubbed out his cigar, strode into the pavilion and slammed shut the door.

A short while later the door reopened. A fine white horse, with an elaborate silver-studded bridle, a very posh saddle and lots of tinsel tied to its tail emerged, led by a fantastic figure in a wonderful costume.

This fantastic figure wore an enormous turban, bedecked with glittering gemstones and floating ostrich plumes. A voluminous black gown of embroidered velvet trailed down the pavilion steps behind him. A silk blouse was gathered at the waist by a cummerbund of purple brocade. Floppy trews of powder blue were secured at the ankles by tasselled cords. Persian slippers with curly toes, worn over lurex socks.

The fantastic figure's face was somewhat fancy. It

was stained a violent orange, which clashed a tad with his bright green beard.

And if the fantastic figure's face was fancy, then no less were his fingers – fabulously estooned with fifteen fashionable finger rings. Phew.

Maxwell grinned (ferociously) beneath his false whiskers. The morning he'd spent in the props cupboard of the university's amateur dramatic society had been well worth while.

And so to PHASE ONE of his FOUR-PART MASTERPLAN.

Maxwell climbed carefully onto Black Bess and gave her a 'giddy up gently'.

As he rode past the ruined airship, Maxwell spied two things that saddened him, yet urged him on his way. The first was the corpse of a skyman, his head twisted around the wrong way.

The second was the coffin of Ewavett, empty, with its lid cast aside.

Maxwell rode on towards the village, breathing easily, keeping his cool.

Into the village he went, head held high, bum bouncing up and down, and horse going clip-clop on the cobbles. As he drew level with Budgen's, Maxwell saw the front door open and a young man in a tweedy suit stumble into the street.

He was an even-featured young man, with swags of yellow hair and, Maxwell knew, as the young man knew, that the young man's name was Dave.

Dave carried two bags of shopping and he limped across the street in front of Maxwell. He hadn't gone but a few limps, though, before an armadillo scuttled from his left trouser bottom, ran between his feet and sent him tumbling to the cobbles. Dave's shopping went every-which-way and Maxwell observed with a rueful smile that it was the self-same shopping he'd helped the lad pick up during their first and fateful encounter.

Maxwell drew Black Bess up short.

Dave lay clutching his ankle and moaning miserably.

Maxwell affected a haughty detachment. He adjusted the folds of his ample gown into a pleasing composition.

'I have fallen,' Dave complained. 'Won't you help me up?'

Maxwell ignored him.

'I've dropped my shopping.' Dave indicated the battered relics of many a previous drop.

Maxwell studied cloud formations.

Dave made a grumpy face and stood up. 'Can I help you at all?' he enquired.

Maxwell glanced down, as if noticing him for the first time. 'Are you addressing me?' he asked, in a deep dark voice of much rehearsing. 'Or are you speaking to my horse?'

'You,' said Dave. Which was a remarkably straight piece of answering, considering his previous record.

'Well don't,' said Maxwell, urging Black Bess, on, 'foul peasant that you are.'

Dave made a face of indecision. He stared down at his decoy shopping, then up at the horse's receding rear end. He dithered.

A small rodent stuck its head out from the top pocket of his jacket and bit him in the ear. Dave ceased his dithering. 'Oi,' he called after Maxwell. 'Come back. Don't go.'

Maxwell rode on up the high street.

Dave caught up with him. He pulled at a curly toed slipper. 'Hold it,' he cried. 'Hold it.'

Maxwell kept on riding. 'What is your name, peasant?' he asked.

'No, it's not peasant,' said Dave, pulling once more. 'And neither is it bastard, though many err in this regard. It's Dave.'

'Well, Dave,' said Maxwell in his deep dark voice. 'I am The Honourable Eddie Von Wurlitzer, Duke of Earl, and emissary to his marvellousness, The Sultan of Rameer, and if you don't get your bleeding hand off my slipper, folk will henceforth know you as "headless".'

Dave removed his hand.

'Now bugger off,' said Maxwell.

And Dave scampered away. Maxwell had a busy day planned for the professional shopping-dropper. But first . . .

As Maxwell approached the manse of MacGuffin, his stomach began to knot and his ring-bedazzled fingers to tremble violently. Maxwell hastily pulled a couple of valium from his pocket and tossed them down his throat. He'd liberated them from the medicine cabinet of the late count. And though, ultimately, drugs never really help you, that's no excuse for not taking them.

Maxwell also took a deep breath. He climbed down from Black Bess, tied her reins to a hitching post, pushed open the front gate and marched up MacGuffin's garden path.

The milk bottles were still on the step, but Maxwell supposed that this was *not* because MacGuffin was asleep. He took another big breath, squared up before the front door and then knocked a great knock on the knocker.

A moment passed. And then a moment more.

Maxwell stood a-trembling. And then he knocked again.

Another moment passed and then a window flew open above.

MacGuffin stuck his big red head out. 'Who dares disturb me from my business?' he shouted.

Maxwell took a step back and rolled up his eyes. The evil one glared down upon him. The pig's bladder face with its beady black eyes was contorted with rage. Maxwell saw that the golden nose-ring was gone. The count's magic had truly died with him.

'Who the devil's arse-wipe are you?' demanded MacGuffin.

Maxwell stared him eye to evil eye. Hatred roared through Maxwell's brain. The red mist, that powerful symptom of his soulless state, blurred his vision. Maxwell's mouth was dry, but he steeled his nerves and drew in another breath. 'Good day to you, sir,' boomed Maxwell. 'I am The Honourable Eddie Von Wurlitzer, Duke of Earl, and I would have a moment of your time.'

'You would *what*?' roared MacGuffin.

'A matter of great urgency. You are the master of this squalid little village, I presume.'

'And much more now besides.' MacGuffin drew in his head and slammed shut the window.

Maxwell stepped forward and applied himself once more to the knocker.

The window flew open again. 'Away with you!' bawled MacGuffin. 'Or I'll cast a spell of scorpions at your scrotum.'

Maxwell held his ground. 'If it please you,' he said politely, 'I am the emissary of his magnificence, The Sultan of Rameer.'

'The Sultan of Rameer?' MacGuffin cocked his big head on one side. 'Wait there a minute. I'm coming down.'

Maxwell waited, nerves jingle-jangling. The front door opened and MacGuffin stood there, filling up most of the opening. He stood in huge and horribleness, a monstrosity made flesh and made from plenty of it. He wore nothing but a red string vest and a pair of unspeakable red Y-fronts. Maxwell viewed with revulsion the bulge of a stiffy in MacGuffin's underpants.

But not a particularly big one.

MacGuffin glared at Maxwell.

And Maxwell stared right back at him.

He was now once more face to face with the beast who had taken his soul. Maxwell chewed upon his bottom lip and fought with the terrible compulsion to leap at the magician and tear out his heart. A compulsion which would surely end with a word or two of magic and Maxwell's hideous death.

MacGuffin struggled into a red satin dressing-gown, garishly adorned with lime green silhouettes of well-hung men and fat-bottomed girls splitting the old bamboo. He knotted the sash about his wandering waistline and glared further glares towards Maxwell. 'This better be very important,' he said.

'Oh it is,' grunted Maxwell. 'It very much is.'

'Follow me.'

MacGuffin led Maxwell through the hall. Its walls were made gay by numerous paintings of sparsely clad women who displayed an unseemly fondness for their dogs. Maxwell turned down his eyes from them and chewed once more on his lip.

In order to conceal his tremblings, Maxwell took to blundering about. Making flamboyant gestures and bluff swaggering movements,. He bumbled after MacGuffin, knocking into things and generally making a nuisance of himself.

'Be careful.' MacGuffin raised a big fist. 'My collection is priceless. If you damage one single item, I will boil your cods in cockroach oil.'

Maxwell moved a little more carefully.

MacGuffin led him through the room of obscene animals, down the hall of obscene statuary, up the sweeping staircase and into the wonderful circular room, with its incredible *trompe-l'œil* ceiling and its crystal-topped table with the incredibly obscene centre support.

MacGuffin indicated a knackered old bentwood chair which stood by an open window. 'Won't you sit down?' he said.

'I would prefer to stand.'

'As you wish.' MacGuffin seated himself in his big red throne-like chair and drummed his fingers on the table top.

Maxwell glanced about the high-domed room. He could not see the cabinet of souls, but he could feel its nearness, almost as if it called to him. Of Ewavett and Aodhamm there was no sign, but Maxwell knew MacGuffin would have them in some safe and private place.

As for Rushmear the horse trader. If Maxwell had been a betting man, he would have wagered all the money he had, that the big man's corpse now lay in MacGuffin's cellar, possibly pickling, prior to the removal of its skin for mounting in the mage's understairs collection. And if Maxwell had got good odds and had any money to wager, he'd have really cleaned up on that one.

'Hurry now.' MacGuffin's big fat fingers went drum drum drum. 'Tell me what you want.'

'As I said, I am the emissary of the Sultan of Rameer.'

'And how is the dear Sultan?' MacGuffin asked. 'In the best of health, I trust.'

'On the contrary. He is quite dead.'

'Dead?' MacGuffin feigned a face of abject sorrow. 'How did this happen? An accident perhaps.'

'An assassination,' said Maxwell. 'By a hired killer named Rushmear.'

'Rushmear?' MacGuffin shook his great head. 'I have never heard of such a man.'

'And why should you have? Rushmear escaped in one of the Sultan's many flying ships. We followed him to this very village.'

'We?' MacGuffin asked.

'Myself and a legion of one thousand knights who now surround the village.'

MacGuffin glanced towards the open window.

'Masters of camouflage,' Maxwell told him. 'Now obviously I have no wish to lay waste to the village and slaughter all its inhabitants, if this can possibly be avoided. And I doubt that you'd appreciate a hundred or so hairy-arsed knights rampaging amongst your collection. So it's imperative we capture this Rushmear as soon as possible and disarm the dangerous device he absconded with.'

'Dangerous device?' MacGuffin stroked one of his chins.

'A metal woman', said Maxwell, 'created by the late Sultan and some clown of a magician. What was his name now? MacGrubby the Maggot, was it? Or MacMurky the Masturbator? Something like that.'

MacGuffin puffed out his cheeks.

'Anyway,' Maxwell went on. 'It is understood that the assassin was in the pay of this MacMuff-diver, who, when captured, will be put to such extremes of torture that he will yearn to have his cods boiled for a bit of light relief.'

'Magicians are not easily captured,' said MacGuffin.

'My knights wear enchanted armour, impenetrable to magic. They have ways of dealing with any magician.'

'What a pity then that they did not save the Sultan from assassination.'

'They were having a day off. But no matter. If this MacGuffer now has the metal woman, they will have no work to do.'

'How so?'

Maxwell laughed. 'It is a high jest indeed and one you will possibly appreciate. Apparently the late Sultan swore a terrible vengeance upon this Mac—'

'*Guffin!*' said MacGuffin. 'It's MacGuffin.'

'You know of him then?'

'Only by reputation.'

'As you will. So, the late Sultan swore a terrible vengeance on this MacGuffin, over what I do not know. But he swore that one day he would destroy him. Now apparently this MacGuffin owns the male counterpart of the metal woman, and you'll laugh when you hear this.'

'Will I?' asked MacGuffin.

'You will. Apparently the late Sultan, well, this was before he was late, if you understand me.'

'Get on with it!' MacGuffin roared.

'Yes, sorry. Well, the Sultan apparently inserted a quantity of highly volatile explosive, actually up inside,' Maxwell made a suitably obscene gesture with a ring-clustered hand, 'up inside the metal woman. So that if the metal man tries to, you know, have a bit of hanky-panky, the friction will ignite the explosive and—'

'Stop!' MacGuffin fell back in his chair. 'You mean, should the two be physically reunited then—'

'Boom!' Maxwell used both ring-clustered hands to imply a very large boom indeed. 'You have to laugh, don't you?' he said.

The look that now covered MacGuffin's face, gave Maxwell to understand that laughing was something

292

he definitely did *not* have to do at this particular moment.

'By the by,' said Maxwell, 'I really must apologize, but I forgot to ask your name, sir.'

MacGuffin was now breathing heavily. His eyes strayed towards a door on the far side of the chamber. 'My name?' he said, in a distracted tone.

'Your name. What is your name?'

'It's . . .' MacGuffin made a gesture, as if plucking a name from the air. 'It's Carrion,' he said. 'Max Carrion.'

'Not *the* Max Carrion?'

'The?' MacGuffin's eyes had become fixed upon the door.

'The legendary hero,' said Maxwell. 'Spoken of with awe throughout the four worlds.'

'What?' went MacGuffin, his jowls all a quiver.

'What an honour to meet you.' Maxwell reached forwards, grasped MacGuffin's great right paw and shook it vigorously.

MacGuffin dragged his hand away. 'Ouch,' he cried, 'you have pierced my delicate flesh with your geegaw rings.'

'My sincere apologies. So many rings. So generous the Sultan was. I hope his dear son Colin will be so kind when he is formally crowned.'

'Get out of my house!' cried MacGuffin. 'I have pressing business that will not wait.'

'Would that I could,' said Maxwell, sitting himself down upon the knackered bentwood chair. 'But it's more than my job's worth. I must search for the assassin and the metal woman with the explosive snatch box. Perhaps I should begin my search here. What lies beyond that door your eyes seem so drawn to?'

'Enough!' MacGuffin raised his hands and made an intricate gesture.

Maxwell tried to stand. 'My gown appears stuck to the chair,' said he, in a voice of some alarm.

MacGuffin flung his broad arms wide. 'Horse and Hattock, Von Wurlitzer's chair, and carry him off to the moon.'

'To the moon?'

With a mighty whoosh the chair rose up and Maxwell shot out of the window.

27

Maxwell clung on to the flying chair. 'So far, so good,' said he.

So far, so good?

'So far, so good.'

With a careful hand, Maxwell withdrew from a trouser pocket MacGuffin's magic pouch. He gently eased one foot into it and then the other. With no less care he slipped his shoulders from the voluminous gown that was magically glued to the chair.

Maxwell leapt into the pouch. The pouch fell down and the chair continued on its historic voyage to the moon.

Down and down went the magic pouch, gathering speed as it did so. Inside Maxwell giggled away, as the ground rushed up and up. There was going to be a 'Splat!' coming soon, but Maxwell seemed unaware of this.

Down and down.

Rush ground up.

With the Doppler whistle of a falling bomb, the magic pouch swept down.

Thirty feet from the ground, a pocket handkerchief popped out of it. A piece of string was tied to each of the four corners. The pocket handkerchief became a tiny parachute. The parachute caught upon the air and the pouch slowed its rate of descent. Fluttered upon the breeze and settled gently down onto a grassy meadow a few yards before the cricket pavilion.

Maxwell stepped out from the magic pouch, dusted himself off, returned the pouch to his pocket and blew his nose on the handkerchief.

'So ends PHASE ONE,' he said. 'And now begins PHASE TWO.'

Half an hour later, a golden knight marched into the village of MacGuffin. The golden knight carried a large white envelope and, as his visor was down, he nearly tripped over a young fellow with a swag of yellow hair, who had tumbled in the street and dropped all his shopping.

He *nearly* tripped. But not quite.

'Are you injured, good sir?' asked the knight.

'I've dropped my shopping,' said Dave, for such was the name of the yellow-haired youth.

'I would gladly help you pick it up,' said the knight, 'but I can't bend in this armour. Do you know of anyone who might wish to earn ten gold pieces for delivering a message and returning with a reply?'

'That's hard to say,' said Dave.

'I didn't find it so,' said the knight.

'No, what I meant', said Dave, 'is, it's hard to say who might wish to earn *ten* gold pieces. There are some, I'm sure, who might wish to earn fifteen, and others twenty. But then there are probably those who would gladly take on the job for as little as four or five.'

'Perhaps you might suggest the name of one of these,' said the knight, patiently.

'I don't see how that would do any good.'

'Why?' asked the knight.

'Because you specifically said *ten*.'

'Perhaps you might take on the job yourself,' the knight suggested.

'I should be so lucky,' said Dave. 'A job like that I'd do for three.'

'Then your day's blessed, because I have here that exact sum, which I am eager to pay anyone for delivering this message and returning with a reply.'

'I thought you said ten?'

'That was a different message,' the knight explained.

The knight issued Dave with *specific* instructions and handed him the large white envelope. Dave hurried away and the knight watched as he ran towards the manse of MacGuffin, falling only once, when a civet sprang out of his right trouser bottom.

A while passed. It was neither a long while nor a short while, but one in between. When it had passed, Dave returned.

He handed the knight a small brown envelope. The knight peered at this through his visor and made approving sounds.

'Might I have my three gold coins now?' asked Dave.

'*Three?*' asked the knight. 'Did we agree three?'

'We did,' agreed Dave.

'Three is a paltry sum. Ten is much fairer. You should have asked for ten.'

'You're right,' said Dave, 'I should. Next time I will.'

'Quite right too,' said the knight. 'It should be ten or nothing, don't you agree.'

'I do.' And Dave agreed once more.

'So do I,' said the knight. '*Nothing* it is then. A pleasure doing business with you.'

And with that he turned about and marched away.

The knight marched out of the village and returned to the cricket pavilion. Here he tore open the brown envelope and examined the contents. A letter, penned in Maxwell's handwriting.

It read.

FOR THE EYES OF EDDIE VON WURLITZER ONLY

Dear Eddie,
The apothecary has just arrived at the camp with the special elixir you ordered which will neutralize the explosive in the metal woman. Do you want me to dispatch a bottle directly to where you are now? If so then just return this note to the messenger, sealed for security in the enclosed envelope.
The knights will remain in hiding awaiting your orders.
Yours, Captain Beefheart of the magic guards.

Maxwell screwed up the message and tossed it into a corner. 'PHASE TWO completed,' he said, 'and now on to PHASE THREE.'

Somewhat after lunch-time, a stooped figure, wearing the distinctive red-and-white striped gown of an apothecary, with the cowl drawn low across his face, shuffled into the village.

And here he met a young man with a very glum face who had just fallen down and dropped his shopping.

'What ails you, young man?' asked the apothecary in a creaking ancient voice.

'I've fallen down,' said Dave.

'You've an infestation, I believe.'

'I have?' said Dave. 'I mean, yes you're right, I have. How did you know?'

'I saw the weasel that sent you flying.'

Dave made a glummer face still.

'I have a potion that could cure that,' said the apothecary.

'You have?'

'I have. But it would cost you three gold coins.'

'Damn,' said Dave.

'However, you might earn three gold coins from me.'

'I might,' said Dave. 'I only wish I knew how.'

'I have a bottle of elixir that must be delivered to the manse of MacGuffin the mage. I would pay three gold coins. The bottle is full right up to the top, so you must not spill a single drop.'

'I'm a very careful fellow,' said Dave.

'You are nothing of the kind, and you know it. Walk very carefully with the bottle. I will have my eye on you all the way.'

'Rely on me,' said Dave, receiving the bottle and bearing it away with a great show of care.

And he didn't spill a drop.

Which made him doubly sad when he returned to find that the apothecary had gone.

The apothecary sat in the cricket pavilion with his feet up and a drink in his hand. 'PHASE THREE completed', he said. 'Which leaves just PHASE FOUR to do.'

It was around five of the afternoon clock when Maxwell returned to the village. This time he wore no disguise. This time he wore a yellow bowling shirt, a really nifty dove-grey zoot suit and his fine substantial boots (which due to their fine substantiality, had survived the stamping he gave them in MacGuffin's pouch). The suit and shirt had been gifts from Sir John (nice thought).

Maxwell sauntered into the village, his hands in his trouser pockets, he was whistling.

He was just passing Budgen's, when he came across a young man carrying two shopping bags. He was a very dejected-looking young man. Very down at the mouth.

'Wotcha, Dave,' said Maxwell. 'Careful how you go now. You don't want to trip over.'

Dave stared, open mouthed at Maxwell. Then he managed a blank, 'Hello.'

'Do you have a decent ale house round here?' Maxwell asked.

'Sadly no,' said Dave. 'All I have is a little private house.'

Maxwell smiled upon Dave. 'Let me put it this way then. Do you know of a decent ale house, that you would recommend to a thirsty traveller?'

'Yes,' said Dave, 'I do.'

'And?' Maxwell asked.

'And, what?'

'And what is its name?'

'Fangio's Bar,' said Dave.

'Would you care to join me for a drink there?'

'I certainly would. It's a shame it's closed for renovations.'

'There's an ale house over there.' Maxwell pointed.

As this was a statement, rather than a question, Dave was somewhat stuck for something to say.

'That's where I'm going,' said Maxwell. 'If you join me I will buy you a drink.'

Dave mulled the concept over. 'You will buy me a drink, simply for joining you in a walk across the road?'

Maxwell shook his head and strolled off to the ale house.

It was one of those sleepy little country pubs. The ones with the copper bed-warming pans, the toby jugs and horse brasses. The ones with the reproduction Windsor chairs, the shove-halfpenny boards and the old boy with the gammy leg who talks about the Somme. The ones—

'Out you!' shouted the barman.

'Me?' asked Maxwell.

'Not you. Him.'

'Me?' asked Dave.

'You,' said the barman. 'Last time you came in here we had bloody okapi running all over the pub.'

'I told you I wasn't lying about the okapi,' Dave told Maxwell.

'Bugger off,' said the barman and Dave buggered off.

'Now, sir,' said the barman to Maxwell, 'how *exactly* may I help you?'

'Drinks all round,' said Maxwell.

'Drinks all round what?'

'Drinks for everyone in the place, at my expense.' Maxwell cast a fistful of golden coins onto the counter.

The barman stared hard at Maxwell and opened his mouth to ask questions.

'As many drinks as the money will buy. Begin by offering each customer one drink of his or her choice. I'll explain what to do with the change.'

'Very well, sir. *Lads*,' the barman called out, 'this gentleman is offering to buy everyone in the place a free drink.'

A brief moment of silence was followed by a great trampling of feet and a surge towards the bar. The barman did the business.

'I'll have one myself also,' said Maxwell. 'From that pump there, in a pint glass, full up.'

The barman finished doing the business.

'And one for yourself.'

The barman finished doing the extra bit of business. 'Are you celebrating something, sir?' he asked.

'Very good,' said Maxwell. 'That's what I'm doing and I want you all to celebrate with me.'

'Celebrate what?'

Maxwell spoke in a good loud voice. 'The death of MacGuffin,' he said.

There was that sharp intake of breath. There was that spluttering sound of beer going up noses. There was a terrible gasping and somebody fainted.

'Before this day is through', said Maxwell, 'MacGuffin will be dead and you will all be free men.'

'MacGuffin dead?' The barman's jaw hung down to his chest.

'Dead.' Maxwell drew a finger across his throat. 'And you will be free.'

'You are clearly insane,' croaked the barman. 'Kindly leave the premises.'

'Remember my name, for I am your deliverer. It is Carrion. Max Carrion, Imagineer.'

'Mick Scallion?'

'Don't even think about it. *Carrion's* the name. And now, farewell.'

Dave sat in the gutter outside. He looked up at Maxwell. 'That was a quick drink,' he said.

Maxwell smiled down at Dave. 'Dave,' said Maxwell. 'Dave, it would probably be best for you to leave the village for a while. I am going now to the manse of MacGuffin. Within the hour he will be dead. It is a well-known fact that when dictators are overthrown, those who collaborated with them often end up swinging from lampposts.'

Dave did not reply to this. But he stood up and he walked away. And he didn't take his shopping.

Maxwell strode along the high street. The whistling strains of *High Noon* were more than he could resist. It was showdown time. The big confrontation. The moment he had waited for. The moment he had dreamed about. The moment he had planned.

Black Bess still stood at the hitching post. Maxwell

untied her reins. 'Go along,' said he, patting her rump. 'You are liberated. Gallop free.'

Black Bess whinnied, tossed her mane about, then sauntered away up the street.

Deep-breath time once more. Maxwell took it, pressed open MacGuffin's gate, strode up his garden path and knocked hard upon the door knocker.

No reply.

Maxwell put his ear to the front door.

Only silence.

Maxwell pushed the front door. It swung slowly open.

Maxwell hesitated. Perhaps he should have brought Dave along to take that first step over the threshold. No, it was all down to he alone. Just go for it.

And Maxwell went for it. He stepped into the hall. 'MacGuffin,' he called. 'MacGuffin, are you there?'

No reply.

Maxwell crept along the hall. Something might spring out. Something horrible. And what to do if it did? 'Run,' Maxwell told himself.

Along the hall and into the room of obscene animals. Did those glass eyes watch him? Maxwell shuddered. No, of course they didn't.

Out into the hall of statues. 'MacGuffin,' called Maxwell. But there was only silence. Apart from the beat of Maxwell's heart and the tread of his substantial boots.

Up the staircase. One step at a time. Slowly. Slowly. Maxwell's hand ran lightly up the banister. Sticky-palmed it was. 'MacGuffin.'

Maxwell heard a distant sound. A low growl? Or a groan? Maxwell continued up the stairs. He approached the doorway of the wonderful circular room. Another low growl. Maxwell stopped, breath caught in his throat. Another sound.

Maxwll entered the circular room.

The crystal-topped table was laid out for a feast: bowls of brightly coloured sweets, decanters of wine, platters of biscuits and cakes. Another sound.

Maxwell passed by the table and stared down.

And then he began to smile.

MacGuffin lay on the floor. He was twisted into an unnatural posture: his knees drawn up to his chest, his fingers bent back upon themselves. His big head was on one side. Yellow slime dripped from his mouth.

'MacGuffin,' said Maxwell, 'whatever has happened to you?'

The beady black eyes were glazed, but they flickered towards Maxwell and fixed him with a stare of unutterable loathing.

Maxwell pulled over MacGuffin's big red throne-like chair and sat down upon it. 'You are clearly quite poorly,' said Maxwell. 'In fact, you are about to die.'

MacGuffin tried to speak, but no words came to him.

'You have lost your voice,' said Maxwell, 'and the movements of your hands, no more to utter curses or fling magic. How has this come about?'

Maxwell rose to his feet and stood over the dying magician. 'It has come about', said he, in a vicious tone, 'because I have poisoned you. Three times over, this single day. How did I do this, I feel you might ask. Well, I shall tell you. I acquired Count Waldeck's medicine cabinet. A great man for poison, was the count. He once had someone poison me. You never forget a thing like that. It's the kind of thing you'd wish upon your worst enemy. And you are *my* worst enemy, MacGuffin.'

A spasm of pain shook the magician. His black eyes rolled up into his head.

'Oh, don't die quite yet,' Maxwell told him. 'You'll miss how I did it. And I shall so enjoy telling you.

Firstly, I poisoned your blood, with a ring coated in venom. Secondly, you poisoned yourself, by licking the gum on the brown envelope I enclosed with the bogus message. And thirdly,' Maxwell kicked the prone figure, 'the elixir I sent you to apply to Ewavett. I'll bet you enjoyed applying it, you filthy creature. It could not harm her metal body, of course, but it soaked into your rotten flesh.'

The black eyes rolled down and crossed, more evil slime leaked from the flaccid mouth.

'So I have killed you,' Maxwell said. 'You die for all those you have sent to their deaths, all those you have enslaved. You die because you are not fit to live.'

A rattling sound issued from MacGuffin's throat, he jerked his head from side to side. Maxwell walked calmly to the table and looked over the colourful fare. 'A succulent feast,' said he, picking up a sweetmeat and putting it to his mouth.

The black eyes fixed him with a baleful stare.

Maxwell dropped the sweetmeat to the floor and hastily wiped his fingers. '*Touché*,' he said. 'A poisoned feast for the victor, I should have expected no less.'

The black eyes closed. MacGuffin lay still.

Maxwell sank into the big red throne-like chair.

It was done. He had taken his revenge. MacGuffin was dead.

Maxwell began to shake and then he was violently sick.

28

Maxwell wiped a sleeve across his mouth. It was not altogether done. There was the matter of his soul. A very grave matter indeed.

Maxwell climbed to his feet. 'Come, cabinet,' he shouted.

No cabinet came. Well, it was worth a try.

Maxwell glanced across the room to the door which MacGuffin had stared so hard at when last they met. In there, perhaps?

Maxwell crossed the room and pushed open the door. A bedroom lay beyond. A marvellous bedroom. The kind of bedroom Maxwell had always fancied: big round bed, with a white lamb-skin cover; deep pile carpet; mirrored ceiling; full range of marital aids on the dressing-table. Maxwell cast the eye of interest over these. Then his eye of interest returned to the bed. On this, side by side, sat Aodhamm and Ewavett.

Still without any clothes on.

Maxwell viewed the beautiful couple. The bronze man, with his peerless physique. The perfect golden woman.

Maxwell cleared his throat. 'Excuse me,' he said.

Aodhamm looked up at him, stared a blank stare.

'You are free,' said Maxwell. 'MacGuffin is dead. I, Max Carrion, have killed him. You are liberated. You may go your way.'

Aodhamm's stare remained blank. His bronze lips moved. 'MacGuffin has defiled Ewavett,' he said.

'Er, yes.' Maxwell scratched at his chin. 'That was my fault, I'm afraid. But the way I see it, one small defilement is better than a lifetime of enslavement.'

'It's not the defilement,' said Aodhamm. 'It's the fact that she enjoyed it.'

'I did,' said Ewavett, grinning hugely.

'Good grief,' said Maxwell, gaping hugely.

'Aodhamm's no good at it,' said Ewavett. 'He makes clanking noises when he comes and he can't keep it up for more than an hour.'

'I think I must be going now,' said Maxwell.

'You look like a bit of all right,' said Ewavett. 'How about splitting the bamboo with me for a couple of hours?'

'You trollop,' said Aodhamm.

'You wimp,' said Ewavett.

'Goodbye,' said Maxwell, closing the door.

'Come, cabinet,' he called. Well, it was always worth a second try. No cabinet came (clanking or not).

Maxwell sought another door. One other remained in the room. Maxwell stalked over and threw it wide. Beyond lay the cabinet of souls, hovering in the air. Maxwell pulled it into the high-domed room. It moved without weight. Maxwell swung it around. 'Open up,' he told it.

The cabinet did not open.

Maxwell applied himself to the lid. 'Carefully does it,' he said. The lid shifted a mite, then dropped back. Maxwell dug in his fingers. As he pulled up the lid, the cabinet rose with it. Tricky.

Maxwell climbed onto the floating cabinet and pushed it down to the floor. There'd be a knack to this. If only he knew some magic word.

Some magic word.

Maxwell stood up from the cabinet and ran his hands over the lid. Some magic word? Maxwell's hands froze. *Some magic word?* The cabinet still floated, kept aloft by the magic of MacGuffin. And when a magician dies, so too does his magic.

Which meant . . .

Maxwell spun around.

MacGuffin's body shook and shivered. MacGuffin was *not* dead.

Maxwell sought something to finish the job. The big red throne-like chair – dash out his brains. And dash them out now.

Maxwell struggled to lift the chair. The chair would not be lifted. Something. Anything.

MacGuffin's body jerked like a puppet on strings. It flapped from the floor, dropped back. Flapped up again. The great arms falling wide, trailing about, bending at strange angles in all the wrong places. The big head lolling this way and that.

Maxwell looked on in horror. Something very bad was about to happen.

Something very bad indeed.

MacGuffin's body rose, swung erect. But he was not standing. His feet scarcely touched the floor. Something other than MacGuffin was working the mage.

Maxwell backed towards the door, pushing the cabinet of souls.

His MASTERPLAN had ended with PHASE FOUR, it did not run to a PHASE FIVE. Maxwell, however, felt well disposed to run.

'Stay. Stay.' The magician's mouth was moving, but the voice wasn't his. It was soft, pleading. 'Stay, Maxwell,' it said.

'No chance of that.' Maxwell had the cabinet almost out of the door.

'Then I must make you stay.'

MacGuffin's mouth stretched wide. Revolting sounds came from his throat. Something vivid red sprang out, a twisting tentacle. The thing thrashed about, another joined it, whirling from the magician's mouth. His chest heaved, then split. MacGuffin collapsed to the floor.

And something stood over the body. Something that had come from within. It was no human something.

Bright red it was, as red as blood. Two horns upon its head. White pointed teeth and slitted eyes. A tail and wings upon its back.

'Aw shit!' said Maxwell, as you would.

'Quickly now,' the creature said. 'As you have slain my host, so now it is that you must carry me within.'

'No fucking way!'

Maxwell snatched a decanter from the table and flung it at the creature. The thing swept it aside and advanced upon him.

'I must come into you now. At once.'

'Who are you? *What* are you?' Maxwell tried to push the cabinet out of the door, but somehow he'd managed to wedge it.

'You have seen the new Adam and the new Eve. Now you behold the new serpent also.'

'The Devil?'

'MacGuffin conjured me, but I possessed him. I guided his hands to conjure Ewavett and Aodhamm, so that I might rule over the new Eden. The Garden of Unearthly Delights.'

'Every bugger wants to rule,' Maxwell struggled to shift the cabinet. 'Still, it's good to get these things out in the open. It helps tie up all the loose ends.'

'I must enter you now.'

'I'd rather that you didn't.'

'MacGuffin dies. At the moment of his death his power will be yours. But only for a moment. If I am

309

within you I can hold the power. Together we can do many things.'

'You really must be joking.' The window above was open. Maxwell wondered if he could leap through it.

'Now, Maxwell, let me come inside.'

'Here,' said Maxwell, 'have this.'

He swung a fist and smacked the creature in the gob. It was somewhat like hitting a rock.

Maxwell howled and as he howled the room began to rock. It was nothing to do with his howling though. It was all to do with MacGuffin. The magician clawed at his hollowed chest, gave a howl of his own and fell dead.

'Now!' The creature flung himself at Maxwell. Maxwell ducked aside. 'Open, cabinet,' he shouted. The lid swung open and Maxwell snatched out the glowing sphere that held his soul.'

'Inside!' The creature threw itself once more at Maxwell. Clutching his soul to his chest, Maxwell ran around the crystal table, the creature in pursuit.

'Quickly, quickly,' it screamed. 'I cannot survive outside a body. We will lose the magic. Quickly.'

'Quickly it is then.' Maxwell turned to face the creature. 'Horse and Hattock, this whole bloody house!' he shouted. 'Then to Hell with MacGuffin's magic!'

'No!'

But it was *yes*.

And chaos was the order of the day.

The house shook and trembled. Slates flew from its roof. The crystal table tipped and smashed. In rooms and halls beneath, showcases shattered and statuary toppled. Rude pictures fell from the walls and broke. And the manse lifted into the air.

As it ripped itself from its foundations, MacGuffin's magic burst out like water from a fractured main.

It boiled about the village, tearing up the cobblestone and frightening the horses.

Dave, who had been packing his suitcase, was flung from his feet. His trousers shredded and a hydra (many headed) rose out of his underpants and went for him something cruel.

Maxwell clung to the obscene table support as the room now spun around him. He tried desperately to keep a grip on the crystal globe, but he could feel it slipping from his fingers.

The creature was upon him. It clung to his leg and Maxwell tried to kick it away. It leered at him and laughed. 'You're all mine now,' it said.

'I'm not done yet,' and Maxwell kicked and kicked.

Things smashed and crashed and windows broke and columns fell and magic roared and raved.

Ewavett's voice could be heard above the maelstrom, coming from the bedroom. 'Yes, yes,' she cried. 'Do it to me, Aodhamm. Do it to me. Yes, yes, yes.'

'I shall do it to *you*,' cried the creature, curling about Maxwell's leg, a horrible blood-red serpent.

'Oh my Goddess.' The crystal globe slipped from his grip and bounced across the room. Pain tore into Maxwell from every direction. The creature rolled itself into a ball and shot towards his mouth.

'No!' Maxwell ducked his head, the thing flew past. It circled round in the spinning room and flew at him once more.

And it was now or never.

Maxwell didn't want to do it, but he knew he had no choice.

Dragging the very last piece of mileage that could possibly be dragged from a single item, he tore the magic pouch from his pocket and held it open in front of his face. The creature swept into it and Maxwell drew the draw string tight.

And then MacGuffin's magic faltered, coughed and died.

And went to Hell.

The manse hovered a moment in the air.

Maxwell scrambled up and dived towards the crystal globe.

And then the manse plunged down.

It missed its former foundations and fell upon Budgen's.

Which cushioned its fall. Though not by a lot.

The roof caved in, the dome collapsed, columns buckled, walls bulged and burst. Dust and bricks and rubble, falling timbers, ruination, mangled bits and bods and bodies.

And then just a bit of a hush.

They dug Maxwell's corpse from the wreckage. There was no way he could have survived. They hauled him into the ruined high street and stood about, making respectful faces and wondering who would be the first to say what a good fellow he'd been and so lay themselves open to standing the cost of the funeral.

Not Dave.

He was going through Maxwell's pockets.

'He owed me three gold coins,' said the lad, who had worked a few things out for himself. 'Hello, what's this?' He prised a crystal globe from Maxwell's dead fingers and held it towards the light.

A tiny Maxwell stared out at him and waved its hands about.

'Aaaaagh!' went Dave, dropping the globe to the ground.

There was a crash, a flash and a sound like rushing wind.

Maxwell's soul swept from the fractured globe and shot back up his left nostril.

Maxwell's eyes blinked open. He coughed and groaned and breathed the air. 'I am alive,' he said, which was reasonable enough. 'And I am whole. I have my soul, I can feel it, I can feel it. Praise the Goddess. Praise the Goddess.'

And in the rubble something stirred.

Though nothing nasty.

Something somewhat Goddess-like raised its golden head from brickdust. 'Oh Aodhamm,' purred Ewavett, 'did the earth move for me that time, or what?'

29

They carried Maxwell shoulder-high around the village. Young women threw petals and kisses. Old folk cheered and children danced a jig.

There was laughter, there was joy.

Maxwell was the hero of the day.

And he'd really done it. All on his own with no-one to help him. He had triumphed.

He had scored the winning goal.

Max Carrion, Imagineer.

'I love you all.' And Maxwell waved and folk waved back and cheered some more.

'I'm his closest friend, you know,' Dave confided to a young waving woman who looked like she might settle for second best.

'Piss off!' said the woman. For looks can sometimes be deceptive.

Hoorah and cheer and clap.

'Max-well. Max-well. Max-well.'

Oh happy day.

And folk came running. Men in farmers' smocks.

'Stop!' they shouted. 'Hold on, stop.'

Maxwell waved and called, 'Hello, hello.'

But, 'Stop,' they shouted. 'Cease all this at once.'

'Whatever is the trouble?' Maxwell asked, and he was not alone in this.

'MacGuffin's magic is no more,' cried the farming types.

'Too right,' called Maxwell. 'I have slain MacGuffin. His magic has died with him.'

'Then we are all doomed,' the farming types called back.

'Oh yes and why?'

One farming type held up a withered parsnip. 'MacGuffin's magic made the land fertile. Now the crops perish and rot.'

'You will grow new crops,' Maxwell called. 'You are free men now and you may grow whatever you will.'

'Not round here, mate. Even the grass where your pavilion landed has turned to brown. It's wasteland here. We are doomed.'

'Nonsense,' said Maxwell, as he was dropped from shoulder height. 'Don't you understand? You are free now, free from enslavement. No more the chattels of MacGuffin.'

'Better a chattel with a full belly than a free man free to starve,' called someone, who favoured a nice turn of phrase.

'Oh come off it. I have saved you all. Rejoice that the wicked magician is dead.'

'I quite liked him actually,' someone said.

'Me too,' said someone else. 'When my cat had the mange he prepared me a magic potion.'

'He cured my warts,' said someone else again.

'He bonked my wife,' said yet another someone. 'You couldn't help liking him though.'

'Too right. Too right.'

'No,' cried Maxwell. 'This is madness. I have saved you all. You are free men. Free men, do you hear?'

'Maxwell has destroyed us all,' cried several farming

types in unison. 'Slay the assassin who has wrought
this ill upon us.'

'No,' said Maxwell. 'No.'

But it was *yes*.

'Slay the assassin.'

'You ungrateful bastards.'

And someone threw a stone.

Maxwell ran, the villagers in hot pursuit.

But Maxwell was well practised in the art of running, and he soon left them some ways behind. He
turned and shook his fist, raised his hands to the sky,
shook his head and then ran on once more.

This time towards the east.

30

It was hardly a 'feel good' ending.

And this was hardly fair.

Over yonder hill ran Maxwell and down the other side.

And here he came upon Aodhamm and Ewavett, walking hand in hand. And still with not a stitch on.

'Ahoy, Maxwell,' called Aodhamm.

'Now listen,' said Maxwell, 'if you mean to set upon me because of what MacGuffin did to your girlfriend, forget it. I'll fight you if I must, but I'd rather run. It's been a trying day.'

'He doesn't want to fight,' said Ewavett. 'He just wants to say thank you. And so do I.' Ewavett kissed Maxwell on the cheek, which made the lad go wobbly at the knees.

'My pleasure,' said Maxwell. 'I'm glad I've made someone happy.'

'You have,' Aodhamm smiled. 'But what of you now? Where are you going?'

'I think I'll just run on for a bit. The villagers will shortly be saddling horses, I've been through this before.'

'Come with us,' said Ewavett. 'We travel to the world of the silver sun. That's where MacGuffin and Count Waldeck snatched us from by magic. You'll be made welcome there, hailed as a hero.'

'A hero?' said Maxwell.

'And there are many women there who will be eager to make your acquaintance.'

'Golden women?' Maxwell asked. 'As beautiful as you?'

'Me beautiful?' Ewavett laughed. 'Where I come from I'm considered rather plain.'

'So what do you say?' asked Aodhamm. 'Will you come with us, or what?'

Maxwell grinned and nodded. 'Rock 'n' Roll,' he said.

THE END

A SELECTED LIST OF FANTASY TITLES
AVAILABLE FROM CORGI AND BLACK SWAN

THE PRICES SHOWN BELOW WERE CORRECT AT THE TIME OF
GOING TO PRESS. HOWEVER TRANSWORLD PUBLISHERS
RESERVE THE RIGHT TO SHOW NEW RETAIL PRICES ON COVERS
WHICH MAY DIFFER FROM THOSE PREVIOUSLY ADVERTISED IN
THE TEXT OR ELSEWHERE.

☐ 14802 4	MALLOREON 1 : GUARDIAN OF THE WEST	David Eddings	£5.99
☐ 14807 5	BELGARIAD 1 : PAWN OF PROPHECY	David Eddings	£5.99
☐ 14256 5	SWORD IN THE STORM	David Gemmell	£6.99
☐ 14257 3	MIDNIGHT FALCON	David Gemmell	£6.99
☐ 14274 3	THE MASTERHARPER OF PERN	Anne McCaffrey	£5.99
☐ 13763 4	THE ROWAN	Anne McCaffrey	£5.99
☐ 14478 9	AUTOMATED ALICE	Jeff Noon	£6.99
☐ 14479 7	NYMPHOMATION	Jeff Noon	£6.99
☐ 14614 5	THE LAST CONTINENT	Terry Pratchett	£5.99
☐ 14615 3	CARPE JUGULUM	Terry Pratchett	£5.99
☐ 13681 6	ARMAGEDDON THE MUSICAL	Robert Rankin	£5.99
☐ 13832 0	THEY CAME AND ATE US, ARMAGEDDON II: THE B-MOVIE	Robert Rankin	£5.99
☐ 13923 8	THE SUBURBAN BOOK OF THE DEAD, ARMAGEDDON III: THE REMAKE	Robert Rankin	£5.99
☐ 13841 X	THE ANTIPOPE	Robert Rankin	£5.99
☐ 13842 8	THE BRENTFORD TRIANGLE	Robert Rankin	£5.99
☐ 13843 6	EAST OF EALING	Robert Rankin	£5.99
☐ 13844 4	THE SPROUTS OF WRATH	Robert Rankin	£5.99
☐ 14357 X	THE BRENTFORD CHAINSTORE MASSACRE	Robert Rankin	£5.99
☐ 13922 X	THE BOOK OF ULTIMATE TRUTHS	Robert Rankin	£5.99
☐ 13833 9	RAIDERS OF THE LOST CAR PARK	Robert Rankin	£5.99
☐ 13924 6	THE GREATEST SHOW OFF EARTH	Robert Rankin	£5.99
☐ 14211 5	THE MOST AMAZING MAN WHO EVER LIVED	Robert Rankin	£5.99
☐ 14213 1	A DOG CALLED DEMOLITION	Robert Rankin	£5.99
☐ 14355 3	NOSTRADAMUS ATE MY HAMSTER	Robert Rankin	£5.99
☐ 14356 1	SPROUT MASK REPLICA	Robert Rankin	£5.99
☐ 14580 7	THE DANCE OF THE VOODOO HANDBAG	Robert Rankin	£5.99
☐ 14589 0	APOCALYPSO	Robert Rankin	£5.99
☐ 14590 4	SNUFF FICTION	Robert Rankin	£5.99
☐ 99777 3	THE SPARROW	Mary Doria Russell	£6.99
☐ 99811 7	CHILDREN OF GOD	Mary Doria Russell	£6.99

All Transworld titles are available by post from:

Bookpost, P.O. Box 29, Douglas, Isle of Man IM99 1BQ

Credit cards accepted. Please telephone 01624 836000,
fax 01624 837033, Internet http://www.bookpost.co.uk or
e-mail: bookshop@enterprise.net for details.

Free postage and packing in the UK. Overseas customers allow
£1 per book (paperbacks) and £3 per book (hardbacks).